C000069434

I Spy th

Also by Stephen Davis

The Tsar's Banker

I Spy the Wolf

Stephen Davis

I Spy the Wolf © Stephen Davis

ISBN 978-0-9955423-0-3
eISBN 978-0-9955423-2-7

Published in 2017 by Peakes Place Publications

The right of Stephen Davis to be identified as the author
of this work has been asserted by him in accordance with the
Copyright, Designs and Patents Act 1988.

A CIP record of this book is available from the British Library.

Printed in the UK by TJ International Ltd, Padstow, Cornwall

Dedication

To my family and everyone who embraces the flag of freedom and equality

**The Nazis knew that in all capitalist countries there were
men ready to betray their own people, so they could save
their own property and privilege.**

'The Chosen Few' 1940

William 'Willie' Gallacher
Scottish trade unionist and Member of Parliament for East Fife.

Chapter One
Zeppelin Field

Nuremburg, Germany September 1937

As Michael Tagleva sat in the area reserved for distinguished foreign visitors and looked out at the huge arena below him, little did he suspect that, in the next few months, his adventure would turn into a nightmare.

The last week had been the most exciting and fascinating of Michael's life. Blond, square-jawed and athletic, he had easily blended in with the crowds of young men and women, sometimes twenty deep, who watched the parades pass the townhouses bedecked with flowers and garlands from roof to pavement, flags fluttering from every window. After the parades, he'd drunk steins of free beer in the medieval *Hauptmarkt* and watched women in traditional folk dress and men in lederhosen dance around the square. It seemed that the entire population of Bavaria was having a good time at the festivities. *Truly*, Michael had thought, *Hansel and Gretel would feel right at home.*

Now, on this final day of the festivities, he had a clear view from his seat of the two hundred thousand soldiers, Reich Labour Service labour corps and party faithful in massed ranks.

The man next to him leaned over. 'Tell me, young man, d'you know Heinrich Himmler?' he asked in an American accent.

'No, I'm afraid we've not met,' replied Michael.

'No? Such a shame. If you get the chance, you should. I've met him twice. You really ought to know Heinrich. He's a great man, a real decent fellow.'

Before Michael had time to question him further, a member of the Hitler Youth, dressed in his brown uniform and proudly wearing the long knife engraved with the inscription *Blut und Ehre*, 'Blood and Honour', showed a visitor into the small gap

1

between Michael and the American. Without hesitation, the grey-faced, bespectacled man whose waist flowed over his trousers thrust a bulky rump between them, cutting off any possibility of further conversation.

The fleshy cuckoo, oblivious to the disruption he was causing, simply looked straight ahead and consolidated his massive frame on the bench. Michael muttered an inaudible curse as he lost more precious inches of seating. In his pale podgy hands, the man held an envelope with 'ENGLAND' written in blue pencil on the front. Michael was about to ask if he were English, when hundreds of loudspeakers around the stadium began to blast out martial music.

Ignoring the lump of flesh next to him as best he could, Michael surveyed the vast crowds eighty feet below him. He felt a heightened sense of anticipation race through the tiered seats as, below them, one hundred thousand people moved into position to create a living chessboard. Eventually the stadium was full. From his vantage point high up in the stadium, Michael watched as, far in the distance, a minute black car came into sight and glided towards the dais. Another arrived, then another and another, until a whole string of them appeared. The thousands of spectators stood and cried out, and a wave of noise swept round the stadium and continued to swell. The cries were not so much a roar as an expression of eager gladness – a happy welcome to the figure standing in the front of the first limousine. It slowly transported him, like a deity, to the dais from where he would address the adoring crowd. Like the hundreds of thousands of others in Zeppelin Field, Michael Tagleva stood and saluted the Führer with an outstretched right arm.

Michael had planned to reclaim a few inches of lost territory when he sat back down. The man next to him, however, had anticipated his intentions and returned his ample posterior to the bench before the final 'Seig Heil!' had subsided. He then leaned comfortably backwards and spread his knees wide. Frustrated by his lack of success, Michael thought he would at least get a picture of the massed ranks before him, so he rose and aimed his camera at the scene. A podgy finger was pushed into his ribs and a voice said, 'Can't see through you.'

Muttering an apology, Michael sat down hastily, furious at the thought of spending the next couple of hours watching the parades while being robbed of any possibility of comfort by the oaf who had enjoyed a lifetime of too much *Apfelstrudel* and steins of *Bier*.

Turning his attention to the scene before him, Michael noticed Hitler had arrived on the dais and was surveying the throng. The crowd fell silent. The Führer folded his arms. The crowds thought he might begin to speak, and many leaned forward in anticipation. Hitler remained silent and unfolded his arms. Surely he would begin to speak now. Instead, he took a sip of water from a glass on the table to his left. He surveyed all before him and still said nothing. Three hundred thousand people were silent, motionless, charged, ready to explode, waiting for their Führer to begin.

From hundreds of loudspeakers the words finally echoed around the stadium.

'When I took power, there were more than six million unemployed and Germany seemed doomed to decay. Today there are none. You must admit that I have fulfilled my promises to you.'

Released from their tension, the crowds stood and roared their approval with outstretched arms and cries of '*Seig Heil!*'

Once more, Hitler paused for silence.

'Germany's sovereignty and equality in Europe has been restored. I hope that the intelligence and good will of all responsible European governments will result in preserving peace in Europe. Peace is Germany's dearest treasure...'

The crowd roared its approval once more, and Michael, along with everyone else in the Zeppelin Field, was mesmerised.

The speech lasted for almost an hour, and when Hitler finished, the crowds went wild. They cheered and cheered as the Führer saluted his adoring disciples. For the next few hours, Wagnerian overtures played, martial songs were sung, parades of tanks rumbled and columns of soldiers goose-stepped past Hitler, and hundreds of planes roared overhead.

As dusk settled over the stadium, one hundred and fifty-two searchlights cut the gloom and threw vertical beams of light into the sky, surrounding the Zeppelin Field and producing the effect of the stadium being enclosed by walls. Michael was sure that, like him, the thousands of people there had never seen anything so spectacular. As columns of soldiers carrying flaming torches marched up and down, the crowds roared their approval and sang the 'Horst Wessel Song'. The festival concluded with a massive fireworks display.

A few hours after the end of the rally, Michael's chauffeured car swept into the long drive at his temporary home in Regensburg. He was able to recognise the familiar large house from its rejection of all unnecessary decoration, a reflection of the new and entirely Germanic approach to life.

He was met at the door by his host, SS-Standartenführer Rudolf Bauer: '*Heil Hitler.*'

'*Heil Hitler,*' responded Michael raising his right hand in salute.

'Did you enjoy the final day of the rally?'

Michael's eyes shone. 'It was fantastic. I can't remember seeing anything so impressive. When the Führer spoke I was so moved. No British politician commands the people's respect like him. I could have cried at the disappointment of not being German.'

Rudolf Bauer smiled. 'It's late. You had better go upstairs to bed.'

'I will, I'm quite tired. Good night, Standartenführer,' said Michael.

Bauer watched Michael climb the stairs to his bedroom and then walked to his study. Picking up the phone, he ordered the operator to be connected to the *Gauleiter* of Regensburg.

His superior answered on the third ring.

After the usual greeting, Bauer relayed Michael's enthusiasm. 'When young Tagleva returns to his family, I'm convinced he will find what we want. The plan is moving forward.'

'Very good, I'll tell Heydrich, but keep me informed of progress. *Heil Hitler.*'

The phone went dead before Bauer could respond.

Chapter Two
A dinner party

Ten months previously

The gloved hand moved the fork just a millimetre to its perfect position on the dining table. The butler, Williams, made one final inspection and looked with satisfaction at the blue and gold Sèvres porcelain dinner service, silver cutlery, cut-glass wine goblets, ornate table centrepieces and arrangements of white roses. He nodded his approval. Except for the red wine stain on the carpet in front of the fireplace, everything was as it should be. Williams sighed. Despite the perfection of the table, he feared the evening would be a disaster, ruined by family conflict. He hadn't experienced such discord in the family since beginning work for the Count and Countess Tagleva many years past. The cause was Michael's shocking announcement two weeks before, and it made Williams more determined that everything to do with the dinner would be as it should be.

Satisfied with the dining room, the butler walked down the servants' stairs to the kitchen and the butler's pantry. Despite his best attempts to prevent it, the atmosphere above stairs was affecting the smooth running of the household below stairs. Among the servants, the family's argument had become the only topic of conversation. Even the boot-boy had an opinion. On more than one occasion in the past two weeks, Williams had cause to admonish a valet or a maid from gossiping and not paying attention to their duties. Now, arriving in the kitchen, he was pleased to see it was a hive of activity.

Williams walked over to the kitchen table and picked up the card that detailed the instructions to the staff for the evening, information that he himself had distributed. He sensed the cook eying him as he looked down the list of guests, where they were to be seated, how they were to be addressed, and the menu in French and English together with the wines to be served.

'Is everything all right?' asked the cook in a slightly irritated tone.

'I trust so, Mrs Banks.'

He put down the card, sighed and walked to his pantry, the command centre of the house. He decided to put his worries behind him by inspecting the champagne that the guests would drink upon their arrival and by spending a relaxing hour decanting the wine to be served with the meal.

He didn't have time to take off his jacket before the housekeeper knocked on his door. 'Mr Williams, can I disturb you, please?'

'Of course, Mrs Frobisher.'

Just as the butler was the eyes and ears of the master, the housekeeper was the mistress's voice and despite being unmarried, Mrs Frobisher was accorded the title of 'Mrs' as a mark of respect of her position in the household. Being a steady middle-aged woman, greatly experienced in her profession and with a tolerable if limited knowledge of the world, Mrs Frobisher fitted the requirements of housekeeper perfectly.

'Millie's been unable to remove the wine stain from the carpet,' she said.

'The one from last night?'

'Yes, that's the one,' replied the housekeeper.

'I had noticed. Just for this evening, let's hide the offending stain by placing a small rug over it. Instruct one of the maids to have another try tomorrow. The rug in the study would be best. I'll tell the footmen to be careful not to trip over it during dinner service. By the way, how is the Countess?'

'Still fretting over Mr Michael; he seems determined on upsetting her.'

'I just hope the argument doesn't boil over and spoil the dinner when we have such distinguished guests in the house.'

Mrs Frobisher left to arrange for the rug to be moved.

The butler walked over to the table where a dozen bottles of Mouton Rothschild Pauillac 1920 stood. Using his butler's knife, he removed the capsule around the neck of one of the bottles. Lighting a candle, he positioned it behind the decanting cradle so he could watch for any sediment that might find itself flowing into the decanter. He placed the bottle into the cradle and began to turn the handle, it slowly tilt. Ten minutes later the decanter was full of clear wine, with half a glass of sediment-laden liquid remaining in the bottle. Once all the bottles had been decanted, the sludge would be handed to cook, who would then add the liquid to the gravy to be served with the *noisettes de chevreuil sauce aux airelles.*

****

Upstairs, Count Philip was stood in Countess Sophie Tagleva's dressing room and watched his wife's reflection in the mirror as she brushed her hair with energetic sweeps.

'I can't understand Michael,' she said. 'How can he delay working with you at the bank, to go to Spain of all places? To think of going to Spain to fight in their civil war... He's always hated violence... The problem is that he believes what's printed in the newspapers, too prepared to believe people and want to help them... It's not even as if he speaks the language. He was such a gentle boy... The twins are upset... They've always looked up to their older brother... Remember when they were very small? It was always Michael they would turn to first for comfort... Halinka's cried all day at the thought of him leaving.' She took a breath, then added, 'Do you think it's our fault somehow? Have we done something... Perhaps we've overprotected him from the dangers in the world?'

Philip looked at his wife and watched as the hairbrush moved through her long golden hair with increasing speed. He'd fallen in love with this beautiful woman twenty years ago and would do anything for her. Not since they had narrowly escaped from the Bolsheviks in Russia after the revolution had he seen her so anxious, and it upset him. When his son had announced a couple of weeks ago that he intended to go and fight for the democratic cause in the civil war in Spain and would delay joining the family bank for a year Sophie had forbidden it, Michael had objected to being forbidden and the arguments had raged at every mealtime. Things had come to a head when the young man had dashed his wine glass to the floor.

At breakfast the following morning, Sophie had slammed her knife onto her side plate, smashing it and cutting her little finger. She wasn't badly hurt, but blood had spilt onto the white tablecloth, the twins had rushed away to the drawing room and Halinka had buried her face in a cushion to hide her tears.

For the first time in his marriage, Philip didn't know what to do. He was angry at Michael because he knew that, if he forbade his son, it could create a rift between them, but if he supported him, he would upset his wife. The argument was made more painful because he felt he had always had a strong bond with his son. When Michael was very young, they had solved puzzles, played chess and bridge and regularly visited the theatre together. He had proudly watched as the boy excelled at school, rode horses, skied and danced better than his father – *Which wasn't difficult*, thought Philip.

He had explained to his son that the civil war in Spain was a foreign affair, that Michael was too young to fight and that it would be dangerous. He'd even reminded Michael of his mother's brother, who lost both an arm and a leg in the Great War fighting the Germans. If any reminder of the dangers of war were needed, Michael had only to look at the high-backed wheelchair his Uncle Sergei had used and which now stood in a corner of his mother's dressing room. Philip knew Sophie dreaded the thought of seeing Michael with only one leg and one arm, sitting in the chair like her brother.

In desperation, Philip enlisted the help of Jean-Claude Moreau – Michael's adopted uncle and Philip's oldest confidant – to try to dissuade him, but Jean-Claude's intervention had come to nought. The more they pleaded with Michael not to go to war, the greater seemed his determination to do so.

Philip knew Sophie wasn't looking forward to the dinner party that night. She was already tired, not having slept properly for the last few nights. The dinner guests were due to arrive in a few hours, and they would expect her to be the sparkling hostess.

She put down the hairbrush.

'Damn Michael for being so difficult! I think I'll try to get an hour's rest before the guests arrive. I'm beginning to get a headache.'

****

In St James's Park, Michael Tagleva was taking a walk to clear his head. He adored his parents, but he was determined to go to Spain. He was appalled at the brutality towards civilians by the Falangists led by General Franco. Supporting the Republicans fighting against him seemed only right. His parents needed to understand that he was grown up, a man now, and like them held principles and had a conscience – and besides, he craved an adventure. The bank would still be there when he returned from Spain and settled down to a lifetime of investments, stocks and bonds. It wasn't as if his parents hadn't had their own adventure. They had travelled across Russia from St Petersburg to Yalta during the Russian Revolution, escaping from the clutches of the Bolsheviks, and fled from Russia with members of the royal family, survived an assassination attempt, frustrated conspiracies and established the Bank of Tagleva. Had he not spent his childhood evenings, in pyjamas and dressing gown, sitting in front of the fire listening to their tales of grand dukes, princes and princesses, afraid of the villains they encountered, wide-eyed at the plots and the deceit of their enemies?

Is it so strange that I should want my own adventure?

He looked at the ground and kicked some dead leaves. His mother was afraid he might be killed. The prospect of death didn't worry him; he couldn't imagine death. He could only imagine how proud of him they would be, and how he would thrill his own children as they listened to his own tales before they went to bed. He slumped down on a bench and stared at the swans on the lake.

A Norland nanny passed, wheeling her charge in its perambulator. Michael was distracted for a brief moment as he looked at the fawn coat that hung to just below the calf, the woollen gloves, the felt hat with the distinctive 'N' embroidered onto the hatband. He thought how lucky she was. The girls from Norland College provided nannies for the British aristocracy and royal family and were constantly reminded that they were not lowly servants, but something more important. *How lucky she is to have a purpose in life that she can be proud of.*

Michael looked down at his shoes, mentally repeating his argument with his parents. An idea entered his head. Mr Winston Churchill would be at the dinner that night. He would ask the great man his opinion at dinner. After all, Churchill himself had gone to South Africa as a special correspondent when not much older than himself. Captured by the Boers, he had gained glory when he escaped the prison that had held him. The whole world had followed his adventure in the newspapers, and when finally he returned to England a national hero, it had propelled him into Parliament. Churchill would support him, Michael felt sure of it.

A gust of wind wrapped a page of a newspaper around Michael's legs. He pulled it free, scrunched it into a small ball, stood up and walked over to a waste bin and dropped it in. He shivered as the chill of the air hit his bones – *Compared to England*, he thought, *Spain will be warm* – and began to walk briskly back to the house.

****

Sophie looked up the table as the crayfish and lobster mousse tartlets were being served. There was Robert Worth Bingham, the American ambassador to the Court of St James; the foreign secretary Anthony Eden and his wife Clarissa; Winston Churchill and his wife Clementine; Noël Coward; some of the bank's directors; and a few friends, including Jean-Claude and Sébastien. In the centre of the table, sitting opposite Winston Churchill was Michael. Sophie smiled at her guests while trying to concentrate on the conversation, willing Michael to behave, hoping her headache would not return.

'I loved your play *Private Lives*,' said a female guest to Noël Coward.

'I'm so pleased. After writing it I knew it would be a success,' replied Coward, waving one arm as if tossing any doubt aside.

'But your plays always have such short runs. I find it difficult to find time to see them before they disappear,' said another woman.

'My dear, I so dislike long runs. They're exhausting, and, I've made it a rule of mine that, when I star in a play, it will run no longer than three months. You must arrange your calendar accordingly.'

One of the men changed the subject, loudly asking Anthony Eden his opinion on the crisis that had filled the front pages of every newspaper for the past week.

'Foreign Secretary, do you think this ghastly American, Wallis Simpson, can be allowed to marry the king? Surely he can find someone more... suitable?'

He appeared to suddenly remember the American ambassador at the far end of the table and quickly spluttered, 'My apologies, sir... That's not to mean I consider all Americans are ghastly... just this particular one, you understand.'

A couple of the diners giggled at the man's discomfort and pretended to wipe their mouths with their napkins.

The American ambassador smiled. 'No apology needed, sir. In America, any man can become president, but since we'll never have a ghastly woman as president, it would seem only natural they come to England in the hope of becoming your queen.'

Once the laughter subsided, Churchill said in his deep voice, 'Whatever you may think, it must be admitted that King Edward has conformed more strictly to the spirit of the Constitution. I suggested to the prime minister that there is one solution that would enable the country to keep the king on the throne and allow him to marry Mrs Simpson. That would be if she became Duchess of Cornwall, rather than queen.'

A few of the guests nodded their approval, and the table conversation flowed from politics to racing and the social calendar. Sophie continued to smile and make polite chit-chat. As charming as she seemed on the outside, though, she was churning inside, hearing little of the talk and dreading the time when Michael might use the opportunity to gain support for his adventure.

She didn't have to wait long before a guest addressed Anthony Eden. 'So tell me, Foreign Secretary, what's your opinion on the Spanish conflict?'

Hidden from view, Sophie wrung her hands under the table.

'On the question of the Spanish War, I'm promoting the idea of non-intervention. Despite the fact that Germany, Italy and the Soviet Union are all involved, Britain will not come to the aid of either side.'

'But isn't it important for people to fight for democracy, against the injustices of Franco's Nationalists?' enquired Michael.

Before anyone could answer, he turned to Churchill. 'You yourself, sir, went to South Africa and ended up fighting against the Boers and found glory and fame – and I intend to do the same by going to fight in Spain.'

The table went quiet and all stared at Michael.

Sophie throttled her napkin.

She glanced over at Philip, who was looking with concern at his wife from the far end of the room. The butler picked up a claret jug, and she hoped he might distract the guests by pouring some wine.

Churchill looked at Michael. 'Yes, I did, young man, but as for finding fame and glory, history, on that matter at least, has been kind to me.'

'But then, you did write it,' interrupted one of the guests.

'Quite so,' replied Churchill.

Everyone laughed.

As the laughter died, Sophie hoped Churchill would realise that he was being used to reinforce Michael's argument with his parents.

Churchill looked at Philip and then at Sophie. Then at Michael over his glasses, an expression everyone knew he employed when he needed to inject gravitas into a debate in Cabinet or the House of Commons. His voice deepened. 'However, young man, the Spanish War contrasts with the Boer War that I fought in… in that… it is of no concern to the British empire and therefore there is no reason for anyone to join in the fight.'

Michael looked, by turns, deflated, annoyed, embarrassed. It was obvious that the support he had hoped for was not forthcoming, and he remained quiet for the remainder of the meal, much to Sophie's relief.

At the end of the evening, Sophie said goodbye to her guests. Winston and Clementine Churchill were the last to leave. After thanking his host and hostess for a magnificent evening, Churchill looked at Michael.

'Are you really determined to seek fame and glory, young sir?'

'I am, sir,' replied Michael.

'Admirable in a young man, and quite right, too. And is it your wish at the same time to serve your country in this… adventure of yours?'

'Yes, sir, of course.'

'Then I would suggest that result can be achieved in a much more satisfactory manner than by becoming cannon fodder in Spain. Bring your parents down to my home at Chartwell this coming weekend. We'll talk then. I have a proposal where you can be of great service to the British Empire and to me.' He then whispered audibly in Michael's ear so that both his parents could hear: 'And give you the adventure you crave.'

Churchill gave Sophie a kiss on the cheek, shook Philip's hand in a final farewell and winked at the count and countess.

****

The following weekend, Michael and his parents travelled to Chartwell. On arrival, the young man thought the house was of no great architectural merit, but it did command a spectacular view across the Weald of Kent.

Winston's favourite aperitif of Johnnie Walker Black Label was served and afterwards, Clementine ushered Philip, Sophie and Michael into the dining room. The meal was plain: consommé followed by roast chicken and concluding with Stilton. When the dishes had been cleared away, Churchill turned to Michael. 'It's time I fed the fish their own lunch, and I was hoping that you might like to help me.'

'I'd be delighted to help you, sir,' replied Michael.

Churchill threw fish food onto the surface of the pond, the golden carp rose from the bottom to suck in their meal. Michael waited patiently until the old man began to speak.

'For years I've been watching political events in Germany with increasing concern,' he said, casting another handful of fish food onto the waters. 'I fear that the Nazi regime aims to destroy not just German democracy but also the democracy of other nations. I've been urging the government to prepare for war, but it's been deaf to my pleadings. Yet if war is declared too soon, any preparations for our defence will be too late.' Churchill watched the fish feed for a few minutes, then turned to Michael and looked him straight in the eye. 'I was hoping, young man, that you could help me to learn more of what's happening in Germany.'

'I would welcome the opportunity, sir.'

'I do not expect you to take any unnecessary risks, though I daresay the task I'm asking you to undertake wouldn't be without certain dangers. Totalitarian regimes do have an aversion to people watching them.'

****

An hour later, as Churchill and Michael walked back to the house, the latter's thoughts of the war in Spain were already a distant memory.

After his son returned to London, Philip and Michael walked into Philip's study where they remained for the next two hours. A week later an application for a visa was sent to the German embassy. The count also sent a message to a friend at the Reichsbank in Berlin asking if he could find a 'good German family' that Michael would be able to stay with. Within a couple of days, he received an invitation for Michael to visit Germany as an honoured guest, to see all that was 'best in the German Reich'.

Chapter Three
Rudolf Bauer

Ten months later: September 1937

As usual, Rudolf Bauer was up early, dressed in the most glamorous and feared uniform in Nazi Germany. The single oak leaf embroidered in silver thread on the collar denoted his rank of SS-Standartenführer, the equivalent of a Colonel in the British army. Embroidered on the left sleeve were the words 'Adolf Hitler', identifying him as a member of the elite unit that was the Führer's bodyguard.

Bauer liked the effect the uniform had when he walked into a room. The men were afraid. The women would study his blond hair, blue eyes and square jaw, the black uniform and wonder how they could smuggle him to their bedroom. When they did, he was often amused when his female conquests begged him to make aggressive love to them while wearing his jackboots and cap with the death's-head badge. He always obliged.

Bauer was a success, but it had come after too many years when triumph had eluded him. After Germany had been defeated in the Great War, his father, a minor official in local government, had lost his job, yet another casualty of the crushing armistice forced upon the country by France and Britain. The family struggled financially in the inflation and economic depression that followed. Bauer remembered his parents being forced to sell their valuables and take loans from a money lender to keep food on the table. Each week the bespectacled money lender with his long beard and outstretched hand called to collect the interest, shaming and angering the young Rudolf. Somehow his father had managed to keep him at school and his grades were good, but he had dashed his father's hopes of a career in banking when he enlisted in the German army three days after his eighteenth birthday. Within a year he was dishonourably discharged after beating up a non-commissioned officer who had reported him for being off camp without permission.

An unemployed civilian, he was without a job or the prospect of finding one. It was inevitable, then, that he was drawn to the National Socialists. The Nazi party promised employment and prosperity. And revenge on those who had betrayed Germany – namely, the republicans, Marxists, Bolsheviks and Jews.

Once the Nazi party had identified him as a hard and ferocious street fighter, Bauer was recruited into the SS and soon came to the notice of Reinhard Heydrich, Himmler's second-in-command. He was chosen to be part of the special unit that, on the 'Night of the Long Knives', had arrested and executed those who dared to dream of replacing Adolf Hitler as leader. His delight at hunting down the traitors had been matched only by the enjoyment he'd felt when carrying out some of the one hundred and seventy–seven executions that destroyed all opposition to the Nazi party. His ascent up the ranks was inevitable because he was an energetic and imaginative workaholic who understood the implicit intentions of his superiors and, more importantly, knew how to transform their visions into policy.

Soon after the Nazis had won the election that brought them to power, Heydrich appointed him to lead the SS finance unit. Its task was to exploit every avenue of finance that would benefit Germany and the Nazi party. His orders were to identify wealthy companies, institutions, foreign organisations, banks and individuals that might be useful or exploited to serve the Nazi cause. When Bauer was informed that Michael Tagleva, the son of the Bank of Tagleva's chairman, had applied for a visa to visit Germany, he sent a personal invitation, via the German ambassador, inviting Michael to be his guest. Within days, the invitation had been accepted.

Bauer settled down to read the file on the House of Tagleva sent to him from SS headquarters in Berlin.

Bank of Tagleva /Count Philip and Countess Sophie Tagleva and family

Main office:	France: Rue Pierre Charron, Paris
Country offices:	England: St Mary Axe, London EC
	United States of America: Fifth Avenue, New York
Main directors:	Count Philip Tagleva, chairman *(English?)*
	Jean-Claude Moreau , managing director *(French)*
	Countess Sophie Tagleva *(Russian)*
	Tobias Meijers, chief accountant *(Dutch* J*)*

The origins and meteoric rise in influence and wealth of the House of Tagleva and its investment house are shrouded in mystery. What is known is that the bank was registered in Paris in 1919 by the Count and Countess Tagleva.

Rumours persist that the bank's wealth is founded on a large amount of jewels and secret papers smuggled out of Russia by the Count and Countess on behalf of the Russian imperial family. If these items exist, it is assumed that they are lodged in the vaults of the Tagleva offices in Paris or London.

It should be noted that Count Philip Tagleva may not be a noble as no record can be found of his birth in Russia. It is rumoured that he is, in fact, English (name of Cummings and one-time employee at the Bank of England). The title of 'Count' seems to have been adopted by him after the death of his wife's brother.

Countess Sophie Tagleva is a member of the Russian aristocracy. She is head of the Sergei Tagleva Foundation, an extraordinarily wealthy charitable organisation dedicated to helping the underprivileged. The Foundation endows schools, hospitals and charities in France, UK and the US. The Tagleva family have large homes in both Paris and London.

Heirs
Michael Tagleva (eldest son, approx 20 years old)
Matislav Tagleva, Halinka Tagleva (twins, both children)
The family are known to speak French, English and Russian fluently. The eldest son also speaks German.
Political leanings and attitudes of the family are unknown.

Assessment
The Tagleva family is one of the wealthiest in Europe. Their political and business connections are wide ranging and include heads of government, government ministers in Europe and the US and mark them out as important and influential. Our assessment is that the Tagleva family, and its bank and foundation, could be a valuable source of influence and finance to the Reich.

Note:
The Tagleva Foundation owns a valuable art collection, much of it decadent. It includes works by Raphael, Van Dyck, Clésinger, Chagall, Matisse, Turner, Picasso, Rodin, together with rare medieval illuminated manuscripts, including one that is believed to be the only copy of a life of the life of the first Saxon king Heinrich.

Bauer took a blue pencil and circled the final paragraph, closed the file and sat back in his chair. He smelt the aroma of fresh coffee wafting from the dining room. Carefully locking the file in the safe, he placed the key in his jacket pocket and walked to the dining room. There he found his wife and Michael Tagleva being served breakfast by the maid.

'Looking forward to the day after tomorrow?' he said to Michael as he entered the room.

'I am, sir. It will be the proudest day of my life!' came the excited reply.

Chapter Four
Rue Pierre Charron

The same day

In Paris, the government district around the Champs-Élysées and the financial district along the Avenue George V is connected by the Rue Pierre Charron. Midway along the length of this street is a building with highly polished double wooden doors. Behind them is the headquarters of one of the most successful private banks in Europe.

Established in 1919, the Tagleva bank has five floors where 103 staff manage the usual activities of international financing, corporate investment, real estate, trade finance, issuing letters of credit, international fund transfers, trade consulting and co-investment in projects of one form or another.

On entering the bank, a liveried doorman will raise his top hat and bid the visitor *'Bonjour!'* and it is not unknown for visitors to mistakenly walk into the bank believing they were entering a smart hotel. Once inside a dark-suited man will politely invite genuine customers to sit on one of the silk-covered chairs until the time comes for them to be escorted to the lift and be transported to the appropriate floor for their appointment.

Customers who wish to access their safe deposit boxes, will find themselves taken to the basement, where the protection of their most important valuables is guaranteed by the presence of armed guards twenty-four hours a day. The safe deposit boxes are located on either side of the bank's twenty-four-bolt Diebold vault. The sight of the large polished steel door, proudly displaying the bank's crest is designed to instil confidence that their treasures are in good hands. The vault also stores a fabulous collection of jewellery brought out of Russia by Philip Tagleva, which awaits a survivor of the Russian imperial family to claim it. In addition, it protects some of the world's most precious art treasures, bought by the Tagleva Foundation and stored in their own individual boxes. These items include a nineteenth-century German cup made out of rock crystal and gold and enamelled by Reinhold Vasters, an emerald and diamond tiara, a gift from Napoleon Bonaparte to his second wife, and a prayer book once owned by Catherine de' Medici.

Leaving the vaults and riding the lift to the first floor, customers will find the various administration departments that enable the bank to function.

On the second and third floors, visitors will find the two main lines of banking, referred to as the 'buy side' and the 'sell side'. The buy side offers advice to individuals, institutions and governments wanting personal investment services and help in acquiring companies or property. The 'sell side' trades securities on behalf of clients. The second and third floors are supervised by Tagleva's chief accountant, Tobias Meijers.

The chairman and the other directors have their offices on the fourth floor. Each office is oak panelled and furnished with an antique two-pedestal desk, a meeting table surrounded with silk-covered salon chairs, a thick Persian carpet, a gilt mirror above the fireplace, and various works of art on loan from the Tagleva Foundation collection.

The fourth floor is also where the Foundation is managed by Countess Sophie Tagleva. Not strictly part of the bank, it is a charity that receives 5 per cent of the bank's profits. Over the past twelve years the Foundation has financed the building of schools and hospitals, and supported impoverished coal miners in South Wales, needy families in the north of England, farmers suffering in the American Midwest that, through drought, had become an enormous dust bowl, and hundreds of wounded soldiers from the Great War.

The fifth floor holds a vast card index system. Supervised by Katherine du Bois, it provides the bank and its directors with up-to-date information that might influence the bank's investment policies.

****

Jean-Claude Moreau, the managing director, is sat at his large mahogany desk. He looked at the French ormolu mantel clock fashioned by the Paris clockmaker Balthazar Martinot. The hands showed the time to be one minute to ten. Whenever the Chairman was in Paris they met on a Thursday morning to talk about business and Jean-Claude knew that Count Philip Tagleva would be on time; he always was. Walking over to the side table, he began to pour two cups of coffee from the pot that his secretary had delivered a few minutes before. He smelled the coffee's aroma, heard the clock begin to strike, and before the soft chimes had subsided, the oak door opened and Philip Tagleva walked in.

'Good morning,' said Jean-Claude without looking up from pouring the coffee.

'It is,' replied Philip, 'but I must warn you, my friend, that my wife's given me strict instructions not to spend too long talking with you. I'm informed we're meeting friends to show them around the International Art and Technology Exposition and then to see the new painting by Picasso she's bought. It's being unveiled to the press this evening.'

'Sophie's keeping you well occupied,' joked Jean-Claude.

'Life with my wife is one round of parties and social engagements. It's why I look forward to our Thursday meetings, the single morning of sanity in the week.'

Jean-Claude smiled. He knew his friend was joking. He and Sophie had been inseparable ever since they had met in St Petersburg during the Russian Revolution, twenty years earlier.

'Have you been to the Exposition? It's certainly bringing in the crowds,' enquired Philip.

'Sébastien and I went last week. He liked the Canadian pavilion with the twenty-eight-foot sculpture of a buffalo, and I loved the Spanish pavilion. The worst pavilion is the British – it's just a large white box.'

Philip laughed. Jean-Claude expected him to jump to Britain's defence, a reflex he adopted whenever his homeland was criticised. 'On this one occasion, I'll disappoint you, my friend. I must agree. I thought it bizarre to see that the major exhibit was a giant photograph of Prime Minister Neville Chamberlain fishing. In comparison with some of the other pavilions, it's... positively peaceful and boring.'

'You must mean the German pavilion,' smiled Jean-Claude.

Philip nodded. 'That pavilion certainly makes a statement. I'm told it's meant to show off German national pride and achievement, though I thought its tall chimney-like tower, topped by the eagle and swastika, makes the structure cold and forbidding.'

'I don't like the two nude males, clasping hands and standing defiantly either side of the front doors,' laughed Jean-Claude.

'I would have thought those strong Teutonic male statues would have made that pavilion a favourite part of the entire Exposition for you, maybe reminding you of Sébastien?'

Jean-Claude smiled at Philip's reference to his lover of the last five years. 'Sébastien's a handsome man indeed, but his features are softer and kinder than those of the Germanic statues, which display no emotion at all. No, I think I prefer the statue atop the Soviet's pavilion of the male worker and female peasant with their hands joined, thrusting a hammer and a sickle into the air. It's a far more wholesome vision for a red-blooded Frenchman.'

Philip smiled broadly at his friend: 'I'm properly admonished. I shouldn't tease you.' And he sat down in one of the silk-covered chairs.

Jean-Claude had taken no offence. Over the years, he had grown to enjoy the gentle teasing from his mentor, the man he trusted and respected most in the world, the person who knew his innermost secrets and who'd asked him to be godfather to his eldest child. In any event, Jean-Claude was more than able to tease Philip back, when the opportunity allowed.

'So, what's news at the bank?' asked Philip.

'Wealthy Germans continue to transfer funds to us for the same reason that we discussed at our last meeting.'

'You're referring to the Nazis closing all businesses with a capital below $40,000 and making it almost impossible to invest in one's own expertise.'

'Exactly,' said Jean-Claude. 'It's had the effect of making the small business owner an extinct species in Germany. Everyone is forced to work for large organisations.'

'Makes it easier for the Nazis to control the economy,' said Philip.

'However, there's been a new development. In recent months, those who *have* managed to open a business are now being asked to make "special contributions" to Nazi party funds.'

'Demanding those is nothing less than a protection racket, so it's not surprising business owners want to protect their money by moving it somewhere,' said Philip. 'How much money has been deposited with us?'

'Nearly two million dollars this past month, mostly in gold bullion.'

'Good grief, that much?'

'Two incidents occurred here at the bank last week. The first was a German depositing a few thousand francs in various denominations, including a number of forged British five- and twenty-pound notes. They weren't good forgeries, certainly not good enough to get past the cashier. But what was interesting was that the businessman said he'd been given them by the German government in payment for goods,' Jean-Claude continued. 'The second happened a few days ago. Another businessman arrived from Munich and asked if he could hire a safe deposit box to store the tool box of spanners from his car. They were covered in oil and grease and the clerks weren't sure what to do, but the man insisted, and I was called from my office to speak with him.'

'What did you do?' asked Philip.

'It turned out the toolbox was made of platinum, and the tools were solid gold and covered in silver. I authorised the safe deposit box.'

Philip laughed. 'I'm uneasy about having such vast amounts of gold, silver and platinum in the bank. Germany's restricting imports, controlling prices and company dividends and building factories to make steel, produce synthetic gasoline and rubber. It seems to me that Germany is building up its financial reserves in preparing for the isolation of its economy. It means just one thing—'

'That Germany's preparing for war,' interrupted Jean-Claude.

'Exactly. Half of Europe's politicians are of the same opinion. The other half have their heads firmly buried in the sand. In the circumstances, I think it isn't sensible to have too much gold in Paris. Not that I expect Germany to win a war, but having our client's gold deposits in a more stable place might be prudent.'

'Then I'll move as much gold as I can to London and New York.'

Philip nodded his agreement.

****

An hour later, their meeting was finally over. Jean-Claude picked up the files from his desk and, following Philip into the outer office, found his secretary, Nicole Labranche, typing a letter. Handing her the papers for filing, Jean-Claude turned to Philip.

'By the way, how's Michael enjoying Germany?'

'Too much, I suspect. My son's letters home are full of praise for the achievements of the Nazis, what they have done, how well they run the country and how much the rest of the world could learn from Adolf Hitler.'

'He's an intelligent boy,' said Jean-Claude.

'That he is.' Together they walked down the corridor towards Philip's office to meet Sophie.

Sophie was in a royal blue silk dress with a white rose pinned on it with a diamond clasp just below her right shoulder. Jean-Claude walked over, kissed her on both cheeks, stepped back, and extended both hands, 'Sophie, you're a vision of beauty, lovelier every time I see you.'

'The two best cities in the world are London and Paris and I love having a house in both,' said Sophie with a broad smile, 'London has the theatres and excitement, but in Paris, a woman is told how beautiful they are by every Frenchman they meet, even when they don't mean it,' and she playfully flicked Jean-Claude's chest with her gloves.

'Are you accusing me of insincere flattery?' he protested.

'Jean-Claude, I've known you for eighteen years, and you've always been a flatterer. But don't let me stop you – you're a master at it.' Sophie blew him a kiss as she walked over to a chair and sat down.

'Will you two stop flirting! We've business to talk about,' Philip interrupted.

'You see, Jean-Claude, talking business is my English husband's idea of unbridled passion,' and she gave her husband a wink.

They all laughed and the two men settled down in the silk-covered armchairs.

Sophie began: 'Now, to be serious, I want to talk to you both about the Tagleva Foundation. As you both know, the Foundation's been working to help people in Germany – particularly Jews deprived of their citizenship. But things are getting worse. New laws forbid them from working in the civil service and in farming, teaching, the law, medicine and banking, too. I'm told that many shops have notices above the doors stating "Jews not served". Mothers are prevented from buying milk for their children and pharmacies won't sell them drugs or medicines. Yesterday I was told that signs are being erected outside German villages saying, "Jews enter this place at their own risk," and in Ludwigshafen there's a sign that reads, "Sharp curve. Drive carefully. Jews 120 kilometres an hour"… It's horrible.'

Sophie continued: 'It's the children I feel especially sorry for and I've been talking with a few friends of mine in London and Paris. We want to extend our help to Jewish families who want to leave Germany to live in France, Britain and, possibly, America.'

'How can I help?' said Jean-Claude.

'To make the arrangements, the Foundation will need additional funds,' said Sophie.

'I'll arrange to release funds to the Foundation's account. Would 25,000 francs be enough for you?'

'That would be wonderful,' said Sophie.

'I'll arrange it today. Now you two go off to the Exposition Internationale and enjoy yourselves.'

They all stood up, and Sophie kissed Jean-Claude on both cheeks. 'Give my love to Sébastien,' she said.

Chapter Five
No. 9 Carlton House Terrace

The same day

Carlton House Terrace is a street in the district of Westminster in London. Its principal architectural feature is two rows of white stucco-faced houses with imposing Corinthian-columned façades on the side of the buildings that overlook St James's Park. No. 9 Carlton House Terrace is the location of the German embassy.

On his appointment as ambassador to Britain in 1936, Joachim von Ribbentrop felt the existing embassy was insufficiently grand and insisted that the interior be modernised to reflect Germany's new importance, and so that he could host extravagant parties to celebrate the coronation of George VI. One hundred and forty-five German craftsmen toiled night and day to complete the work. A magnificent staircase was constructed, and on the first floor, interior walls were demolished to create a ballroom and one reception room had a vast swastika made up of mosaic tiles laid into the floor.

****

Most embassies have intelligence officers attached to them for the purpose of spying on the host nation. The resident spy at the German embassy is the commercial attaché and he has a meeting with a contact that, for obvious reasons, doesn't want to have in the embassy. Leaving the building – and making sure he was not being followed – he walked over the road to St James's Park.

Christopher Hatton was waiting for him on one of the park benches. Hatton was there to collect his monthly expenses, made up of crisp new five-pound notes, and to deliver some information in return.

The file at the embassy told the German that Hatton had been an easy recruit for the Nazis. He had had a miserable childhood and blamed his misery and lacklustre career on his parents and others he felt had held him back. Hatton's family lived in a two-roomed cottage in the Nettlebridge valley in Somerset. His father was a saddle-maker, devout Christian and member of the Plymouth Brethren, but also a bully – and with six children to be fed, the family lived in poverty. When it was time to pay for the education of Christopher, the youngest child, Hatton's father considered it an unnecessary expense. Despite this, or possibly because of it, Christopher felt an irresistible attraction to books and the knowledge they contained. He taught himself to read, but with no money to buy books, he was forced to steal them from the local bookshops.

At the age of fourteen, his father found Christopher a job at the local colliery. The first time he walked into the cage that lowered him into the dark abyss 1,200 feet below ground, he threw up. For "aving no backbone,' he was nicknamed Jellyfish by the other miners. He suffered the name-calling in silence, remembering the source of each slander and swearing that a time would come when he would repay every jibe.

If he was miserable and lonely at work, his social life was no better. He had no close friends and the girls in the area teased him about his weight and acne. Each rejection was another insult to be repaid. The loneliness built into a frustration he found difficult to control, and two years after starting work at the colliery, he was caught exposing himself to a nine-year-old girl. The Plymouth Brethren put him 'under discipline' for sexual immorality. He left Somerset and moved to the anonymity of Wales where he found work at the South Wales Miners Federation, known to everyone as 'The Fed'.

Considering his impoverished upbringing, it was perhaps inevitable he found himself attracted to the ideology of Nazism. For Hatton, National Socialism represented much more than a political movement. It provided a vehicle for his hatred and his ambition. He rejected the view, held by those with no vision, that Nazi ideas comprised a grotesque hodge-podge of half-baked ideals. He admired Hitler for changing the cultural landscape of Germany, restoring its traditional values, ensuring that talent ruled over privilege. He saw no contradiction that Nazi ideals were, at the same time, modern and anti-modern, dynamic and utopian, that they harked back to an idyllic and romanticised past. He dreamed of the day he could bring Nazism to Britain.

Using the pseudonym of C Carson, he sent articles to the fascist periodicals *The Blackshirt* and *The Fascist Quarterly*, and was delighted when they were published. Within months 'C Carson' came to the attention of someone in Berlin, and he was approached by a contact at the German embassy. The embassy arranged for him to leave The Fed in South Wales and, using their own secret contacts, secured him a job as a researcher at the House of Commons and also paid for his membership to the Anglo-German Fellowship, under the name of C Carson.

Reaching Hatton in the park, the commercial attaché sat next to him. 'Sorry to have kept you waiting,' said the German. 'Have you managed to get any information regarding the plans for improvements to the British army?'

'Seems like there's proper resistance in Foreign Office and the Treasury to rearming the army. Foreign Office's opinion is that rearmament would cause pointless complications in its negotiations with Germany, and Treasury believes it's unaffordable.'

'Very good,' said the attaché.

'In addition, I've persuaded some important people in the Anglo-German Fellowship who also sit in Parliament to support keeping things as is.'

'Are you sure they will do that?'

'They are frightened of Communism. By supporting co-operation with Germany they hope to avoid it. To the British aristocracy, Communism means confiscation of their estates, loss of their titles and their privileges. I have another meeting with them tonight.'

'Very good. It's important that England does nothing to oppose Germany's ambitions... One more thing: I must get a message to someone who works at the Bank of England. I have no reason to visit the bank myself, even as a commercial atta-ché, but you can arrange for delivery of the message.'

The attaché handed Hatton a brown envelope, inside was his money and the message for the man at the Bank of England. The meeting over, Hatton pocketed the envelope and left the park, walking through Horse Guards Parade towards the Houses of Parliament.

Hertfordshire, England: that night

Brocket Hall is the home of Arthur Ronald Nall Nall-Cain, the second Baron Brocket. As in many of the great houses in Britain, the décor is built for show and Brocket Hall is no exception. The marble chimney pieces, designed by Robert Adam, are adorned with mirrors by Thomas Chippendale, the ceilings covered with geometrical patterns in baby pinks and blues and turquoise. If the interior is exotic it's the bedrooms that have caused the scandals. One of the earliest residents was the first Lord Melbourne whose wife was the Prince Regent's mistress. In the early days of their affair, Lady Melbourne was inconvenienced by having to reach her lover's room via her husband's bedroom. To rectify the situation, she had a door-way constructed onto the landing from her own chamber, thus giving her easier access to the Prince languishing in his suite nearby.

The second Lord Melbourne's wife scandalised society by introducing England to the waltz in the Brocket Hall ballroom. A further scandal was created when Lord Palmerston, twice prime minister, expired suddenly of a heart attack, aged eighty-one, on Brocket Hall's billiard table while explaining the more subtle rules of the game to a chambermaid.

In the drawing room Lord Brocket's butler was serving brandies to his guests, all members of the Anglo-German Fellowship. The start of their meeting had been delayed by the late arrival of one of the members. His lateness irritated the guests, whose time was too precious to be wasted. The door opened and Christopher Hatton's porcine frame entered the room.

'Evening,' he said.

The others looked with disdain at Hatton's round bespectacled red face, thinning hair and gold chain adorning the waistcoat stretched over his stomach. He was late because, after he left St James's Park, he'd seen to some of his duties as a trustee at an orphanage in Poplar. Afterwards, he had given some 'personal tuition' to a pretty young orphan girl, a practice he carried out regularly. Dot – he assumed the name was short for Dorothy – was a pretty young thing, dressed in her cream-coloured dress with blue ribbons decorating the bodice and hem, and skin that was like silk to the touch. The hour he'd spent with her had been more than satisfactory, and on leaving, he informed the nurse that he'd be back the same time the following week and would like to see Dot again.

Without any apology for delaying the meeting, he squeezed himself into the vacant salon chair, which audibly complained at the weight it was now being asked to accommodate. The butler finished pouring the last brandy and left the room, closing the door silently behind him. Christopher looked around the table at the other members of the fellowship. There was Frank Cyril Tiarks, a director of the Bank of England; George Geoffrey Dawson, the editor of *The Times*; Archibald Ramsay MP; and the 8th Duke of Buccleuch, a member of the king's household.

He looked at each in turn. With no power or title of his own he knew they looked down on him. It was them, and their kind, that had held him back all his life. Had things been different and he had been awarded the scholarship to the Central Labour College he deserved, it would have propelled him into the upper reaches of the Labour party, perhaps becoming a parliamentary candidate. They would then be looking on him as an equal. Instead the scholarship had been given to a boy named Aneurin Bevan.

For years, Hatton had hoped that, one day, he might be selected as a candidate for Parliament, but quickly discovered that people within the Labour party laughed at his ambition. He struggled to understand it. Perhaps it was because he was fat, or didn't speak posh. Or was it because those in charge of the Labour movement were Jews? He didn't know, and because he didn't know, he burned with hatred for, collectively, those who ran the Labour party, the ruling classes, the wealthy mine owners, the Jews, the bankers, the aristocracy. He loathed them all, but the day he dreamed of was fast approaching. He might have no title, be low-born, they may not know his real name, believing him to be C Carson, but he knew he was now more important to the *Realpolitik* of the situation than all of them.

'*Now* we are all here we should get started – there's a lot to discuss,' began Lord Brocket.

****

The following morning Michael glanced up from his breakfast at the clock on the wall. It wasn't even nine o'clock yet. He sighed. The house was quieter than a crypt. The Standartenführer was at a meeting in Nuremberg and his wife had left the house early to go shopping and wouldn't return for hours if past experience was to be relied on. The only other person in the house was Kurt, the house steward, who now walked into the room to clear away the breakfast things. He looked at Michael as if he'd smelt something unpleasant. Michael decided he didn't want to have Kurt as company and left the house to walk in the garden.

He felt the cool breeze on his face as he walked between the apple trees in the orchard. He reflected on the things that Bauer had shown him and what he'd tell Mr Churchill on his return. He would tell him of the new roads, the fine buildings and the happiness of the people and what the German people thought of Hitler. It amounted almost to worship. He remembered the men he'd met who had told him that they did not know what the country would have done without the Führer. There had been some criticism and some people were inclined to blame his supporters for things they did not approve of, but there had been no whisper of criticism of Hitler himself. *It's just like our own motto: 'The king can do no wrong,'* he thought.

****

At the far end of the orchard was a line of fir trees that was the boundary between the house and the fields beyond. Michael noticed some movement among the trees and walked over to investigate. A blackbird was caught by its leg in a piece of wire fencing and hanging upside down. As Michael approached, the bird began to flap its wings in panic. Speaking softly he took the bird into his hand and began to free the tiny leg from the wire. Somehow the blackbird sensed it was being rescued and ceased struggling. Michael felt the bird relax in his hands.

After two minutes the bird's leg was free, though bleeding. Michael placed the bird on the ground and walked away. The bird seemed to wait to get its bearings and after a few seconds flapped its wings and rose into the sky. Michael watched it circle above his head a couple of times as if giving some sort of thanks for its rescue and freedom. Once the bird had disappeared, Michael turned to walk back to the house but noticed a wooden building nestling behind the fir trees. Strange that he'd not seen it before. It seemed to have been purposely hidden from view. It was too large for a garden hut. Intrigued, Michael decided to investigate. There were no windows in the structure. At the far end, he found a door and pulled on the handle. It was not locked. Michael walked inside. Except for some benches around the side and a small desk in one corner, there was only one piece of furniture in the centre of the hut.

Almost three feet in height, it was made entirely of wood. The top had eight slats and one end was around six inches higher than the other. At the end nearer the floor was a plank with two holes cut into it. Michael approached it and looked at it more closely. He ran his fingers up the two-and-a-half feet of its length. To one side of the contraption was a leather belt. On the other side a buckle obviously designed to hold something down. Suddenly its purpose became clear and the horror of it paralysed him. He couldn't believe it, didn't want to. Even in his worst nightmares he'd never seen anything like it. But its purpose was clear.

The holes in the plank were designed to hold someone's feet so a person, stripped naked and bent over the bench, could be tied down with the leather belt. In such a positon they would be unable to struggle. Michael looked at the wall. There hung a variety of whips, canes and paddles – some leather, some wooden and even one made of metal. His gaze was drawn to the ceiling to hooks and metal bars. He imagined victims being suspended from their wrists as they were interrogated. The visions of what happened in this place accelerated inside his head. He wanted them to slow down so he could breathe, but they didn't. In the silence he could hear the screams, the eyes wide with terror, the mouth rigid, the teeth grinding together, the fists clenched with blanched knuckles and the nails digging deeply into the palms. Michael's breaths come in gasps; he felt giddy. His heart hammered inside his chest, the room spun, he felt sick. He ran back to the house, sweating and trying to control his breathing. As he ran up the garden he didn't notice Kurt watching him from Bauer's office.

Chapter Six
Wewelsburg Castle

Nuremberg, two days later

That night Michael did not sleep well. What he'd seen in the hut at the bottom of the orchard returned to him in his dreams and haunted him. He thought of all the impressive things he'd been shown by his German host, Munich, Berlin, the fun he'd had drinking steins of beer and flirting with the girls in Nuremberg, the inspiring rally at Zeppelin Field. Each of these memories was now invaded by what he'd seen at the bottom of the garden.

He rose early and, to drive away the tiredness, had a cold shower. Afterwards he stood looking at his reflection in the mirror. His nakedness stared back at him. Looking at it he knew any German would assume he was a perfect example of the Aryan race. His thoughts went back to the Nuremberg rally where he had witnessed Germany's new religion. A religion with a creed that dictated how its followers must think, feel and act. Where black- and brown-uniformed priests controlled every aspect of life – art, entertainment, leisure, sport – and destroyed anything the religion disapproved of. Today he was to be admitted into the new religion, today would be his baptism when he would become an apostle of the priesthood and he would be one of them.

Michael dressed and went downstairs to find Bauer in the hallway in his black uniform. On the bottom step, Michael stood to attention, raised his right arm.

'Good morning, Standartenführer. *Heil Hitler!*'

His host returned the salute. 'Good morning, Michael. Did you sleep well?'

'I did, thank you.'

'This is a very special day for you. Are you ready for it?'
'I am, sir.'

****

One hour later Michael and Bauer were at Nuremberg airport boarding a Junkers Ju 52/3m, a three-propeller snub-nosed transport plane, for the short flight to Paderborn airport. As the plane approached its destination, Michael looked out the small window at the rivers, grassland, forests and lakes that lay between the Eifel hills and the Teutoburg Forest.

Michael's first view of Wewelsburg Castle, with its distinctive round towers and massive defensive walls forming a triangle, was from the aircraft just before it came in to land. As soon as they landed, a black Mercedes sedan came along side to carry them the ten-minute drive to the castle. After climbing the steep hill, it sped through the entrance and into the courtyard where a small group of SS officers had gathered to greet them.

Alighting from the car, the usual salutes were made. Rudolf Bauer told Michael that he was to attend an important meeting. 'Lieutenant Schneider will look after you and give you a tour of the building.'

The lieutenant stepped forward, shook Michael's hand, and the tour began.

'To understand the castle, one must understand Reichsführer Himmler's vision. That is that each new world order cannot thrive without the destruction of the old. Therefore destruction is as healthy, as is the restructure that follows. The SS has taken all that is Aryan and good from the old ancient order and fashioned it into the new.'

The lieutenant walked into the castle. Michael followed.

'To reflect the old order, our study rooms are named after King Arthur, Henry the Lion, Christopher Columbus, Aryan, Teutonic Order and so on. Appropriate names, you're sure to agree.'

Michael nodded his head in agreement.

'One day, very soon, this castle will hold the ancient records of the German race, plus the Holy Grail and the Spear of Destiny, and once all these ancient treasures are at Wewelsburg it will truly be the centre of the world. From this castle, the magic that is the power of Nazism will radiate out.'

Michael followed Schneider as he climbed the spiral staircase.

'You are now entering the most important room in the castle, the Obergruppenführers Hall, where ceremonies and meetings of the leadership are held.'

As Michael's eyes slowly adjusted to the gloom, he could make out twelve columns and, between them, twelve windows that let in no light. Around the ceiling was written: 'Great questions will not be resolved by talk, but by iron and blood.'

Schneider pointed towards the centre of the white marble floor, to a dark green sun wheel where a small eternal flame bathed the room in a golden glow. 'The axis of the sun wheel consists of a circular plate of pure gold,' said Schneider. 'It's the centre of the castle and thus the centre of the entire Germanic world empire. You are to stand behind the flame. This is where you will take your oath.'

Michael did as he was instructed and his guide left the room.

There was no sound, but Michael had a sensation of being watched. He remained at attention for what seemed like an age.

From hidden niches around the walls appeared twelve members of the SS, each representing one knight of the ancient Round Table. Over their uniforms, they wore black cloaks lined in white that reached from their shoulders to the floor. Each held a sword in his left hand. One of the knights placed a cloak over Michael's shoulders and attached the clasp, fashioned in the shape of a wolf's head, to hold it in place. The group encircled Michael and raised their swords so that the points met above his head. He was handed a jewelled chalice of wine and told to drink. When the chalice was empty, Michael felt light headed.

The room began to fade into darkness, the black uniforms disappearing into the gloom. He started feeling warm, the kind of warmth that you experience when you're cold and someone gives you the most comfortable blanket you've ever felt. All at once a thin shaft of golden light from the domed ceiling pierced the gloom. In defiance of gravity, Michael felt as if he were being taken up into the shaft of light, and he watched as silver thunderbolts, oak leaves, death's-head images and a dozen pairs of eyes danced around him.

Michael heard a deep voice that echoed time and again: 'Your sacred oath is...?'

After hearing the question put to him a dozen times, Michael answered each of the knights with one sentence, 'I vow to you, Adolf Hitler, as Führer and chancellor of the German Reich, to give unquestioned obedience and loyalty to the leader closest to my heart. So help me God.'

'This is your sacred oath?'

'It is... upon my life!' shouted Michael.

The light faded, the swords were lowered and Michael could see clearly once more. As he recovered his senses, he was surprised to find himself now with the eternal flame behind him.

Rudolf Bauer stepped forward and shook his hand.

'Michael. Now that you have given your oath it gives me great pleasure to present to you an honorary membership card of the German National Socialist Workers Party. It's awarded to few foreigners, so you are very privileged. In addition, for the future services you will give the Reich, I'm authorised by Reichsführer Himmler to present you with this dagger.'

Michael took the weapon. Imbedded in the ebony at the top of the grip was a distinctive symbol: an eagle holding a wreath that contained a swastika. He pulled the blade from its scabbard to reveal the inscription: *Meine Ehre Heist Treue*, 'My Honour is Loyalty'.

'It's also my pleasure to present you with this very special gift.' Bauer handed Michael a black leather-bound book. 'Open it,' he said softly.

Opening the cover Michael read the title *Mein Kampf* and, below it in black ink, the signature 'Adolf Hitler'.

'What can I say?' said Michael. 'These gifts will always remind me of this day and my sworn duty.' He raised his right hand. '*Heil Hitler!*'

'*Heil Hitler!*' responded the twelve knights in unison.

The assembled party were delighted with the ceremony and all shook hands. Michael was ushered from the chamber, and once they were alone in the corridor, Bauer smiled and said, 'Your oath has been made and we will now discuss how you can serve the Reich. I am sending you to Berlin where you will be trained so that you can fulfil your sacred oath. Go to the courtyard and wait for me in the car.' Michael walked down the stairs.

Once Michael was out of earshot, Bauer was approached by one of the knights. 'Can we trust him to do what we plan?'

Bauer looked at his superior officer. 'We'll know soon enough. He begins his training in the next few days. His instructors will keep us informed.'

'Remember he *is* half Russian.'

'I haven't forgotten.'

Chapter Seven
Tirpitzufer, Berlin

One week later

The Treaty of Versailles that was imposed on Germany after the Great War prohibited the establishment of a German intelligence organisation. Despite this, the number of people attached to the Abwehr, the Nazi's military intelligence unit, had increased from less than two hundred to nearly a thousand. The section responsible for recruiting and training those prepared to spy on Germany's potential enemies – France, Great Britain and the Soviet Union – was located at the Abwehr's Berlin headquarters at 76/78 Tirpitzufer.

****

Michael's day started at six, and over the following weeks, he learned the basics of espionage – how to recruit sources to give up their secrets, how to lie and how to spot when someone else was lying. He practised the techniques of concealing a message in a newspaper, an overcoat and other everyday items. He learned to pass information to another agent in a public place, such as a café or railway station, and make it seem like a natural encounter. There followed intensive instruction in using a miniature camera to take photos of documents and lessons on sending a coded message using a popular book.

'Your message is created by using groups of three figures, such as 24 18 5,' said his instructor. 'Together, the three numbers refer to a specific word in a particular book. For example, '24' means that you open the book to page 24, then count from the top to line 18 and the fifth word in that line is the first word of the message. As you continue to find word after word, a whole sentence can be strung together. Both parties, the sender and the receiver, must use the same book and the same edition to ensure the code uses the same words.'

Finally, Michael was shown how to use a radio transmitter.

'We thought very carefully about your code name and chose, "FAOLAN". Start every message with it. Can you remember that?' his instructor asked.

'Of course, but what does it mean?' asked Michael.

'*Faolan* is Irish Gaelic. It means "little wolf". If MI5 happen to listen to your message, they are likely to assume that you are Irish and probably a member of the IRA. Clever is it not?'

Once Michael's training was complete, the Abwehr sent Bauer a detailed report.

He read that Michael had been considered a highly satisfactory student: a fast learner with an intelligent mind who expressed great enthusiasm for everything Nazism wanted to achieve and, importantly, according to his instructors' assessment, he would be willing to take risks.

After reading the report, Bauer telephoned his superior. 'Everything is proceeding according to plan,' he said.

Once he replaced the telephone into its cradle, Bauer sat at his desk, looked out of the window and rubbed his chin gently. He hadn't shared his unease with his superior.

Chapter Eight
Helmut

November 1937

Rue Le Tasse is a quiet private street in a very nice neighbourhood of Paris. Confirmed by a sign with white lettering on a blue background attached to one corner of a building: '*Les chiens ne faire pas leurs ordures* – an instruction that clearly but politely informs all dogs that they are prohibited from 'doing their business' on the street.

To find Jean-Claude's apartment, one enters through the wrought-iron and glass front door into a white marble-clad lobby with a high gothic-like ceiling. Then you take the lift – only large enough to accommodate two people – to the fifth floor. Once inside the spacious and comfortable apartment, most visitors can't resist spending some time admiring the view from the sitting room that overlooks the Jardins du Trocadéro with their dramatic fountains and, beyond them, the Eiffel Tower.

Jean-Claude watched Sébastien pass cups of coffee and plates laden with *mille-feuille* and *Saint-Honoré* pastries to their guests. He never tired of looking at his handsome lover, the dark brown hair that fell over his forehead, the hazel eyes, and the slightly tanned skin. They had met when Sébastien had interviewed Jean-Claude for his weekly column in the magazine *L'Illustration*. A month later Sébastien moved into the apartment.

Their two friends, Alain and Luc, took a pastry each. They, too, were lovers, both from the German-speaking part of Alsace-Lorraine, and had met while studying at Heidelberg University. There they had rented a spare room in a house owned by a philosophy student called Oscar. Alain and Luc were discreet about their relationship, managing to keep it a secret from their classmates. Oscar, on the other hand, had been unable to hide his homosexuality. Life started to become difficult for him when the leader of the German Students' Association, an ardent Nazi, took a dislike to him. Whenever he arrived in class, the Nazi would loudly refer to Oscar as *e Tunte*, 'the fairy', or *Schwuchtel*, 'queen'.

After a few months of verbal abuse from his persecutor, Alain and Luc noticed that Oscar rarely left the house and then only to attend lectures. His loneliness seemed to eat him alive, feasting on any youthful hope and happiness he had once had. On more than one occasion, Alain and Luc had heard Oscar sobbing in his room. They tried to help, give advice on coping with the bully's abuse, but nothing seemed to make things better.

One evening, as Alain and Luc walked into University Square, they found their classmates and friends, encouraged by a group of Hitler Youth, singing incantations and hurling 'un-German' books into a huge bonfire. They were mesmerised by the frenzied scene as the works of Victor Hugo, Ernest Hemingway, Helen Keller, D H Lawrence, H G Wells, Aldous Huxley, Fyodor Dostoyevsky, Leo Tolstoy, Albert Einstein, Friedrich Engels, Sigmund Freud, Franz Kafka, Heinrich Mann, Karl Marx and Stefan Zweig were looted from the university library and classrooms and consigned to the flames.

Shocked, not understanding the scenes they were witnessing and not wanting to be any part of book burning, they hurried back to their accommodation, past a group of brown shirted storm troopers shouting obscenities near Oscar's house.

The cries from the street were so loud they could still be heard behind the closed front door. They found Oscar in the kitchen. Hanging at the end of a rope attached to a meat hook. In disbelief they stared at their friend. They read the note on the table – how he was a cancer within society, how he couldn't cope any more, how he had finally chosen to flee from the condemnation of society and his classmates. The final line begged the Church and his parents' forgiveness for the sin of taking his own life.

Once they had recovered some of their composure they discussed what to do next. Deciding that they may have failed to protect him in life, in death they were determined to make some sort of amends by giving Oscar as much dignity as they could. Alain collected a carving knife from the drawer, and together they cut him down and laid him carefully on the kitchen table. They washed his face, combed his hair, dressed him in his best clothes and placed a pillow under his head. Collecting a rosary and a Bible from his bedroom, they wrapped the rosary around his hands and laid the Bible on his chest. Finally they placed candles at each corner of the table.

Looking at the scene, Luc asked, 'What should we do now?'

Alain had always been agnostic, but if there was a God then surely he would be waiting for Oscar and Alain wanted to ask God to care for him. 'I think we should say a few prayers,' he said.

Luc collected the prayer book from Oscar's bedside table and Alain read some prayers for the dead. At the end of the final prayer, Luc's cheeks were moist with tears. 'I wish we'd done more. We should have done more, been braver, saved our friend,' he said.

Hearing the baying crowd outside in the street, 'What could we have done against those beasts?'

Luc muttered, 'They'll come for us, too, if they can.'

'No, they won't, we won't let them. One day we'll be able to grieve for Oscar properly, but first we must look after ourselves. Oscar would want that,' replied Alain.

That night they each packed a small suitcase and, abandoning most of their possessions, left Germany by the night train.

****

The only other person in Jean-Claude's sitting room was Helmut Becker, who'd been smuggled across the German border the previous night in a false compartment that Alain had built under the back seat of his car.

Sébastien passed him a cup of coffee and the plate of pastries with a reassuring smile.

47

'*Danke*,' said Helmut almost inaudibly, picking up one of the pastries as if he'd been ordered to do so.

Once they were all settled, Jean-Claude spoke: 'I think we should begin by asking Helmut if he could tell us his story.'

Helmut took a sip of the coffee. Jean-Claude looked at the young man in his late twenties and noticed his hand shake very slightly as he replaced the cup on the table in front of him. Helmut nervously rubbed the little finger on his left hand.

'Forgive my poor French as I explain. I thank you, with all my heart, for getting me from Germany. I know it was big risk to you all. You know, after I leave university, I can only find work in hotel in Berlin. I work hard and two months ago the hotel director promoted me to reception manager. Another employee hoped for job. He was very upset when he did not get the promotion. He was a platoon leader in Hitler Youth and in anger tells Gestapo that I am homosexual. You can see by the way I am it's difficult to deny.'

Helmut forced a smile before continuing.

'My boss tells me to leave hotel before I am arrested. I have no time to pack my things… I just go to this friend of mine, he allows me to sleep a few days on his floor… After that, my friend tells me that my room at the hotel has been entered by the Hitler Youth, my things smashed and my clothes thrown out of the window and burned, even a picture of my dead mother destroyed. It was the only one I had. Then my old boss sends a message that Alain is coming and you help me get out of Germany.'

A tear fell from Helmut's eye and cascaded down his cheek. He wiped it away with the back of his hand.

Jean-Claude, Sébastien, Alain and Luc looked at Helmut in silence.

'Sorry for my crying,' said Helmut.

'Take your time. We're all friends here,' replied Jean-Claude.

Helmut smiled again and after a short pause continued. 'In Nazi Germany, homosexuality is degenerate behaviour. They say it threatens… disciplined masculinity. They say it's… *non-Aryan*. Propaganda minister Joseph Goebbels says Germany must exterminate such people root and branch – the homo-sexual must be eliminated.'

Helmut paused, cleared his throat, and wiped away another tear. 'Paragraph 175 of penal code has been changed so that it say… '*any unnatural sexual act*' is to be punished with prison.'

He paused again, rubbing the little finger on his left hand. 'What is *unnatural act* is decided by Nazi courts… men like me are arrested. The Gestapo hunts out homosexuals – they say it is contagious disease. Now they have new law, "The amendment for the prevention of offspring with hereditary diseases". It says homosexuals are threat to moral purity of the Reich. If people are guilty under this law… a judge orders castration.'

Helmut paused to contain himself once more. 'Hundreds of men are being arrested. I'm so grateful to you. If they caught me, I know I would be in prison, then they castrate me. I would not live a week if they castrated me, I know I wouldn't… I have two friends that have been castrated and sent to mental hospi-tals to be *cured*… I haven't heard from them since their arrest.'

The four looked at Helmut. He was as white as a sheet and shaking.

'Well, you're safe now,' said Luc. 'The next task we have to do is to arrange passage for you to the United States. We have friends there who will look after you, find you a job and make sure you settle.'

'You have all been so kind. I will never be able to thank you enough,' replied Helmut as more tears flowed down his face.

****

An hour later, Helmut had gone to the guest bedroom to rest and Jean-Claude was saying goodbye to Alain and Luc.

'There are so many like Helmut. The Nazis make themselves popular by playing on old prejudices. The Germans are told that certain groups of people contaminate society. That they must be removed and when they are, then everything will be better. For those that don't belong to a persecuted group it's easy and convenient to turn their backs and ignore what's going on. So many need our help,' said Alain.

'We'll find a way to help as many as we can,' replied Jean-Claude.

Once Alain and Luc had left Jean-Claude walked to his study, picked up the telephone, and asked the operator to connect him with Countess Sophie Tagleva.

'Sophie, how do you fancy dinner at Le Procope on Thursday next week?'

'Oh, how lovely, one of my favourite restaurants! Will Sébastien be coming?'

'No, just the two of us.'

'You're plotting something,' said Sophie.

'See you next Thursday at eight.'

Chapter Nine
The list

Three days later

Bauer was at the desk in his study reading a letter of complaint received from the American embassy about the treatment of American citizens in Germany. Since the US embassy was seeking financial damages against the Nazi party on its citizen's behalf, it had landed on Bauer's desk for him to compose a diplomatically acceptable reply.

The undisputed facts were that a young American called Philip Zechman and his German-born wife were on vacation and visiting relatives. They had been walking in the town centre of Mannheim one Saturday afternoon at the same time as a parade of SA storm troopers was marching through the town centre.

> *At one-thirty, a small group of storm troopers broke off from the parade and were in Planken Street. Deciding the Zechmans were Jews, the storm troopers knocked them to the ground and kicked and punched them. Mr Zechman and his wife were hospitalised. Mr Zechman suffered injuries to a kidney from which he might never fully recover. Mrs Zechman lost her unborn baby, and has, since returning to the United States, discovered that her womb had been removed during the operation in the Mannheim hospital and she will not be able to conceive again.*

Bauer sighed. Replying to a letter about two Jews being beaten up was a waste of his time. He was tempted to inform the ambassador that the fault lay with the Jews for stupidly walking around the town at such a time. However, he penned a reply more in keeping with correspondence with a diplomatic legation. Once he had finished it, he read it through:

> *The incident is being investigated. If found, the perpetrators will be severely punished. It would be helpful if the Zechmans could identify those responsible by providing the names of their attackers. Failing that, could they identify the SA unit collar patch each would have worn?*

Satisfied, he placed the note in the tray for typing. If the Zeckmans did identify their assailants' collar patches, any subsequent investigation would discover the storm trooper unit wasn't in the town that day.

Bauer now drew a thick file towards him and leafed through it. He read through the papers methodically, making appropriate comments in blue pencil on some. He paused, took a sip of his coffee and looked at his watch. The time spent replying to the American embassy had taken longer than he'd wished and he was now late for his morning exercise. He always looked forward to riding around the park on his favourite horse. Bauer in his black uniform astride the grey that would prance along the bridleway with its ears straight forward, nostrils flaring, tail up, head pointed down on arched neck always attracted admiring glances from the young women in the park.

He looked at his watch again. He would come back to his paperwork after his ride. As he picked up the pile of folders, a number of loose papers cascaded onto the floor. *'Fluch und Spreng!'* he cursed and knelt down to retrieve them.

He stuffed them back into the folder. They were muddled up, it couldn't be helped – he would sort them out on his return. He thrust the folders into the safe, closed the door, locked it and departed for the stables.

****

Michael had returned from his training in Berlin the day before and had slept late. After dressing, he was walking across the hallway on his way to the kitchen to get some coffee when he glanced out of the hall window to see the postman walking up the drive. Opening the front door, he took the bundle of letters addressed to the Standartenführer from the postman. He placed the bundle on the desk in Bauer's study. As he turned to walk out, he noticed a piece of paper peeping out from under the desk. He bent down and picked it up and read through the list of names:

Archibald Ramsay MP
Duke of Westminster
5th Duke of Wellington
22nd Earl of Erroll
Marquess of Graham
Duke of Buccleuch
Lord Londonderry
Lord Redesdale
Lord Brocket
Samuel Chapman MP
Ernest Bennett MP
Montague Norman, governor, Bank of England
Frank Cyril Tiarks, director, Bank of England
George Geoffrey Dawson, editor, *The Times*

Michael read through the paper twice before carefully replacing it underneath the desk. Leaving the study, he closed the door gently.

'What were you doing in the Standartenführer's study?' said a loud voice that startled Michael. He turned to find Kurt standing by the front door, his eyes boring into him.

'The post arrived and I put the letters on the desk.'

The house steward scowled. 'The post is my duty. In future, remember that the Standartenführer's office is private, forbidden to you, you understand? *Verboten.*'

'As you wish,' said Michael.

The house steward watched as Michael brushed past him, opened the front door and walked into the garden. He then went into the study and looked around. Everything seemed to be in order, the post lying neatly on the desk. As the steward was about to close the door, he noticed a piece of paper peeping out from under the desk...

****

Michael walked through the orchard. The list of names perplexed him. What was its significance? What did it refer to? It must have fallen from a file and landed under the desk. It couldn't have been left there for him to find – no one could have anticipated that he'd collect the post and put it on Bauer's desk. As he walked in the garden, he knew that he had to find the meaning of the list and there wasn't much time. He was leaving Germany in a few weeks, returning home. It would be risky. If he was caught searching through Bauer's papers by Bauer or the suspicious Kurt, he could expect to be dragged to the hut in the garden.

He pictured himself being stripped naked and strapped to the flogging bench and Bauer interrogating him. Once the latter had extracted the information he wanted, Michael imagined being hung from one of the hooks in the ceiling. Eventually his broken body would be returned to Paris with much ceremony. His grieving parents would be told that the death was accidental, or if Bauer felt particularly malicious, that the suicide of someone so young and talented was a tragedy. The largest wreath at his funeral would be Bauer's.

Chapter Ten
Café le Procope

Francesco Procopio dei Coltelli established his coffee house in the Rue des Fossés Saint-Germain in Paris in 1686. It quickly established itself as the meeting place for intellectuals, and everyone else with the slightest reputation in the arts or politics – and those who hoped to gain one.

Voltaire, Rousseau and Victor Hugo had all been regular customers. It's said that Diderot and Benjamin Franklin argued the finer points of science over a dish of tripe in white wine. Even the turmoil of the French Revolution did nothing to dent its popularity, and Robespierre and Marat consumed dishes of veal sweetbreads as they drew up lists of aristocrats' appointments with Madame Guillotine. It's even said that a Lieutenant Napoleon Bonaparte had to leave his new hat as a pledge after being presented with a bill too large for him to pay.

The private salon on the upper floor afforded the privacy that Jean-Claude needed. Sophie glanced at him over the top of her menu. Being invited to dine alone in a private salon with a man would usually result in a proposal of a love affair. She giggled inwardly at the thought and wondered why the mystery. She didn't have to wait long to find out. Over aperitifs, Jean-Claude recounted the details of Helmut Becker's escape from Germany. Sophie listened attentively.

'There are so many people like Helmut in Germany. I was hoping I might help some escape Germany using the resources of the Foundation,' concluded Jean-Claude.

'Why do you think helping people like Helmut is your responsibility?' asked Sophie.

'Perhaps because if I were in their position, I'd hope someone would help me. Perhaps it's because there are things in my past I'm not proud of, and I remind myself that, while I can't undo my misdeeds, I can make amends.'

'We all have those,' smiled Sophie.

Jean-Claude looked down at the table. 'There's one particular event I'm making amends for. In my youth, I destroyed a man. I thought it was justified revenge for the wrongs he'd done to my parents. Afterwards I realised that my revenge wasn't for my parents but for me, to calm my own anger. Ever since I've regretted it, and I've never quite forgiven myself for what I did. He thought of me as his friend and, in reality, I liked him, too. So I should have saved him from himself but I didn't, and it's haunted me ever since. Despite being a long time ago, my remorse for what I did seems to cut me deeper as time passes. Philip warned me that I might regret what I'd done, and he was right.'

Jean-Claude looked up at Sophie, who was playing with her knife. She looked at him and then back down at the knife and then back at Jean-Claude.

'I'd like to help, but our work with Jewish children takes all our resources,' she said softly. She smiled. 'I apologise – that's no reason at all. We both know it. The Foundation is short of neither money nor resources. You deserve a better explanation.'

Sophie leaned over and touched his hand in the way close friends do when giving bad news. 'I do sympathise with your problem. So I'll explain some of the difficulties and frustrations we have when we try to bring a Jewish family out of Germany. You'll have the same problems with the people you want to bring out. Firstly there's the documentation. Each person leaving Germany needs a passport, then a certificate from the local police noting the formal dissolution of their residence. After that, they need to obtain a certificate from the Reich Ministry of Finance approving emigration, which requires payment of an emigration tax of twenty-five per cent of their total assets valued at more than 50,000 *Reichsmark*.'

She withdrew her hand and took a sip of wine.

'Then they must supply an itemised list of all gifts and property made to third parties since January 1931. If the value of those gifts exceeds 10,000 *Reichsmark*, the total is added into the calculation of the emigration tax. Following that, a certificate must be obtained from the local tax office stating that there is no outstanding tax due. Then, a certificate from a currency exchange office must be obtained stating that all currency regulations have been followed. If the family intend to take personal and household goods out of Germany, a customs declaration, dated no earlier than three days before departure, is needed. This declaration must include a list, in triplicate, of all personal and household goods. The list must identify items acquired before January 1933, and it must detail those items acquired afterwards. The value of each item must be specified, and written explanations given for the necessity of taking them out of Germany. The list must be attached to a certificate from a currency exchange office permitting the export of all personal and household goods, dated no earlier than fourteen days before departure. Even with all those documents, emigrants can't leave Germany with more than 2,000 *Reichsmark* and they must hold valid travel papers and an entrance visa for another country.'

'My God,' said Jean-Claude, 'that's almost impossible.'

'Exactly,' said Sophie. 'That's why so many leave with just a suitcase – and some with nothing at all.'

She took a sip of wine. 'However, that's not the only hurdle they have,' she said. 'There's a myth that Britain's doing all it can for people fleeing Germany and that it always admits genuine refugees. But Britain has introduced a strict quota for refugees entering the country. The government says it's to exclude bogus applicants, but it grants entry to Jews *only* if the Jewish community guarantees there will be no drain on the public purse. The result is that since the start of the persecution, Britain's taken in fewer than 5,000 Jewish refugees. France has admitted even fewer: just 600.'

Sophie was unconsciously wringing her napkin as she spoke. 'I apologise. That information's not helping you with your problem,' she said.

'Actually, it is. It tells me it will be impossible to get people like Helmut out of Germany legally. Britain will accept a few thousand Jewish children because it's politically popular, but Britain considers homosexuality a crime. As criminals they would not be allowed entry into Britain, and if they did and were later discovered as homosexual, they would be deported back to Germany, to prison or worse. We'll have to find other ways to help them.'

'I wish I could help, but the Foundation can't assist you in smuggling people out of Germany considered to be criminals. If we were to be found to be breaking the law, the British and French governments might stop us bringing the Jewish families and children out of Germany.'

'I do understand and wouldn't ask you to risk anything that might compromise what you're doing for the children,' answered Jean-Claude

The door opened. Their first course of pan-fried foie gras with prunes had arrived.

Once they were alone again, Sophie paused for a moment, then whispered in case someone might be listening: 'There is one thing I could do for you, however. Some months ago we brought out a family from Munich by the name of Finkenberg. They arrived with just one small suitcase and two of the sweetest children you can imagine. The Foundation put them up in an apartment in Paris, near the Porte de Montreuil Métro station to be exact. We gave the husband a small grant to set up a business. He's a printer by trade and prints the usual visiting cards and letterheads.' Lowering her voice even further so Jean-Claude had to lean in close to hear her, she continued: 'From the conversations I've had with him, it seems that his real speciality is producing... how can I describe them... "official documents".'

'You mean he's a forger?' asked Jean-Claude quietly.

Sophie giggled. 'Would you like to meet him?' she asked as she carried the tiniest forkful of foie gras towards her lips.

****

A week later Jean-Claude was standing in Samuel Finkenberg's workshop near the Porte de Montreuil.

'My father was an artist, but no one bought what he painted,' said the printer. 'To put meat on the table he created works by the Old Masters. He sold lots of those – a few even hang in the best museums in Europe. He taught me three things. Firstly, you must know your chemistry; secondly, if people want to believe they're looking at a valuable painting by Van Dyke, they'll convince themselves that they are; and finally, always have a sense of humour.'

Samuel passed Jean-Claude a mug of steaming coffee and became serious, 'Have you heard the story of Hitler and Göring standing on top of Berlin's radio tower?'

'No.'

'Hitler says to Göring that he wants to do something to make the people happy. "Then why don't you jump?" says Göring.'

Samuel rocked with laughter and despite hearing the joke before, Jean-Claude found it too infectious not to join in. Still with a smile on his face, Samuel walked over to a workbench and motioned Jean-Claude to follow.

'If we are to make a forged document, the first thing to decide is whether to alter a real one or create a completely new document. Whichever we choose we have to be careful. Make a mistake when altering an original document and it'll be as obvious as a rabbi at a Nazi party rally.'

Samuel laughed again and pulled out a towel and a sheet of paper from underneath the bench and placed them next to each other. 'When making a new document, it's important they look as if they are the correct age and as worn as they naturally would be. Let me show you how I age paper. We'll need two-and-a-half teaspoons of ground coffee beans, which we place it in the centre of the towel, like so. We then fold over the edges of the towel to trap the coffee in the centre.'

He walked over to the sink and poured the contents of a kettle of boiling water over the towel. Once satisfied the colour draining from the towel was correct, he squeezed out the excess liquid.

'Now we take the towel and gently stroke the paper with it until we have the correct colour.' After a few strokes, the paper took on a soft brown hue and Samuel seemed satisfied. 'We must let it dry before we repeat the process on the other side.'

Samuel reached up to a shelf and pulled down a tin, opened it and removed some documents and placed them on the workbench.

'You've asked me for some German travel documents. Having an original document from which to copy is always helpful, but you must make sure it's the correct one. The Nazis have issued two designs. The earliest type had the old Weimar eagle on the front cover and the Nazi eagle and swastika stamped on the inside. In May last year, they changed the design. The Weimar eagle was replaced with the Nazi eagle holding a swastika. Notice, too, that in the newer version it's positioned between the words *Deutsches Reich* at the top and the word *Reisepass* at the bottom. All officials have seen and handled so many, they will easily detect a poor copy.'

Samuel looked at Jean-Claude. 'However, a passport will be useless on its own. You'll also need the *Arbeitsbuch*.'

'What's that?'

Samuel pulled down another tin, opened it and produced two crimson-covered booklets, each with a silver eagle and swastika on the cover.

'This is the *Arbeitsbuch*, a work permit. German law requires all workers to carry them. The purpose is to document the work history of each German citizen. In reality it's an effective tool for the police to see if a worker is far away from their employment town or village. It's a simple means of citizen control.'

'That's clever,' said Jean-Claude.

'The Nazis are clever and you will do well to remember that. Never underestimate them.'

Samuel placed the two booklets side by side on the workbench. 'There have been various changes in the cover of the *Arbeitsbuch*. This one' – he pointed to one of the booklets – 'is for German citizens only. Foreigners working in the Reich have to carry a similar book that's printed on a different colour paper and includes a photo of the owner. No photo is required for the German worker. The ones you've asked for will be for German citizens, and so will not contain photographs. That'll make it easier for you to use them time and again.'

Samuel picked up one of the booklets and stroked it lovingly and held it up to his nose and breathed in deeply. 'This is one I made a few weeks ago and it's so perfect it even smells of Nazi' and he laughed once more.

Samuel picked out two more German work permits from the tin and passed them to Jean-Claude.

'Now, tell me, which is the forgery?'

Jean-Claude studied both documents. He felt the paper, held them up to the light. 'I'm not sure,' he answered, 'They both look the same. The one in my left hand,' he said firmly.

'Wrong. It's the one in your right,' came Samuel's response.

'How can you tell so easily?' asked Jean-Claude.

'I always put a tiny mark on the cover, like a water stain, so that I never lose the original. The last thing I want to be doing is to forge a forgery. Any mistake simply gets repeated.'

'It's all brilliant,' said Jean-Claude. 'How soon can I have the documents we discussed?'

'I have everything I need, so let's say two to three weeks.'

'That would be perfect.'

Walking over to the shelves, Samuel pulled down another metal box, opened the lid and extracted a card.

'There is one more thing you might find useful – a Nazi party membership card. This one was issued to an Eduard Kolle, a teacher from Heidelberg visiting Paris for the weekend. He carelessly lost it in the Métro when he bumped into a friend of mine. You see the card's embossed with the seal of the Nazi party's official initials on the lower left. Show this card to almost any German official, and generally they won't ask for any other documentation. I could have some made up for you and your friends.'

'It could prove to be useful. Add whatever cost on to the account and I'll settle up when I pick up the documents in a few weeks,' said Jean-Claude.

Chapter Eleven
Flood and fire

Three weeks later

For the past two hours, Bauer had been working in his study. The quiet and solitude of the early mornings allowed him to work uninterrupted.

He picked up the draft paper entitled *The War and British Attitudes*. With satisfaction, he read that the new British prime minister, Neville Chamberlain, was taking a more active part in foreign affairs than his predecessor and seemed to have a tolerant attitude towards Germany's need for expansion. Bauer read the final line that concluded: 'The British are anxious to avoid any sort of conflict.' With his blue pencil he wrote at the bottom of the page:

> Britain is not prepared for war. Its desire for tranquillity in Europe is great. It would be useful if we could discover what England would be prepared to pay for such tranquillity. We should encourage our contacts in Britain to promote Germany's freedom of action in Eastern Europe.

Bauer was distracted by a slight rustle, then another. He looked at the two water droplets that had appeared on the file in front of him. The impertinent interruption confused him: where had they come from? Then another fell onto the paper. He looked up at the ceiling and saw a damp patch forming above his desk.

'*Gott in der Hölle!*' he swore. He quickly swept up the papers to protect them from the increasing waterfall and moved them to a side table. He rushed out of the study and towards the stairs.

As he did, Michael appeared from the dining room, ham sandwich in his hand. 'Anything wrong?' he asked.

'Water's coming from upstairs! Tell Kurt to close the stop-cock.'

Bauer climbed the stairs two at a time and Michael hurried towards the kitchen. Kurt was standing at the stove heating some oil in the large frying pan ready to brown the onions and ground beef for a *bierock* casserole.

'There's water flooding into the study – turn off the stop-cock!' Michael shouted.

Unaccustomed to noise in his kitchen, Kurt took a second to register what the English boy was urgently shouting. Hearing the word 'stop-cock', he threw the dishcloth he was using as an oven glove onto the kitchen table and rushed out of the kitchen, into the garden.

As Michael watched him leave, he saw the oil gently warming in the pan. He walked over to the stove, turned the gas on full, and left the kitchen. On the way out, he picked up an empty fruit bowl and the cloth from the kitchen table. In the hallway, he heard Bauer shouting at his wife and her protestations of innocence. The slap she received sounded like a hard one.

****

Kurt located the stop-cock underneath the metal grill near the back door. He turned the handle; it was stiff. He cursed. The last time Bauer's wife had left the tap running in her bath, he had made sure that the valve was only just closed. Now it was taking all his strength to turn it. He cursed again, changed hands and tried to turn the handle once more. *Damn the bitch for leaving the bath to overflow. The Standartenführer will be in a foul temper for the rest of the day.* Kurt strained at the stiffness of the metal tap and cursed again.

****

Entering the study, Michael knew he had but a minute before Bauer returned downstairs and discovered him in the study. Scattered all over the side table were files and papers. Michael began to leaf through them. What he was looking for, he didn't know, and even if he found it, would he recognise it? There were notes from generals Keitel and Beck. He picked up a file entitled *The German Jewish economy* and a report from the chemical manufacturer I G Farben headed *Synthetic oil production*. Michael gritted his teeth. The papers were in a jumble and he felt sweat begin to form on his brow. His hands began to shake as he leafed through more files, including one named *Money as a weapon of war*. It was not what he was looking for. He moved on to the next file.

He heard Kurt's cry from the kitchen. The steward had obviously managed to close the stop-cock and returned to his kitchen to find the fat in the pan had caught fire. Flames were licking the ceiling and the smell of smoking oil was drifting into the hallway and upstairs to the bedrooms. Michael froze as he heard Bauer curse and the sound of his boots on the staircase. The steps followed the source of the fumes coming from the kitchen. There were more curses and shouts as Bauer and Kurt tackled the flames that were now singeing the ceiling and which had set alight the dishcloths near the stove.

Michael lifted another paper and read the heading:

German Foreign Office, Political Department and Finance
The preparations and assessment for mobilisation of German armed forces.

Two eventualities for war are to be considered and plans are to be drafted for both eventualities.

Case Red: War on two fronts with the main struggle in the West. Include the French staging a surprise attack on Germany with the Reich employing its main forces in the West.

Case Green: War in the East. To begin with a surprise German operation against Czechoslovakia to parry an imminent attack by a superior enemy.

Michael read through the one page of instructions and then the note at the bottom, in Bauer's hand:

The necessary conditions to justify such actions as Case Green, both politically and in international law, <u>must</u> be created beforehand. It is essential that England remains neutral. Our friends in

England will be instrumental in persuading their government of the legality of Germany's actions and in neutralising any opposition. The Führer has stated that the Reich must be ready for war by 1938, at the latest by early 1942.

****

The fire was out. Bauer was now in a rage. His hands and face were dirty from the fire, the ceiling was singed, the house smelt of burnt oil, and upstairs his wife tearfully nursed the cut lip that would confine her to her room for the remainder of the day. He left the kitchen cursing the carelessness of his wife and the incompetence of his house steward. Walking into the hallway, he opened the front door to let the smoke out and then went to his study.

Opening the door, he saw a bowl on his desk collecting the last droplets of water falling from the ceiling. Michael was kneeling on the floor mopping up water with a cloth. At first, Bauer was annoyed to see him there, a place he had no permission to be in. Yet the boy was doing his best to clear up the mess, to make good the problems caused by his stupid wife and Kurt.

Michael looked up. 'I don't think there's much damage.'

Bauer looked at the papers on the side table, gathered them up, walked to the safe, opened the door, bundled the papers inside, slammed the door shut, locked it and walked out of the house. In the orchard, he relieved his frustrations by stomping the molehills flat.

****

Michael finished mopping up the water and walked to the kitchen to return the bowl and cloth. Kurt was smarting over the reprimand he'd received from the Standartenführer and was still confused over the stiffness of the stop-cock. He was also sure he hadn't had the gas on the stove turned up full.

When Michael walked into the kitchen, the steward gave him an accusing look. Michael smiled back at Kurt, placed the bowl and cloth on the kitchen table, and left. Kurt muttered another curse under his breath.

Chapter Twelve
Jean-Claude's plan

10 December 1937

The champagne cork flew out of the bottle and Jean-Claude began to fill the glasses. Sébastien, Alain and Luc were at Rue Le Tasse celebrating that, the previous day, Helmut had boarded a ship bound for the United States.

'The State Department doesn't allow anyone to enter the United States without a valid immigration visa and that takes months to arrange. How did you manage it so quickly?' enquired Alain.

Jean-Claude smiled, 'A client of Tagleva's is private secretary to William Bullitt. I asked him for a favour.'

'Bullitt, the American ambassador?' asked Luc.

Jean-Claude nodded. 'When I told my friend about Helmut's plight, he was very sympathetic. A couple of days after our discussion, he told me he'd gained a quiet nod from the ambassador, and a few days after that the visa arrived.'

'We can't expect your contact to help all the people we hope to rescue,' commented Luc.

'No, we can't, particularly as my friend goes back to the United States in a month. Helmut is the only one the American embassy will be able to help.'

'So we have to go back to smuggling out one person at a time in the back of the car,' said Alain.

Jean-Claude emptied his glass. 'More champagne anyone?' he asked.

'You seem very pleased with yourself,' said Alain, 'Let me guess – you have a plan.'

'As a matter of fact, I do.'

They began to listen attentively to Jean-Claude.

'Germany began broadcasting television pictures during the Berlin Olympics and has been developing television ever since. It currently broadcasts for ninety minutes, three times a week, from the Paul Nipkow television station in Berlin. Like German radio and newspapers, television's used for Nazi propaganda and controlled by the Ministry of Public Enlightenment and Propaganda under Joseph Goebbels.'

The three looked blankly at Jean-Claude, wondering when he would get to the point.

'To film a parade, Nazi rally or any other place they want to broadcast, they use large television trucks to move the cameras and boxes of equipment to the location. Most television vans have a crew of six: a camera operator, two technicians, an announcer, director and someone to drive the truck.'

'You're about to suggest we smuggle people out of Germany in a television truck?' said Alain.

'Yes,' replied Jean-Claude as he took another sip of champagne.

'You're mad. Buying a television van will cost us a fortune, even if we could find one,' said Luc.

'But we don't need to. People don't know what a television van looks like. Our truck only has to look like one enough to convince a casual onlooker that it's real.'

'It's a mad idea, it won't work, and what about work permits and papers?' said Luc loudly.

'With the correct papers, people – including the police – will accept that the broadcast van is real and official.'

'And where the hell are we to get those?' sighed Luc.

'I think I've solved the problem,' replied Jean-Claude. 'There's a man near Porte de Montreuil who'll be able to supply us with all the travel and identity papers we need.'

'Who?' asked Alain.

'It's best you don't know for the moment,' replied Jean-Claude with a smile.

'With the correct papers, maybe it could work,' Sébastien said to Luc, unconvinced.

'I'm not so sure,' said Luc. 'A great big television vehicle running around Germany and France will be too conspicuous, too noticeable. It'll stick out like a sore thumb.'

'That's the point,' replied Jean-Claude. 'Who'd suspect a large German television van from Deutscher Rundfunk, stuffed full of expensive equipment to be smuggling people out of Germany?'

'And where are we going to get one of these television vans?' said Luc, shaking his head.

'Leave that to me,' replied Jean-Claude.

'It's a mad idea,' said Luc to Alain.

****

It was Michael's last night in Germany and Bauer had invited him into his study.

He passed a glass of Obstler to Michael, who drank the robust sweet pear brandy. Bauer was sitting behind his desk, one leg crossed over the other, simply watching the young man sip his drink. Then he spoke: 'Have you enjoyed your time in Germany?'

'I have. It's been a revelation,' replied Michael.

'You've taken the sacred oath of obedience.' Bauer chuckled quietly and glanced down at his watch. 'Do you know, Michael, that in Germany there have been many people who have taken an oath to serve the Reich. There have been a few who have betrayed it. Liars and deceitful people who think they can get away with the consequences of such a crime. They never do, of course. They always get caught, always confess their crimes and are always punished.'

Michael's mouth had gone dry and he had an intense desire to lick his lips, but his Abwehr training had taught him that, to do that or run his hands through his hair or shift in his seat would all be taken as signs that he was lying.

Michael looked at Bauer, picked up his glass from the desk and took another sip of the Obstler. 'Do you really think I could betray my oath... your trust in me? If you're worried that I'll fail in my duty because of my youth, I assure you that I won't.'

As Bauer studied his face, Michael looked him in the eye and smiled, thinking that to the Nazi officer it must look as if his smile was pasted onto his face. He felt a bead of perspiration run down his back.

Bauer seemed to relax and smiled back. 'I'm sorry that Kurt has been difficult while you've been here. He's a suspicious man. He thinks you've been spying on us.'

'I know Kurt doesn't like me, but I don't really know why. You must have so many important people to visit, I guess he's been upset at having to look after me, I'm not important enough. He probably thinks it's below his dignity, someone so young, a non-German. When he caught me putting the post on your desk one morning, he was quite angry. He's very protective of his duties. In fact, he's kept a very close eye on me – there isn't anything I've done that Kurt hasn't seen.'

Michael continued to look at the impassive face before him.

'Actually, there would have been something I would have stolen, if I knew where it was kept.'

Bauer raised his eyebrows.

'The recipe for Kurt's Beef *Rouladen* with red cabbage. It's delicious.'

Bauer continued to look sternly at Michael, then suddenly seemed to relax and roared with laughter, slapping his knee.

'You go and pack your things, and I'll upset Kurt further by asking him to write out the recipe for you.'

Chapter Thirteen
Michael's homecoming

Two days later

Matislav and Halinka watched eagerly as the train came to a halt and hissed its last breath of steam. The carriage doors were flung open and the platform began to fill with people. The twins soon saw their older brother climb down from his carriage. Michael's feet had barely touched the platform when they threw their arms around his neck until it hurt.

'What have you brought us?' they asked excitedly.

'Don't worry, I've brought presents for you both,' answered Michael.

'What are they?' they asked excitedly.

'You'll have to wait and see,' replied Michael, knowing he still had to wrap the gifts in the brightly coloured paper he'd bought. He pictured his younger brother, Matislav, marching around the house, wearing the green felt hat with its white feather tucked into the hat band, and his sister, Halinka, cradling the stuffed toy bear with its long skirt and festival garland. Then he smiled as he thought of the cuckoo clock he'd brought for the nursery, and mischievously pictured them sitting in their pyjamas and ignoring Nanny's pleas of 'Go to bed!' as they waited for the cuckoo to appear, just one more time.

****

After dinner, when the presents had been opened and the twins had gone upstairs, Michael sat in his father's study sipping Armagnac. Philip studied his son. Michael had grown up, was more self-assured. It reminded Philip how much he had matured in Russia, during the revolution, when he had met Michael's mother, a lifetime ago.

Michael recounted what he'd seen in Germany, the Nazi party rally at Zeppelin Field, the ceremony in Wewelsburg Castle, how by chance he'd seen the paper under Bauer's desk, had started the flood and the kitchen fire. When Michael had finished, he showed his father the gifts he'd been given after the oath ceremony.

Philip took the dagger with the silver eagle and swastika embedded in the black ebony handle. Pulling it from the scabbard, he read the engraved inscription on the blade. He placed it on the table beside him, picked up the book, opened the cover, saw the signature, closed it and placed it next to the dagger.

Philip looked at his son, Michael averted his gaze, a habit he had adopted during childhood when confessing to some minor misdeed.

'I'm ashamed at accepting such awful things,' he said. 'My time in Germany has confirmed to me that the Germans are drunk with Nazism. In their intoxication, they've consented to its prejudices and hatreds, to be led blindly towards chaos and the abyss. I feel tainted, Father, as if I've spent the last few months in the belly of the beast.'

Michael raised his eyes.

'Yet I can't blame the ordinary people. In many respects, I know how easy it is to be swept up into the madness. When you're in the middle of a hundred thousand people all with their right arms extended as they watch columns of soldiers march past with their flags held high and everyone excitedly shouting "*Sieg Heil!*", it's all too easy to become dizzy with the excitement of it all. In such madness, I know, it's impossible not to do the same.'

Michael paused as if to collect his thoughts. Philip didn't interrupt.

'It was only when I was alone that I could see the dark side. A society where everyone spies on everyone else and reports to the authorities any remark or activity they interpret as being critical of Nazi rule… where jealous neighbours inform on each other for the slightest thing… where your best friend, boss or secretary could be an informer… and you never know you've been denounced until, in the dead of night, there are men at your door who have come to arrest you.'

Michael paused and took another sip of Armagnac.

'But the worst things are the Nazi theories on race. Laws forbid people to work as doctors, lawyers, teachers and actors simply because they are Jewish. Teachers in schools and universities are selected on the basis they teach the lies about the superiority of the German people, and those who don't are denounced by the very students they teach.'

Michael paused again. 'Father, things will soon get worse, I've seen secret papers that Germany is preparing for war against France and Britain.'

'Do you have proof of that?'

'No, I couldn't risk being caught with them, so I memorised them. You know how good I am at that. But there's one other thing that might help prove what I'm saying is true if it actually happens.'

'What's that?' asked Philip.

'When I was in Bauer's office, I saw a timetable for the annexation of Austria. It will start with pro-German riots all over the country. The riots will be used as a pretext to send German troops into Austria with the excuse of preventing bloodshed. I can give you those dates, and if they match up with events as they happen, then Mr Churchill is more likely to accept the other things I say.'

'It would certainly give credence to your other observations. But I have one question. At the castle, you took an oath to serve Adolf Hitler… Why did you agree to that, knowing what you've told me?'

Michael smiled. 'Yes, I did, and I know how much importance you attach to a promise… that such an oath is binding and must be followed. But I thought it was the only way I could get them to trust me and create a way for me to find out what was going on. So, when I said, "I vow to you, Adolf Hitler, as Führer and chancellor of the German Reich, to give unquestioned obedience and loyalty to the leader closest to my heart. So help me God." I had a British postage stamp with a picture of George VI in the left breast pocket of my jacket. My oath was no lie. King George was closest to my heart!'

Philip roared with laughter.

'That list of names you found in Bauer's study. I gave it to Katherine du Bois to see if she could find a connection between them all. It seems the people on the list are all members of the Anglo-German Fellowship and some are members of the Right Club. The first is a group who aim to build friendships between Britain and Germany. The Right Club was founded by Archibald Ramsay, a Scottish aristocrat and parliamentary non-entity. It's a secret society for those with pro-Nazi sympathies.'

'That's interesting,' said Michael, 'because Bauer especially wanted to know about prominent individuals and businesses that you and Mummy knew in Britain. In particular, those close to the government, in Parliament and the media.'

'Did he say why he wanted the information?'

'No, he didn't, but he did say he was very keen that I should start work at our bank. I was told I would be contacted by someone who already works there. I wasn't told who, only that the person will pass on orders from Berlin. One strange thing, though: Bauer was very interested in the Tagleva art collection. On more than one occasion he asked me about specific things that Mummy had collected.'

'Well, never mind about that now. Your German masters will be delighted to learn that you're to start work in Paris *and* in the card index section on the fifth floor. It's where you will have access to all our secrets.'

****

Three days later Katherine du Bois welcomed Michael to the 'Brains of Tagleva' and began to explain the history and impor-tance of the work done on the fifth floor.

'The concept of having a system of card indexing is so that information can be easily and quickly recovered. It's not a new idea. It was initially proposed by a French priest called Jean Rozier in the eighteenth century, and the Tagleva index essentially follows his system. It looks more complicated than it actually is. If you concentrate and follow my instructions, I daresay you'll soon get the hang of it.'

Michael looked at the rows and rows of drawers, each capable of holding hundreds of cards, and wondered if indeed he would ever get the hang of it.

'Cards are stored in steel drawers, which are fire-proof and have a rod through them to hold them in order and prevent them getting muddled up. All the cards are of a uniform size and each card contains a single piece of information. Every card can be cross-referenced by a number to any other card related to a person or subject. Is that clear?'

Michael nodded, hoping that, once he started working with the system, it would make sense.

'The cards are used by Tagleva for a variety of purposes. The most common is to record the names and addresses of account holders and the transactions made on their accounts. Other sections record decisions made by directors or managers regarding loans and investments. A third section holds information on individual political leaders and companies and other economic news that might affect future financial decisions or investments – and so on.'

Katherine became serious and looked over the top of her spectacles at him.

'There is one thing you need to be clear about. I'm very strict about maintaining the index properly. If a card is carelessly put into the wrong place, it creates a substantial problem when we need to locate it. I allow each member of staff just three errors in placing cards into their correct position, after which they are immediately transferred to another department in the building. Do you understand?'

'Perfectly,' replied Michael, thinking that Katherine du Bois was, in her own way, as frightening as Rudolf Bauer.

Having completed her explanation of the system, Katherine told him he was to report to Juliette Villeneuve, who would train him and supervise his work.

Juliette, Michael concluded, was perhaps a year or two older than himself, but it was difficult to tell. She had brown hair, a petite and perfectly formed nose, sparkling eyes and, most of all, a charming smile.

She sat him down at a desk and began showing him how to correctly complete a card with all the information required. Inserting one into a typewriter, she began to type data from a sheet of paper onto the card, pointing out what information was relevant and what information should be put onto another card. Once done, she asked him to complete a card himself, pointing out where he had done it correctly and where he had made a mistake. After an hour Michael felt he had gained enough confidence to be able to relax a little.

'So what do you like to do after work?' he asked Juliette.

'We aren't here to talk about me and what I do after work. You have this system to learn – just concentrate on what you're meant to be doing,' she replied curtly.

Michael blushed at being so completely rejected.

At her desk, Katherine du Bois looked up and smiled.

****

Returning home that evening, Michael's mother asked, 'How was your first day at work. Do you think you'll make friends?'

'It was fine and probably not,' replied Michael, looking distracted.

Sophie did not press him further.

Over the next few weeks, Michael got to grips with the card index. What, at first, had seemed a hugely complicated system became an understandable map showing everything that was happening inside Tagleva as well as the world events that might affect clients' investments. Within two weeks, he was able to assemble information on almost any topic concerning economics, politics, and financial risk – and he always replaced the cards in their correct position.

Michael put Juliette's rejection out of his mind. There was no point in brooding over what might have been. Nevertheless, it didn't prevent him stealing the odd look and admiring the Lucien Lelong skirts that fell to just below her knees, the blouses and sweaters tucked into the skirts that showed off her tiny waist, her beautifully manicured nails, and the Mais Oui perfume by Bourjois that lingered long after she had walked past. Despite her smiles being rarely directed his way, he found himself captivated by the dimples in her cheeks. *One day*, he thought, *I might just pluck up the courage to ask her out again.*

Chapter Fourteen
Anschluss

March 1938

Nancy, the former capital of the Duchy of Lorraine, is in the north-eastern French *département* of Meurthe-et-Moselle. Visitors to the city always visit the majestic Place Stanislas with its statue of Neptune, fountains and imposing wrought-iron gates.

Jean-Claude, Sébastien, Alain and Luc were in Nancy, but not to see the sights. Nor did they have a reservation for luncheon at the Grand Hôtel de la Reine overlooking the square. Instead they were standing in a draughty garage on the outskirts of the town.

'There,' said Jean-Claude to the others, 'what do you think?'

The three men stared at the grey van with large white letters on the top of the cab that spelt out the word Fernsehaufnahwagen.

'What is it?' asked Alain.

'It's a German television van,' declared Jean-Claude proudly.

'Where did you get it?' enquired Luc.

'I bought a van in France and had the exterior changed so it's identical to the one in this photograph.' He passed them a photograph of a television van taken at the Berlin Olympics two years before. 'Let me show you the inside.'

He walked to the back and pulled open the double doors. Inside, from floor to ceiling, was an array of electronic equipment covered in knobs and dials.

'We're going to use this van to smuggle people out of Germany,' Jean-Claude announced.

Alain looked at the interior of the van. 'Does the equipment work?'

'No, it doesn't.'

Luc raised his eyebrows, opened his eyes wide and stared at the ceiling.

Jean-Claude continued: 'Let me explain how it would work if it were real. An ordinary film camera would be mounted on the roof of the truck. The camera takes conventional photographic film. The exposed film passes down a light-tight tube into a tank full of developing solution, then into a fixing tank, through a washing tank, a drying process and finally past an indoor television camera that copies the image. A microphone records the sound separately. The film is given an additional drying and wound on to a take-up spool. Other equipment picks up the film from the spool and transmits the image and sound signals. People can be watching the picture on their televisions within sixty seconds of filming the original scene.'

'I didn't mean how the equipment works. I meant how will we use the van to smuggle people, but since you've started giving a lecture, how *does* it move the picture through thin air?' asked Alain.

'Actually, it's quite easy to understand. It's done by scanning the image you're filming in a series of horizontal rows, one after the other, at very high speed, using a rotating disc, called a Nipkow disc. Done fast enough and with enough rows, the full image appears and the dots and the rows aren't noticeable.'

'I don't really understand, but what type of things do people watch on television?' asked Sébastien.

'Nazi rallies, Hitler's speeches, and some entertainment. One of Germany's most popular shows is *An Evening with Hans and Gelli*. It's about the wholesome life of a young Aryan German couple that the rest of the population is meant to model themselves on.'

'You're telling us that Germans spend their evenings watching people acting out ordinary lives?' asked Luc.

'Yes, it's very popular.'

'Sounds utterly boring,' said Luc scratching his head in disbelief.

'So where will the people be hidden?' enquired Sébastien.

'They won't. They'll pretend to be engineers and sit in the van in full view of everyone—'

Luc interrupted. 'But the van will be seen from a kilometre away. It's too noticeable. We'll be caught the minute anyone inspects inside the van.'

Jean-Claude smiled 'That's the beauty of it. All we have to do is to convince people that it's real. If they think it's real, they'll believe it is. No one's going to inspect all this very expensive fragile equipment, knowing nothing about it, if they've been warned that any damage that disrupts filming will be reported to Dr Goebbels personally.'

'But we're bound to be stopped and questioned,' protested Luc.

'I agree but we'll have travel and work papers, and if any-one asks how the equipment works, we'll confuse them with science. Talk about the number of lines on a television set, fre-quency, vision, megahertz and Nipkow discs. They'll soon get bored and walk away.'

'If the equipment doesn't work, that will give us away. Peo-ple will soon see through the deception,' argued Luc again.

'I thought of that,' said Jean-Claude climbing into the back of the van. Reaching over to one of the panels, he flicked a switch. Within a few seconds, lights glowed, needles moved over dials and a humming noise could be heard coming out of the van.

'How did you manage that?' asked Sébastien.

'Batteries hidden behind the control panels make the dials come alive, and the humming comes from a large fan. I've even bought a real film camera we can erect on the roof.'

Alain sucked in his lips before looking at Luc and whisper-ing, *'Tout est possible, tout est possible.'*

****

On the fifth floor of the Bank of Tagleva, Katherine du Bois was supervising the completion of a report that had been requested by Philip Tagleva. It was to be the basis for a discussion on the future of the bank's investments in Austria.

She typed the opening line: 'The Treaty of Versailles (June 1919) forbids both the union of Germany and Austria and the use of the name "German-Austria"...'

What followed was a record of meetings between the chancellor of Austria, Kurt von Schuschnigg, and Adolf Hitler that had led to the annexation of Austria into the German Reich. Katherine picked up one of the cards from the pile detailing the various official communiqués and reports of the meetings as described by one of Austria's negotiating team, who just happened to bank with Tagleva.

'Hitler subjected the Austrian chancellor to an outburst lasting over an hour addressing him as Schuschnigg, instead of the title "chancellor", as diplomatic courtesy required,' Katherine continued to type.

> Chancellor Schuschnigg was presented with a paper by Hitler. It allowed the establishment of the Nazi party in Austria and the appointment of two pro-Nazi ministers. One would be Minister of the Interior, with authority over the police and security, and the other the Minister of War. Schuschnigg was told to sign and was given three days to comply... Schuschnigg signed. On his return to Austria, however, Schuschnigg repudiated the agreement, demanding a referendum on the treaty by the Austrian people.

Katherine typed Hitler's reaction into the report:

> The news that Schuschnigg had torn up the agreement sent Hitler into a fit of fury. Reports we've received from a contact in Berlin tell of Hitler kneeling on the floor of his study kicking and screaming and biting the carpet.

She pictured Philip smiling at the, irrelevant if not incorrect, detail of the German dictator eating carpet. She continued to type:

> Schuschnigg went to bed on 10 March convinced the Nazis would present no further obstacle to Austria's independence. At five the following morning, he was woken and informed that German troops were massing on the border. In the Austrian Parliament, Hitler's supporters forced the cancellation of the referendum. Schuschnigg resigned.

Katherine picked up another card.

The Austrian president Wilhelm Miklas – considered to be ineffectual (many of his countrymen believe his chief accomplishment is being the father of a large brood of children) – refused to appoint a pro-Nazi chancellor in Schuschnigg's stead.

The new German foreign minister, Joachim von Ribbentrop, faked a crisis by engineering a 'plea for German assistance' from inside the Austrian government. On 12 March German troops marched into Austria.

Katherine then typed the second part of the report – the financial results and assessment:

The main reasons for Germany's annexation of Austria may be because Germany has a shortage of steel and a weak balance of payments. The annexation of Austria brings into German control the iron ore mines in the Erzberg area and the financial reserves of the Austrian National Bank of 748 million *Reichsmark*, more than twice that of Germany's.

The final part of the report recorded the international reactions:

(i) On the day Germany marched into Austria, the stock market in New York rose.
(ii) America's CBS Radio broadcast: 'All France believes Hitler invaded Austria to prevent the planned plebiscite.'
(iii) In London, *The Times* commented that, 300 years before, Scotland had been joined to England and that this event was not very different.
(iv) The British prime minister, Neville Chamberlain, told the House of Commons: 'Our ambassador in Berlin has registered a protest in the strongest terms with the German government.'

At their next Thursday meeting Philip discussed the report with Jean-Claude and told him, 'It won't end here. If France and Britain allow Hitler to get away with it, he'll want more.'

Chapter Fifteen
The Russian Tea Room

April 1938

The Royal Borough of Kensington and Chelsea is the smallest district in London. Despite its size, it boasts major attractions – three museums, a university and the department store Harrods. The motto of this highly fashionable borough is *Quam Bonum in Unum Habitare,* which roughly translates as 'How good to dwell in unity'. However, it would surprise its wealthy residents to learn that the area is far from united. Since 1830 it has been a hotbed of international intrigue that began when the Royal Geographical Society's was established in the Borough, its purpose not just the 'advancement of geographical science', but also as a front for spying against Imperial Russia, during the difficult time known as 'The Great Game'. A hundred years later, during the 1930s, the Russian OGPU, the State Political Directorate which later became the KGB, issued a guide to its spies that told them that 'due to its good reputation with the police, South Kensington is a suitable base to undertake clandestine activities'.

Opposite the Underground Railway station in Cromwell Place the Russian Tea Room is well known for its warm welcome, caviar, fine vodka and the lemon tea poured from a silver samovar. The owner of the tea room, Nikolai Wolkoff, had once been an admiral in the Imperial Russian navy, his wife a maid of honour to the Tsarina. At the start of the Russian Revolution, the admiral had been the Russian embassy's naval attaché in London. After the Tsar was toppled from power, the Wolkoff family sensibly decided to remain in England, and to earn a living they opened their tea room. Their daughter, Anna, established an haute couture boutique near Regent Street. After one of her creations was featured in the Coronation edition of *Vogue*, the Duchess of Gloucester and Wallis Simpson both became clients and soon her creations were being worn by the leaders of London society, including the wives of Archibald Ramsay and Arthur Wellesley, the 5th Duke of Wellington.

With their Imperial Russian connections, the family were fierce opponents of Bolshevism and gravitated towards the extreme right-wing views of the Nazis. As a consequence, the tea room always gave a particularly warm welcome to members of the Right Club, and it also acted as a post office for secret messages to and from Berlin.

Christopher Hatton was sitting at a table in the back of the tea room, near the door to the kitchen. The waitress brought him a glass of refreshing lemon tea and a *pryaniki*, a honey and spice biscuit that perfectly complemented the strong Russian tea. Placing a white envelope on the table, he opened up a newspaper and read it while he waited for the tea to cool. Fifteen minutes later, he folded the newspaper, carefully placed it on top of the envelope and left the tea room. The newspaper and the envelope were quickly cleared away with the empty tea glass and taken through the service door into the kitchen. The information contained in the envelope would be read in Berlin that night.

****

Two weeks later, Jean-Claude and Philip were sitting at the table in the chairman's office in Paris as the clock on the mantelpiece chimed nine o'clock. The coffee at the far end of the table was cold, the croissants untouched. Philip's secretary brought in another report to update them on the worsening political situation.

Jean-Claude read it to Philip: '"The governments in Paris, London, Prague and Moscow believe that Germany is about to invade Czechoslovakia. The Czech government has mobilised their army."' He paused. 'Do you think the Germans can be stopped?'

Philip rubbed his chin. 'Probably not after it swalled up Austria with no objections and Neville Chamberlain's comment to

Lady Astor that Britain wouldn't come to the aid of Czechoslovakia if Germany attacked. Hitler will consider that statement an open invitation to invade.'

'Well, everyone believes that an attack by Germany will happen soon,' Jean-Claude said. 'People have begun to cash in on that. The American ambassador in London, Joseph Kennedy, has short-sold Czech stock. He's banking on the fact that, if the Germans invade the Czechs, the stock market will collapse. Kennedy's likely to clear $500,000 profit. I'm told he claims it's "just good business".'

Philip scowled.

Jean-Claude added: 'And the chairman of General Motors has defended a proposed invasion by saying that as GM is Germany's main supplier of military vehicles an invasion would be "highly profitable" for GM.'

'Why is morality always a victim whenever there's a fortune to be made?' sighed Philip.

'What do you think will happen next?' asked Jean-Claude.

'The abiding memory I have of the events leading up to the Great War is that a political crisis has a momentum of its own. It's a confusing fog. Everything happens all at once, and governments find they can't control events – they are controlled by them. For example, before the Great War, stock markets all over Europe fell, with everyone trying to buy gold. The British government tried to prevent a banking crisis by raising interest rates to ten per cent, which only increased the panic. I suspect it will be the same this time.'

They were interrupted by the ringing of the telephone and Philip's secretary saying that Michael had come with an urgent message from the fifth floor.

Michael entered the office and handed over an envelope. Jean-Claude opened it. 'It's from our contact in Berlin. At a meeting today, Hitler told his generals, "It's my unalterable decision to smash Czechoslovakia by military action in the near future."'

Philip took his son to one side.

'Have you been contacted by Berlin to pass them any information.'

'Not yet, perhaps they've decided they can't trust me,' replied Michael.
'Tell me if they do, will you?'
'Of course, father.'

Chapter Sixteen
A television van in Ladenburg

A sleepy town ten kilometres north-west of Heidelberg, Ladenburg is picturesque with narrow streets, cobbled roads and half-timbered buildings surrounding its central square.

The television van parked outside the town hall. Alain walked in and identified himself as leader of a team from the *Volksfernseher* – people's television – and asked to speak to the *Bürgermeister*. Kurt Pohly was not just the town's mayor but also the senior Nazi party member in the area. Once his secretary had informed him of the visitors from Berlin, he immediately told her to admit them to his office.

'Herr *Bürgermeister*, Berlin has decided that Ladenburg is to be shown across the Reich as Germany's ideal small town,' Alain told him. 'You are known in Berlin as an exceptional administrator and we would like your permission to film the town and yourself, its leading citizen, as a model for the rest of Germany to follow.'

The *Bürgermeister* noticed the slight accent showing the man originated from Alsace-Lorraine, he prided himself on noticing such detail.

'Will Reich Minister Goebbels see the film?' enquired Pohly.

'It was the Reich Minister who suggested your town. In fact, it was he who told us about you and instructed us to interview you.'

The mayor pushed out his chest. 'Reich Minister Goebbels mentioned me himself, did he? My wife will be so proud when she hears.'

'It needs to be kept secret,' said Alain firmly. 'That is, until the film is broadcast. If other towns hear we're filming in Ladenburg, every one of them will demand that we film them and feature their *Bürgermeister*. If that happens, it will be difficult to hold up Ladenburg, and yourself in particular, as something special.'

The mayor thrust his thumbs into the sides of his waistcoat and adopted the pose he usually took when speaking to a gathering of the town's citizens. 'Quite right, you can only have one *best* mayor in Germany... When will the film be shown?'

'We don't know the exact date, but we'll let you know. You and your wife will receive invitations to come to Berlin to see the film broadcast, and you'll get to meet the Reich Minister. But not a word must leak out.'

'No, of course not, not a word, you have my promise – not one word will pass my lips,' insisted the mayor.

Over the next half an hour, Alain and Luc set up cameras and lights in the Mayor's Parlour while the mayor was prepared for his big moment.

Alain explained: 'The television camera doesn't pick up the red of the human complexion, which leaves the face flat and unnatural. This special makeup allows the lips, eyes and mouth to appear accurate in relation to the rest of the complexion.'

The mayor's cheeks and lips were coloured a dark olive green; the nose, eyes and throat were painted white; and the eyebrows were transformed into a royal blue.

When everything was ready, the mayor stood in front of the camera and for four minutes addressed the people of Germany, telling them of the beauty of Ladenburg and the industrious, energetic work he unselfishly undertook for the town and the party.

At the end of filming, Alain thanked him. 'Perfect! You were so good, you're a natural.'

The lights, camera and equipment were packed away.

'Now remember, not a word to anyone, not before we tell you the date of the broadcast,' Alain reminded him.

'Not a word will be uttered by me to anyone,' insisted Pohly.

From his office window, the mayor watched the television van drive away. Once it was out of sight, he opened his office door and rushed past his secretary. Her mouth fell open; she'd never seen her boss with a green face.

Striding through the town, Pohly waved to a few of his neighbours and gave a cheery *'Guten Tag!'* to some women gossiping on a street corner.

As he arrived at his house, his wife was removing from the oven the large, heavy pot of *Sauerbraten* she had prepared for guests coming to dinner. As her husband entered the kitchen and she saw his green face, white nose and dark blue eyebrows, she screamed at the terrible vision. She then let go of the pot containing meat, wine, vinegar, spices and herbs, carefully marinated for three days and lovingly cooked for two-and-a-half hours. As the pot fell to the floor, it smashed and the contents spilled all over the flagstones.

Over the following weeks, the topic of conversation among the men in the town's *Bierkellers* was the *Bürgermeister*'s green face, white nose and blue eyebrows. In the cafés, the women whispered to each other that the mayor and his wife were not speaking. The postmistress announced to her best friend that she had been told he'd been banished from the marital bed and was now sleeping on the sofa in his study. No one commented on the fact that a television van had arrived in the town with two engineers and had left with five.

Chapter Seventeen
A paper to Berlin

20 May 1938

Rudolf Bauer was attending the conference chaired by Reinhard Heydrich in Prinz-Albrecht-Strasse in Berlin. The chief of the Reich's main Security Office had been efficient as usual. The meeting had started at the exact minute scheduled.

Heydrich began: 'Now that Germany and Austria are united, we need to consider Case Green as a matter of urgency. I don't need to remind you that Germany's need for living space is greater than other people's. Germany therefore must have living space in the East.'

The entire room knew Heydrich was referring to Czechoslovakia and waited for him to provide the clues to their own contributions that would please their master.

'There are three aspects of an invasion we need to think about: the military one, the political reactions, and the propaganda before and after the event. Taking these three areas in turn, I consider that an unprovoked attack on Czechoslovakia would lead to hostile world opinion. That presents a problem because military action after a period of diplomatic discussions that leads to a crisis is also considered as unsatisfactory, because it would give the Czechs time to take defensive measures.'

Those listening then heard the action they would unanimously support.

'The Führer prefers a third alternative: lightening action resulting from an incident. Of course, the Führer has the following expectations: an assumption that there will be little or no resistance from the Czech military; the outside world seeing the action as peaceful and not a warlike undertaking; and the action being carried out without mobilisation of German armed forces.' Heydrich paused. 'We might start by considering the murder of a German diplomat during an anti-German demonstration, like the one we planned for Austria, though we didn't use it.'

Heydrich looked around the table; there were no disagreements. Everyone in the room accepted that a diplomat sacrificing his life for the greater glory of the Reich was acceptable, even when the diplomat was never asked his opinion of it.

An hour later, back in his own office, Bauer was contemplating the meeting when an orderly walked in and handed him an envelope. Bauer looked through the papers inside. It contained copies of the information that had been left on the table at the Russian Tea Room in Kensington by Christopher Hatton.

Reading the last page he knew the time had arrived when Michael Tagleva must start to become a useful servant of the Reich. He would arrange for a message to be sent to the German contact at the Tagleva bank, ordering contact to be made with Michael Tagleva... and give him his instructions.

****

Every Friday, wherever she was in the world, two dozen white roses were delivered to Countess Sophie Tagleva. Today Mrs Frobisher was passing the time before the delivery of the blooms by sewing name-tags into the family's clothes. She had done this for years so that a garment's owner could be identified clearly, particularly after it was laundered or left around the house.

When the doorbell at the tradesmen's entrance rang, Mrs Frobisher put down her needle and thimble, walked to the door and accepted the box from the delivery boy. She took it straight to the hallway where she knew Sophie would be waiting – the Countess always insisted on arranging the gift from her husband herself.

Sophie had chosen a large cut-glass vase to show the flowers off at their best. She intended to contrast the creamy roses with the richer tones of honeysuckle and the soft coppery-brown of day lilies, Megasea leaves, the fern-like leaf of the giant fennel, and some wild grasses.

Once finished, she stepped back to admire the display and made the odd adjustment until she was satisfied.

The ritual of sending two dozen white roses to his wife every week had its origins in the first night they had dined together in St Petersburg when he'd presented her with a single white rose. She had pressed it into her Bible which was, even now, stored in the desk in her dressing room. He considered the sending of the roses an expression of his undying love for her. Now he walked out to the hallway to admire his wife's creation.

'It looks lovely,' he said.

Sophie plucked a rose from the display, threaded the stem through his buttonhole and together they walked, hand in hand, to the drawing room for coffee and biscuits.

Philip poured Sophie a coffee. 'How are things at the Foundation?' he asked.

'Arranging for Jewish families to leave Germany is getting increasingly difficult. The British government aren't as cooperative as I'd hoped they might be. Everyone seems to be in favour of appeasing Hitler. I don't understand why the world can't see what a nasty little man he is—'

Philip interrupted. 'Did I tell you that I met with Churchill last week? He's sent a letter to Hitler saying that, if German armies cross the Czech frontier, it will bring about a new world war.'

'I'm beginning to like Winston more and more.'

Philip smiled. 'Are you changing your opinion about Winston, my dear?'

Sophie knew Philip was teasing her. 'We might have had our disagreements in the past, and I haven't forgiven him for his awful treatment of the miners during the General Strike. But I do approve of his opposition to Hitler. I suppose he's not such a bad old stick... when you get to know him.'

'Is that an endorsement?' asked Philip.

'Hardly an endorsement. But it's a woman's privilege to change her mind. Do you think he might become part of the government again?'

'If the appeasement fails and we end up going to war with Germany, then his experience as a leader during the Great War would make Churchill an essential part of any government.'

Sophie was about to say something, but bit her lower lip gently as if preventing words from falling out before they were properly ordered.

She looked at Philip. 'If there's a war, Michael will want to fight. He'll be among the first to volunteer, I know he will. He'll see it as another adventure, his duty, and I worry for him. I wonder if we might do something so he's not in too much danger.'

'He's a sensible boy. And we can't stop him fighting for his country – it would be wrong for us to try – and if he found out that we had used our influence to protect him, he'd resent us for it. We can only support him, whatever he does.'

'I know you're right. I just wish he was a little less adventurous. You know he's bound to volunteer for something that'll put him into the greatest possible danger.'

Philip remained silent.

****

Christopher Hatton's ample frame was slumped in the armchair in the office he shared with three other researchers at the House of Commons. He read through the report compiled for the prime minister and which had been sent, out of courtesy, to the leader of His Majesty's loyal opposition.

Secret

The probability is that, following an invasion by Germany, Czechoslovakia's resistance will crumble within weeks and both Britain and France will be powerless to prevent it.

British Foreign Office policy is quite clear: Britain should avoid trouble in Central Europe at all costs. The

Great War, twenty years ago, stands as an awful warning of the failure of this policy.

French policy: France also feels unable to be involved in Central Europe. A major factor is the French republic's unpreparedness for conflict. The most glaring military weakness is the state of France's air force. Its chief believes that it would be overwhelmed by the German Luftwaffe within two weeks of the start of a war.

Hatton read the paper. It was the confirmation he'd been waiting for. Britain and France would not go to war against Germany if the latter invaded Czechoslovakia. Hatton left to take tea at the Russian Tea Rooms in Kensington. The secret report would be read in Berlin a few hours after the British prime minister had read it.

****

On the fifth floor of the Bank of Tagleva, Michael was filling out index cards. He had come to appreciate the value of the 'brains of the bank' to Tagleva's directors and managers. The process both impressed and fascinated him. He was compiling a report that said that the French cabinet were divided on supporting the Czechs if Germany invaded.

Michael had almost finished when Juliette Villeneuve leaned over his shoulder and whispered in his ear: 'How would you like to take me to the cinema tonight? We could go and see *The Awful Truth*. Cary Grant and Irene Dunne are in it.'

'I thought you didn't want to go out with me after work,' replied Michael softly.

'I didn't want you to think that just because you're the chairman's son, I would fall at your feet when you asked me. Besides, you're the only man on the fifth floor to ask.'

Amused at being informed he was the only possible choice of companion, he whispered, 'Would you do me the honour of accompanying me to see *The Awful Truth* tonight?'

'I'd be delighted. Thank you so much for asking me.'

With a smile Michael picked up another card. *Had contact from Berlin been made?*

****

That evening Michael and Juliette arrived at Le Champo cinema in the Rue des Ecoles in the Latin Quarter. The usherette showed them to their seats and, within minutes, the lights dimmed.

Michael was mildly amused at the plot. Jerry, played by Cary Grant, and Lucy, Irene Dunne, are a married couple who doubted each other's fidelity. Jerry suspects Lucy of having an affair with her handsome music teacher. Lucy discovers that Jerry lied about a business trip and has also been unfaithful. The jealous pair agree to divorce and both rush into new relationships. The soon-to-be-divorced husband and wife realise their love for each other has never died and both scramble to spoil each other's chances for newfound romance. The plot reminded Michael of *Much Ado About Nothing*. Juliette enjoyed the farce and laughed a great deal.

After the cinema, they took a cab to Chez André, a new bistro in the Rue Marbeuf. Michael had chosen the restaurant with care. It was inexpensive and the menu included all the traditional French favourites – onion soup *au gratin*, snails in garlic, oysters, veal kidneys with creamed leeks, and duck *confit*.

After the waiter had taken their food order, Michael looked around the dining room and noticed the head waiter showing a man to a table. He looked very like the man he had seen at the cinema, sitting a few seats away from them in the same row. *I must be mistaken*, he told himself and dismissed the thought.

Turning to Juliette, he asked her what she enjoyed doing in her spare time.

'I love jazz.'

'Jazz?' said Michael, captivated by the expression that now lit up Juliette's face.

'There's no better music than jazz. I love the improvisation and the solos. My favourite musician is Django Reinhardt, a gypsy. When he plays the guitar, it's like poetry, it's so romantic.

He's one part of the Quintette du Hot Club de France, you know.'

'So what's your favourite song?' asked Michael

'"Three Little Words" by Harry Ruby.'

'Apart from jazz, what else do you like?'

'Fast cars,' Juliette smiled broadly, 'I love the shape, the noise, the speed.'

'What's your favourite?'

'I love the Delahaye, the car that won the Monte Carlo Rally and Le Mans last year. It's powered by a four-and-a-half litre V12 engine with three camshafts in the block, four overhead rocker-shafts, and triple Stromberg carburettors… a wonderful car.'

Michael stifled a chuckle. He hadn't understood a word.

Juliette looked at his amused expression. 'I'm sorry, I've been talking too much. So, what are your interests?'

'Compared to jazz and fast cars, all very boring. I love chess, reading, solving problems, and puzzles.'

Juliette stared past him and supressed a yawn.

'I do ski, though. I went to the Alpine World Ski Championships to watch James Couttet, and when he wasn't in competition we'd ski together.'

Juliette leaned forward, her eyes sparkling. 'James Couttet! You've skied with the French downhill world champion?'

'Yes, our families sometimes holiday together,' answered Michael offhandedly.

'You've been teasing me. Oh, I'd love to be able to ski. It looks such fun.'

'So, as I'm not so boring, you'll come out with me again?'

'Perhaps…' she giggled.

Chapter Eighteen
The note in the pocket

September 1938

The butler placed the decanter of Taylor's vintage port onto the luncheon table, to the right of Lord Brocket. Pouring himself a glass, he passed the decanter to his left. George Dawson, editor of *The Times*, filled his own glass passing it to Christopher Hatton, who passed it to Frank Tiarks, a director of the Bank of England, who simply looked at it. Seeing the port decanter come to a halt, Archibald Ramsay MP grunted loudly and was relieved to see it on the move once more. Filling his glass, he passed it to Lord Londonderry who didn't want a glass and gave it to the final guest, Arthur Charles Wellesley, Duke of Wellington.

Dawson spoke: 'Did you read the leader in *The Times* about Czechoslovakia ceding the Sudetenland to Germany?'

Everyone nodded.

'An excellent article, I thought. Suggesting that all German-speaking areas belong to Germany seems only sensible to me,' added Dawson.

Again, everyone nodded in agreement.

'On the topic of Germany, I have news,' said Hatton.

The group looked at him expectantly.

'As you know, Chamberlain met with Hitler. A contact of mine at the Foreign Office went with the prime minister as one of his advisors. By all accounts, it was a long and tedious journey. The time allowed my contact to speak with Chamberlain and he put forward our cause and need for appeasement.'

'That Britain must never fight with Germany?' said Lord Londonderry.

Hatton stretched his back, tilted his head back slightly and stared at Londonderry. After a full second, he continued:

'During the journey, Chamberlain looked out of the window as train after train of German troops passed him going in the opposite direction, towards Czechoslovakia. He was obviously affected by the sight, because when he met Hitler, he gave the Führer everything he wanted.'

'That's wonderful,' said Ramsay.

'That's not the end,' replied Hatton. 'Since Munich, Chamberlain met Hitler again, this time at the Rheintotel Dressen in Bad Godesberg. My contact was in that group, too. When the prime minister left the hotel, Hitler told him that it was his last design of territory. It seemed to cheer Chamberlain up.'

Brocket spoke, raising his voice. 'Well, if that's the case, then why has the government mobilised the fleet? I heard it on the radio news last night, and that trenches are being dug in the royal parks in London. What's *that* for if they don't expect war?'

'And I heard there are plans to evacuate the children out of London,' added Dawson.

Hatton raised his hands. 'All this is true, but it don't mean war. It's done to calm the population. I suggest you each use your influence with government to ensure that appeasement continues.'

'Well, if there is a war, it'll be the fault of those who hope to profit from it – the bankers and the fucking Jews,' said the Duke of Wellington.

None disagreed.

Hatton looked around the table. They all wanted peace so that things remained the same, preserving their status, privileges and wealth. To achieve that end they would give Hitler anything he wanted. He was the only one who wanted war, couldn't wait for war so that everything would change. Without war, he would remain an insignificant nobody. But when Germany had its victory, the people around the table would know him for what he was and they would squeal like pigs. He would make sure of it.

****

102

The following day was market day in Trier, a city on the banks of the Moselle and near the border with Luxembourg. The square was full of people moving between the stalls and children playing around the stone cross. Within sight of the square was the Roman Catholic cathedral of St Peter, the largest ancient Roman structure outside Rome. As the television van came to a halt near the west door, a small crowd gathered, pleased to have a distraction from their morning chores. They watched as an engineer set up a camera on the roof of the van and began to film the cathedral. When the director indicated the crowd should form a group so that they could be included in the film, they were delighted. The young boys jostled against each other to ensure they were in the front. Ten minutes later the equipment was being packed away and the five engineers climbed into the van and made ready to drive off.

At the edge of the crowd, a member of the Hitler Youth had watched the proceedings and walked over to a policeman.

'That van arrived with two men and is now leaving with five,' the boy told him.

'What of it?' the policeman replied. He looked at the boy and noticed he wore the insignia of the HJ-Streifendienst, the special patrol force that functioned as the internal political police of the Hitler Youth. Its main task was ferreting out disloyalty, its members denouncing anyone who criticised Hitler or Nazism.

The policeman knew the boy, and that he was more fanatical than most. If this thug thought he'd not done his duty, his superiors would get to hear of it.

'Tell me more,' asked the policeman feigning a respect he didn't feel.

'I've just told you. The van arrived with two engineers and is now about to leave with five. Isn't that suspicious?'

The policeman didn't want any trouble with his superiors, and the adolescent would be more than happy to cause it. He walked over to the driver, followed closely by the boy.

'This Hitler Youth says your van arrived at the cathedral with two engineers and now you have five people in the van.'

Luc looked at the policeman and, behind him, at the teenager dressed in his brown uniform, standing with feet spread wide and hands on hips.

'The others were in the square looking for other places to film. They've just arrived back. We've filmed the best bits of the town, so we're now off to another part of the district.'

'Ask them for their papers,' the boy ordered the policeman.

'I'd better see your papers,' the policeman said apologetically.

Luc called out to everyone in the back: 'We have to show our papers.'

Alain shouted from the rear of the van, 'Let's film the policeman doing his duty. It will make a great addition to the story. They'll love it in Berlin.'

Alain climbed out of the van and quickly set up the camera.

Inside the van, dials sprang to life and the electrical equipment began to hum softly.

Alain shouted out to the policeman: 'I'll signal you when to look at the papers!'

The policeman watched the cameraman.

The crowd fell silent.

The signal was given: 'Camera rolling…'

The policeman leafed through the identity cards, passed them back through the window and saluted smartly.

'Perfect. Berlin will be delighted with that,' said Alain.

Two minutes later the van was driving out of the town. The policeman thought of his neighbours going to the cinema and seeing him on the newsreel before the main picture was shown.

'Well?' asked the Hitler Youth to the policeman.

'Well what?'

'Were their papers in order?'

'Yes, of course.'

The Hitler Youth walked away… he would make a report to his troop leader.

****

Three days later, the heads of the governments of Great Britain, France and Italy again met with Hitler in Munich. In the next room were sitting the representatives of Czechoslovakia, waiting to hear their country's fate. Shortly afterwards, four signatures were placed on the document that gave the German army the freedom to move into Czechoslovakia unopposed.

On returning to Britain, Chamberlain announced that he held the paper that brought 'peace in our time'. The crowds cheered 'good old Neville' and sang, 'For he's a jolly good fellow.'

The following day, *The Times* editorial wrote of Chamberlain: 'No conqueror returning from a victory on the battlefield has come adorned with nobler laurels.'

When Philip Tagleva read the article, he turned to Sophie and said: 'I fear we will be at war with Germany within a year.'

****

That same morning Michael walked through the rain to the Bank of Tagleva and, on arrival, hung his raincoat on the coat-rack near the radiator to dry it out. He took his usual seat and began work. He stole a look over to where Juliette was seated. When the clock above the door said it was ten past nine, Juliette rose and went to speak to Katherine du Bois. After a few words, Juliette walked to the coat-rack, donned her hat and coat and left.

All through that morning, Juliette's seat remained empty and Michael wondered what had happened. He hoped nothing was wrong. He decided to create an excuse to speak to Katherine du Bois. He looked over to her desk. She was talking to Jean-Claude's secretary, Nicole Labranche. He would have to wait. After a few minutes, Nicole left and Michael took his opportunity.

'Yesterday, Juliette mentioned to me that she had something for me to do today. Will she be coming back?

'Juliette's not well. She'll be in tomorrow.'

'Nothing serious, I hope,' enquired Michael.

'No, nothing serious.'

At the end of the day, Michael collected his raincoat. At the door to the street, he saw it was still raining outside. He put on the raincoat, said goodnight to the doorman, thrust his hands in his pockets, his left hand encountered a piece of paper. Pulling it out of his pocket, he founded it was a folded note. It hadn't been there that morning.

Opening it, he read: 'Your friends from Wewelsburg send you greetings. Expect orders to follow soon.' Michael thrust the paper back in his pocket and, oblivious to the rain hitting his face, he haunched his shoulders, fixed his eyes on the pavement and walked home.

Chapter Nineteen
16th day of Cheshvan

9 November 1938

Sophie poured herself a coffee. It had been a good day. The Tag-leva Foundation had arranged for fourteen Jewish children to travel from Germany to London, and they were now enjoying their first evening meal with the families that had volunteered to look after them for as long as was needed.

Philip walked into the drawing room.

Sophie looked at him and his slightly forward tilting head and knew something was wrong. 'Bad news?' she asked.

Philip sat down on the sofa next to her. 'I'm afraid it is. I've just heard from Paris that a junior official at the German embassy has been shot and is likely to die.'

'I don't like the thought of anyone being shot, but why is it important to us?' asked Sophie.

'Because the man who fired the pistol is a seventeen-year-old boy called Herschel Grynszpan. He's Jewish, and the Germans are bound to want some sort of revenge. It may affect the Foundation's work with Jewish children.'

'Oh, God,' said Sophie.

'According to the Paris police, Herschel bought a revolver and ammunition, caught a Métro train to Solférino station and walked to the German embassy. He asked to see the ambassador, but instead was shown into the office of an Ernst vom Rath. Herschel shot him several times.'

'But why?'

'It seems Herschel's family were forced out of their home by German police, and the family's possessions and business was confiscated. They were forced to move over the Polish border, but the Polish government refused to admit them and put them in an internment camp. Herschel's father sent him a postcard begging him to rescue them. Herschel wasn't able to and said

107

his shooting of the diplomat was in revenge. He told the French police he did so in the name of 12,000 persecuted Jews.'

Philip got up and went over to the table and poured himself a coffee.

'It gets worse. I'm told he entered France illegally and has been living with a small Yiddish-speaking group of Polish Orthodox Jews in Paris.'

'How will this affect the work of the Foundation?' asked Sophie.

'I've been told, confidentially, that the French intend to halt any further transports out of Germany. The fourteen children you've arranged to get out may be the last.'

'Oh, God, no, and just as we've got permission to increase the number we can bring out,' groaned Sophie.

****

The German army has always considered the city of Augsburg strategically important. That was why the Wehrmacht had barracks for three army regiments in the city: the Twenty-seventh Wehrmacht artillery and infantry regiments and the Panzerjäger Kaserne tank regiment. With so many soldiers and military administrators in the town, it was very wealthy. The cafés, restaurants and shops were always busy, full of men in uniform.

Luc and Alain hadn't heard about the death of Ernst von Rath. As they drove into the city, Luc and Alain felt increasingly nervous. They had hoped to avoid attracting attention from security-conscious soldiers and policemen by arriving before the sun rose above the rooftops, but as the television van neared the centre of the city, they saw that the streets were full of people. An acrid smell of burning reached them, while a strange red glow lit up the morning sky.

'What's going on?' asked Luc.

'I don't know. But something's not right.'

As the van drove slowly down a road, its headlights lit up two Gestapo agents in their usual green Bavarian garb banging on a door. It was opened by a woman in her night clothes.

'Does Heinz Landmann live here?' Alain heard through the van's half-open window as they passed.

A minute later, they came across the cause of the red glow in the sky.

A synagogue was on fire. Fire hoses weaved a snake-like pattern from the fire trucks and along the pavement to the hydrant. Alain and Luc looked at the scene – it was absurd. Not one of the hoses had its stream of water directed at the synagogue. Instead, the firemen were dampening the surrounding buildings as the synagogue burned in a strangely controlled fashion. In the middle of the road, a group of youths hurled stones at the stained-glass windows. Religious books and Torah scrolls littered the street, forcing the van to drive over the sacred Jewish texts and a calendar recording the day as the '16th day of Cheshvan in the year 5699'.

The van turned left at the end of the street and drove slowly past a police station. Paddy wagons were busy disgorging men who were being directed into the station.

Two streets later, the television van was halted by a group of around twenty youths in the road shouting obscenities at the apartment above a tailor's shop. Alain estimated their average age to be around fifteen. He watched as one of them, smaller than most of the others, picked up a brick from the side of the road and threw it. The missile left the boy's hand, turning and turning almost in slow motion until it reached the shop's plate glass window. The glass shuddered, went still and then, like a waterfall, cascaded onto the pavement and into the street. The youths stepped back to avoid the torrent and cheered. There followed a further volley of bricks knocking a tailor's dummy to the floor, and more whoops of delight as it rolled into the street. The boys launched more bricks at the remaining mannequins as if they were playing a game of knock coconuts at the annual funfair in the summer. Within a couple of minutes, not a single mannequin remained upright. Having wearied of this entertainment, the boys ran up the road to find another window to smash.

Luc felt an icy chill creep over him. The vision of Oscar hanging from the kitchen ceiling returned to him, and without looking at Alain, he whispered, 'I'm afraid. We should turn back.'

Alain looked at Luc, whose face was strained and waxen, and grasped his forearm to give him some strength. 'Me. too, but we can't leave. We've three people to rescue from this madness.'

'Jean-Claude should be with us. He's never here to take the risks. It's always you and me who he puts in danger.'

'You know the reason, we've discussed it before. He doesn't speak German. It would make things difficult if we're stopped. Besides if he came it would mean we could only rescue two people instead of three.'

Luc fell silent as they drove down a couple of streets, past more shops with their windows smashed and a wall daubed with 'Jew bloodsuckers' above a crudely painted Star of David. Ahead of them the road sparkled in the headlights as if it were covered in diamonds. The strange sound they heard was the van's wheels rolling over the broken shards of glass, crushing them into a powder. Alain prayed that the glass would not puncture the wheels. Ten minutes later, Luc parked the van at the appointed place – the medieval Church of St Anne's.

They waited in silence, watching as groups of youths ran up and down the street. They shouted to each other about which shops had been attacked and which had yet to be attended to.

Alain clenched his teeth and Luc his fists so tight that the knuckles had turned white. A police wagon, its windows blacked out, rushed past, its siren blaring.

Luc swallowed hard. 'Where are they?' he said in desperation.

There was a bang on the passenger door. Alain was startled. Through the window he saw a tall blond youth. He slowly wound the window down.

'Why aren't you filming what's happening?' demanded the youth.

Behind him stood a dozen others waiting to hear the answer. Alain looked into their faces. They were flushed with excitement, wide-eyed, deliriously happy, giddy with the exhilaration of the night.

Alain's throat was dry, he could hardly speak. 'We've been ordered not to, not until the end,' he croaked.

'Then you're going to have a long wait,' laughed the boy and the group ran away and up the street.

As he watched them go, Luc exhaled loudly.

'There they are,' said Alain, indicating the corner in front of them. A group of men were walking quickly towards the van.

'But there are five of them!' cried Luc, 'We're expecting only three.'

The back door of the van opened and the five men climbed in and closed the door.

'We were expecting only three of you! Who are the other two?' shouted Alain.

'They are friends, Jews...' said one of the men. 'You have to save them. Can't you see what's happening?'

'We can't take you,' pleaded Luc. 'We've papers for only five people. If we get stopped... it's too many.'

Two of the men looked at Alain and Luc. They had watched from their friend's second-floor apartment as the windows of their shops were smashed, as gangs of youths had run up the street with flaming torches, shouting their names.

Alain looked at them. Their eyes were wide with terror.

One of the Jewish strangers muttered, 'We don't want to get you into trouble. We'll leave. Good luck, my friends, and God be with you.'

Up ahead a policeman turned the corner into the street.

'Stay where you are!' shouted Alain. 'You're here now. It'll be more dangerous for all of us if you're seen leaving the van. We'll manage somehow.'

'We can't,' said Luc, ' We'll be caught.'

'Oh, God, just drive,' shouted Alain to Luc.

The engine came to life, the van moved forward and the policeman saluted as they passed.

In the back, one of the passengers whispered in Hebrew, 'Blessed are you, Lord our God, King of the universe, who bestows good things upon the unworthy and has bestowed upon me every goodness.'

The other whispered the response: 'Amen. He who has bestowed upon us every goodness, may He continue to bestow upon us every goodness.'

****

Ten days later, Bauer was in his study reading the reports of the riots. The first had begun two hours after news of Vom Rath's death had reached Germany.

The SA, SS and Hitler Youth had been ordered to dress in civilian clothes, and armed with sledgehammers and axes, they had soon gone to work. The orders, which were very specific, had come from Himmler himself. Non-Jewish life and property were not to be endangered. Synagogues too close to non-Jewish property were to be smashed rather than burned. Jewish businesses or dwellings could be destroyed but not looted; foreigners, even Jewish foreigners, were not to be subjected to violence.

The police were ordered to arrest as many Jews as the local jails would hold, the preferred targets being healthy young men who could be used as labour for the Reich.

Bauer looked at the report recording the results:

- 200 synagogues damaged or destroyed.
- 29 department stores destroyed.
- 7,500 Jewish businesses destroyed.
- Throughout Germany, Jewish homes ransacked.
- For their own protection, 30,000 Jewish men arrested and are being held in Dachau, Buchenwald and Sachsenhausen concentration camps.
- The number of German Jews killed is uncertain but estimated at 91.

Although violence against Jews had not been explicitly condoned, Bauer was surprised the number of deaths had been so few. There was, however, one distasteful aspect that had spoilt the night. An event that left Bauer feeling disgusted, sick and angry. He had, of course, ordered the immediate arrest of the men responsible. They would be tried for their crime and, when found guilty, would suffer the harshest punishment. Raping a Jewish woman was a crime worse than murder. It violated the

Nuremberg racial laws forbidding sexual intercourse between Germans and Jews. He would see to their punishment himself and would ensure the men would be made an example of.

He put down the paper and picked up the menorah, the ancient nine-branched Hebrew candelabrum, given to him by Heydrich as a memento of his work. He felt its weight in his hand. Although small, it was pure gold. He would have it melted down to make something more appropriate, possibly cufflinks with the eagle and swastika. He placed it in the safe and locked the door.

Two days later, Bauer inspected some of the damage done that night for himself. He noted the ruined synagogues, the uprooted tombstones and violated graves. Some of the fires still burned, fuelled by Jewish prayer books, scrolls, artworks, and philosophy texts. He was satisfied.

Before the riots, Bauer's main concern had been the reaction of foreign governments. As expected, people all over the world read the newspaper reports of the riots, but their leaders did no more than shake their heads. None broke off diplomatic relations.

A week later, the only remaining problem was with the insurance companies. The Jews were claiming four million *Reichsmark* to repair their shop windows. The insurance firms feared that, if they paid the claims, they would go bankrupt, and if they didn't, confidence in German insurance would be harmed.

To Bauer, the solution was a simple one.

The insurance companies would pay the Jews the four million *Reichsmark* being claimed, but the state would confiscate the payment and repay the insurance companies four-fifths of the amount. In addition, the Jewish community would be 'fined one billion *Reichsmark* for their abominable crimes'. Heydrich and the insurance companies were delighted with the suggestion.

As a senior member of Adolf Hitler's bodyguard, Bauer attended Vom Rath's state funeral in Düsseldorf. Hitler and the foreign minister both laid wreaths.

****

113

In London, Sophie read the newspaper reports of *Kristallnacht* to Philip:

> … Mob law ruled in Germany as hooligans went on an orgy of destruction. Our correspondent has observed many anti-Jewish demonstrations in Germany since the Nazis came to power, but never anything as nauseating as this. Racial hatred and hysteria has taken complete hold of an otherwise decent and cultured people. This correspondent witnessed fashionably dressed women clapping their hands with glee and respectable mothers holding up their babies to watch the 'fun'…

Putting down the newspaper, she sighed. 'To read that people are being arrested for the *crime* of being Jewish, being forced to scrub the pavements and tormented by their neighbours is awful. This is worse than any of the anti-Jewish pogroms the tsars implemented in Russia. It has, however, shamed the British government into approving the *Kindertransport* programme for Jewish children.'

'Though I fear the parents will be forced to stay in Germany,' said Philip. 'It's only going to get worse. I should go to Paris. Jean-Claude might need my help.'

'I'll ask Mrs Frobisher to pack our bags. I'm coming to Paris with you.'

'Are you coming to Paris to be with me or because Michael wrote about Juliette in his last letter and you want to… inspect her?'

'I want to be with you, my darling. I have things to organise if the Foundation is to bring as many children as we can out of Germany, but… it would also be nice to meet Juliette at the same time… Do you know her?'

'I've seen her at the bank once or twice. She's very pretty.'

'Do all men measure a girl on how pretty she is?'

'I did when I saw you,' replied Philip, smiling.

'How shallow,' said Sophie, giving her husband a playful slap on the wrist.

Chapter Twenty
La Grosse Pomme

March 1939

The American jazz singer Adelaide Hall shared the top of the bill with Duke Ellington at Harlem's fabled Cotton Club in New York. It brought her wealth and fame, and enough money to buy a home in the all-white community of Larchmont. But the other residents weren't happy with a black neighbour and tried to have Adelaide and her family evicted. Following a mysterious fire at their home, Adelaide, fearing for her loved ones' safety, sold up and left New York for Europe. The family settled in the Paris district of Pigalle, famous for its tourists, theatres and adult shows, and Adelaide opened La Grosse Pomme – 'The Big Apple' – jazz club. It became an overnight sensation, where champagne could be drunk all night and the next table might be occupied by a government minister, wealthy businessman or even a star of the French stage accompanied by his wife... or possibly not. To gain entry into its lively interior, it was necessary to impress the Senegalese doorman who took his responsibility to admit only the best sort of client very seriously.

Michael and Juliette joined the back of the queue. The doorman recognised Michael and immediately called them to the front. The club's door opened and the doorman raised his top hat as Juliette and Michael disappeared inside. A woman in the queue turned to her husband and said, 'They must be somebody. I wonder who they are,' unaware that Michael had given the doorman one hundred francs the previous evening to facilitate their entrance.

A hostess showed Michael and Juliette to their reserved table at the front of the stage. Juliette was wide-eyed with excitement. Every table was full, with those unable to sit leaning against a wall or the bar, and the air was thick with cigarette smoke. Waiters passed between the tables, carrying trays full of sophisticated martini cocktails and fruit-infused vodkas, and the noise of people talking, laughing and enjoying themselves was almost deafening. Michael ordered a bottle of Veuve Clicquot Ponsardin Brut champagne. Juliette, clearly intoxicated by the electric atmosphere, hugged Michael's arm and looked around the club.

She shouted into his ear: 'Isn't that Maurice Chevalier at that table over there?'

'I do believe it is,' replied Michael, remembering that the entertainer was rumoured to be having an affair with Adelaide.

After a few minutes, a spotlight hit the stage. Adelaide Hall, dressed in the most gorgeous costume of floating plumes, made a dramatic entrance down a spiral staircase. As she reached the bottom step, she was joined on stage by twenty other dancers and the band struck up the club's own take on the famous French dance, renamed 'The Canned Apple'. At the end of two minutes of high kicks, splits and cartwheels, Adelaide took her bows and the audience stood and applauded loudly.

Once everyone had caught their breaths, the main event was introduced and the Quintette du Hot Club de France – Stéphane Grappelli, Louis Vola, Django Reinhardt, Roger Chaput and Joseph Reinhardt – took their places. The room went quiet. The band struck up 'Ain't Misbehavin'' and the audience began to follow the swings, rhythms, improvisation and deliberate distortions of the music. Then followed 'Avalon', 'Exactly Like You' and other favourites. Whenever a tune finished, the audience clapped their hands, stamped their feet and shouted for more.

Well after midnight, giddy from the jazz and a second bottle of champagne Michael and Juliette left La Grosse Pomme.

'I've had such a wonderful evening,' she said as the taxi arrived at her apartment.

'I hope we can do it again soon,' replied Michael, regretting the evening had come to an end.

Juliette leaned over and kissed him on the cheek. 'It's been a very special evening. Thank you and, yes, I'd love to do it again.'

He watched her run up the steps to the front door of her apartment building. She turned, blew him a kiss and was gone.

Michael travelled home to his family's house in Boulogne-Billancourt.

All the way home, he could think only of Juliette and the note he'd found in his coat pocket as he'd left the bank that afternoon. He had been tempted to ask her about it but didn't want to spoil the magic he was beginning to feel.

****

At 6 a.m. the following morning, German troops poured into Czechoslovakia.

That evening Hitler made a triumphant entry into Prague, declaring that 'Czechoslovakia has ceased to exist.'

Chapter Twenty-one
The café in Montparnasse

Two days after the jazz club, Michael was sitting in a café in Montparnasse. A Parisian café is one of the few places where every strata of French society can mingle. Sit in any café and you will see the regulars arrive at the same time every day, study the familiar menu for some minutes, order the same coffee and pastry they had eaten the day before and leave at precisely the same time. For many, it is their living room, office and library, where they collect their mail and have business meetings, and where a lunch can last two or even three hours. It is also where a Frenchman feels free to exchange ideas, and as a result draws to it aristocrats, intellectuals, artists, writers and the rabble. The result is that the café has always been a hotbed of political discussion and intrigue. If proof were needed, it is said that Karl Marx met Engels in a Parisian café and over coffee developed the ideas in the 'Bible of the working class', *Das Kapital*.

Michael looked around the café, at waiters in their black uniforms and long white aprons weaving their way between the wicker chairs, delivering cups of coffee, glasses of Chablis, *mille-feuille* pastries and onion soup. He recognised the man in the far corner reading a newspaper and sending a stream of blue smoke from his Gauloises cigarette into the air from his last visit, but he wasn't the man Michael was waiting for.

One of the waiters delivered the black coffee and the slice of *Opéra gâteau* he had ordered. Michael savoured the bitter black liquid and picked up his fork to cut into the elegant cake made up of thin layers of joconde sponge soaked in syrup and layered with coffee buttercream and chocolate ganache. Once finished, he glanced at the slip of paper left in a saucer by the waiter, paid the amount requested, added a few centimes as a tip and got up to leave.

'Excuse me,' asked a man at a table a few feet away. 'Have you finished with your newspaper?'

'I have,' said Michael, handing it to him.

The man waited for a minute, stuffed the newspaper into his bag, and walked into the street, his own coffee half finished. Hidden inside the newspaper was the information the note inside Michael's raincoat pocket had ordered him to acquire. The envelope would be in Berlin before nightfall.

****

Christopher Hatton sat in an apartment close to Carlton Terrace that the German embassy kept for meetings that could not be held on a park bench in St James's Park without causing suspicion. He hoped the meeting wouldn't take up too much time. He'd arranged another hour's tuition with Dot at the orphanage in Poplar.

'I've talked to members of the Anglo-German Fellowship. Some of them have been meeting with the prime minister and encouraging government ministers to do everything to avoid war with Germany. They tell me that the prime minister has shied away from war. He's risked his political career to help Hitler get what Germany wanted in Austria and Czechoslovakia, and he also knows that Britain can't defend a country on the other side of Europe. Also that Britain can't afford a war.'

'Have you any evidence I can pass on to Berlin?'

'This,' Hatton passed his contact a sheet of paper. 'It's part of a report from the Bank of England.'

The German read the paper and its final short paragraph:

> … Unlike 1914, England should not allow itself to blunder into a war that is likely to last years… such is the fate of rich countries; that not even England has the money to fight a world war.

120

'Where did you get this?' asked the German.

'The contact at the Bank of England.'

'Excellent! I'll get this sent to Berlin at once.'

****

Two days later, Rudolf Bauer was comparing the messages left at the café in Paris by FAOLAN and the one given to the diplomat in London by Christopher Hatton. Interesting, thought Bauer, how two reports on the same situation could be so utterly at odds with each other, but which was correct? They couldn't both be.

Hatton's information insisted that England would never go to war with Germany. Finances would not allow it and Britain could not possibly benefit from such a war. Hatton's report also pointed out that the British prime minister had lost a beloved cousin in the Great War and, ever since, had proclaimed that wars have no winners, only losers. Hatton had even included secret communications from Britain's dominions of South Africa, Australia and Canada, indicating their reluctance to sacrifice their soldiers on any future battlefield in Europe.

FAOLAN's message emphatically took the opposite view. It said that, if Germany attacked Poland, both France and Britain would be likely to go to war against the aggressor. It detailed the huge numbers of troops available to the French. Bauer studied the statistics of Michael's paper. It detailed a military force that dwarfed Germany's, facts that Bauer already knew. Nevertheless he read it once more:

> France is prepared for a war with Germany. The French army has in excess of 900,000 regular troops. In addition, there are five million reservists and all have received some military training.

Bauer was aware that Germany's ninety divisions amounted to one-and-a-half million men, one-sixth the size of the French army, and were stationed on the east side of Germany, ready to invade Poland. If, after the invasion of Poland, Britain and

France attacked in the west, Germany would be unable to resist and, within days, would lose a war.

Bauer hoped Christopher Hatton's assessment was the correct one. His was, after all, based on information coming out of the British Foreign Office and would suit Germany's plans best. Yet FAOLAN's report came from one of the best sources of information in Europe, the top floor of the Tagleva bank in Paris. Whichever report proved correct, Hatton's or FAOLAN's, the die was already cast.

Chapter Twenty-two
The last days of peace

July 1939

Michael and Juliette arrived at Saint-Germain-en-Laye.

Walking in the gardens, Michael was in the middle of a lecture on the history of the *château* while Juliette listened attentively, her arm threaded in his. '... From its long stone terrace you can see Paris in the distance—'

Juliette interrupted, 'Tell me: why does the town have a baby's cradle as part of its coat of arms?'

'I don't know,' replied Michael.

'There's no point in me bringing you on these trips if you don't know the answers to my questions!' she exclaimed.

Michael laughed.

Looking into the distance, she said, 'Wasn't it because Louis XIV was born in the *château*, and to celebrate the birth the town included the cradle in their coat of arms. Later, the first Napoleon established his cavalry officers' training school here, and in 1919, the treaty of Saint-Germain was signed at the *château*, officially recognising Czechoslovakia and Poland as independent nations.'

Michael blushed. 'You've known the history of this place all along and you've let me prattle on. Why didn't you stop me?'

'Perhaps I enjoy hearing you prattle,' giggled Juliette.

'I'm sorry – was I being pompous?'

'It's something you men can't help, so I shouldn't tease you.'

Michael blushed even more, much to Juliette's delight. 'Can I make up for it by buying you lunch?' he asked.

'Of course, you can.'

Michael roared with laughter and kissed her on the hand, and arm in arm, they walked towards the restaurant.

After aperitifs, they were served a delicious cream of watercress soup, followed by the *maître d'hôtel*'s suggestion of chicken cooked with snails and served with bread sauce. After the meal, Juliette smiled and, reaching over, touched his hand.

'Thank you for a lovely morning. I've so enjoyed it.'

'We'll have many more, and I promise not to show off next time.'

'Actually, I like it when you show off,' she smiled. Then she paused and looked at him seriously. 'Michael, can I ask – what will you do if there's a war?'

He'd tried to answer the same question for himself. Being eligible to fight for both the French and English, he knew that both countries could conscript him into their army. He'd decided that, if war did come, he would quickly volunteer for the British. He hadn't forgotten that he had taken an oath to serve King George at Wewelsburg Castle.

'I'm sure it won't come to war,' Michael replied. 'Shall we go to see a film at the Cinéma Rex tomorrow evening?'

'I'd love that,' she answered.

****

Jean-Claude and Sébastien were in their apartment with Luc and Alain.

'So far we've brought twelve men out of Germany, but it isn't enough. There are so many more who need rescuing,' said Jean-Claude.

Luc sighed. 'I'll admit that the television van has worked. And despite attracting attention from crowds of people, no one suspects it isn't what it pretends to be. The problem is, the political situation has become too difficult, and crossing the border between France and Germany is now too dangerous.'

'I agree with Luc,' said Alain. 'We've done as much as we can for the moment. The officials on both sides of the border are getting twitchy and suspicious. If we aren't arrested by the Germans, French soldiers are likely to shoot at any German vehicle first and then ask questions. We shouldn't risk our luck.'

Jean-Claude knew that Luc and Alain were right. They took the main risks and it would be unfair to put them in additional danger. Now that they all agreed that it was too dangerous to continue to rescue more people from Germany, Jean-Claude felt an acute sense of failure. A dozen people had been saved, but it was such a small and insignificant number. There were so many more trapped in Germany.

****

At work the following day Katherine du Bois noted that Michael and Juliette ignored each other at work more than was natural. She couldn't fail to notice the lingering looks Michael gave Juliette and the occasional whispered message. Most people at the bank might have expected her to disapprove of their blossoming love affair for some reason, but Katherine didn't have time to be concerned with young love. For the past three years, she'd had her own secret affair – with a married man working in the president's office at the Élysée Palace – to worry about. As long as their love affair didn't adversely affect their work on the fifth floor she was content to ignore it.

'Michael, I've had a message that your father would like to see you.'

Michael took the stairs to the floor below. As his father's secretary had already left for the day, he knocked on the door to the inner office before walking in. His father, sitting at his desk signing papers, looked up and smiled.

'Michael, good evening and thank you for giving up your time to come to see me.'

Michael smiled at his father's politeness. *The quality and mark of a gentleman. He's always polite, even to us children.*

'I'm about to leave to meet someone at the Hôtel du Louvre,' Philip continued. 'Would you accompany me so we can talk on the way?'

The hotel was a favourite meeting place of his father's, for no other reason than Sir Arthur Conan Doyle had featured it in an adventure of Sherlock Holmes. It gave his father a connection to England, if ever so slightly. The walk to the Avenue de l'Opéra was a short one, so Michael assumed the conversation would not be of great importance and was thankful that he would not be too delayed meeting Juliette.

As they set out, neither noticed the man in the trilby hat on the opposite side of the street who also began walking towards the Hôtel du Louvre.

Philip said, 'Michael, I'm going to London for a few days to see Winston Churchill, among other people. He's asked me if you would be coming to London, too. He's anxious to see you. We wouldn't be away for long, three weeks at the most, and your presence would be very useful to me. I'd also enjoy your company.'

Michael's thoughts immediately turned to Juliette. Since their first date, he hadn't been able to stop thinking about her. He got up and went to sleep dreaming of their future together. The talk of war, work at the Tagleva bank and everything else going on in the world was a rude intrusion into the time they could spend together. He delighted in her company – watching as she curled a lock of her hair between thumb and forefinger as she thought and tilted her head when she didn't understand something, and listening to the way she emphasised certain words. Most of all, he loved the way she tossed her head back when she laughed, how she teased him, and the silly gifts they bought each other. Alone in his bed at night, he would read, over and over again, the notes and letters she sent him and carefully locked them away in the antique box he'd bought for the purpose in the Flea Market. Three weeks sounded like a lifetime; it was a lifetime.

Perhaps he could persuade his father to allow him to travel to Paris for a weekend. Three weeks was so long.

****

One of the early notes in Michael's raincoat had told him that, in an emergency, he was to go to 78 Rue de Lille and chalk a 'Z' on the building. The chalk mark could be seen from and would be understood by the German embassy on the opposite side of the road. The day after scrawling the chalk mark, and at precisely six-thirty, Michael walked into Les Deux Magots café on Place Saint-Germain des Prés. The two wooden Chinese figurines of mandarins, which gave the café its name, gazed serenely over the room of people enjoying their after-work coffees and aperitifs. Michael spied a free table and slid onto the red moleskin banquette, placing the newspaper next to him.

A waiter approached to take his order.

Ten minutes later, a man walked into the café and asked, 'Is the seat next to you vacant or is it reserved for your newspaper?'

'It is vacant,' replied Michael, removing the paper to allow the German contact to sit down.

'What news have you?' he whispered quietly to Michael after ordering a coffee.

'I'm to go to London with my father and will probably stay there for a few weeks.'

'What will you be doing there?'

'He has meetings with various government officials and the Bank of England and wants me to be his personal secretary.'

'After you arrive in London, go to the Russian Tea Room in Kensington. Go on a Tuesday evening and ask for Anna Wolkoff. She will be expecting you and will give you a radio transmitter and code book. Use it to keep in contact with us.'

The man got up and walked out of the café.

After leaving the Les Deux Magots, Michael boarded the Métro. He was not relishing having to tell Juliette he was going to England with his father. He would soften the blow by promising to use the boat train to visit Paris at least once. With increasing anticipation, he walked down the Rue des Rosiers into the centre of the Jewish quarter to meet her at a coffee shop.

'I'm sorry I'm late,' he said, kissing her on the cheek.

'I've ordered you a coffee and your favourite pastry.'

'Perfect.'

The coffee and pastries arrived. Juliette knew he had something serious to say, an intuition confirmed when the pastry – folded up with cream cheese and apricot filling and sprinkled with sugar – remained untouched. Usually it would be quickly devoured and then he would ask if she would think him greedy if he ordered another.

'I have something to tell you. My father's going to England and I'm to go with him to act as his personal secretary. It'll mean I'll be in London for a few weeks, three at the most. He's agreed that I can come back to Paris to see you during week-ends... and... perhaps you could come over to England to see me.'

'Three weeks apart won't be such a hardship,' she said.

'It will be a hardship for me!' said Michael. 'You know how much I love you.'

Her little finger touched his and stroked it softly. She was smiling at him. He wanted to pull her close and kiss her but knew she would not be pleased if he did so in the café.

'Perhaps I'll find a nice Frenchman to take me out to dinner now that my Englishman's abandoning me,' she said.

Michael felt his stomach tighten as if a knife had been thrust into him, cutting him to the very core.

'You won't, will you? I'm not abandoning you – it's work.'

'Then I won't but only if you promise to write to me every day via the bank's telegraph,' she said. 'But you'd better be discreet,' she laughed.

'I'll send you a coded message only you can read. It will be made up of a collection of three numbers. Each group will refer to a word in a book. The first will indicate the page, the second the line and the third the word. I'll buy two copies of a book tomorrow to make sure we both use the same edition.'

'And which book do you suggest we use for our secret code?'

'How about Gustave Flaubert's *Madame Bovary*?'

Juliette smiled back at him, 'Trust a man to choose a book that was banned for salacious content. Perhaps I should take note of the novel's cautionary tale of romanticised, forbidden love?'

Michael spluttered: 'I meant nothing by it. I thought it was a good book. Perhaps we should use *Anna Karenina* instead.'

Juliette laughed at his embarrassment and placed her hand over his. Looking into his eyes, she whispered, 'Then, before you depart for England, and perhaps tonight, you should show me some romanticised, forbidden love?'

His mouth fell open. She raised one finger, pushed up his chin and looked into his eyes. 'Well?' she asked.

Michael said nothing. His expression was answer enough.

Chapter Twenty-three
An interview

August 1939

Jean-Claude was in his office meeting with the Bank of Tag-leva's chief accountant, Tobias Meijers. Jean-Claude liked Tobias and appreciated his acute mind and flexible approach to accounting that had, over the years, made him invaluable to the bank. His staff on the second and third floors worked very hard for him, except when his family visited. On those occasions, the female staff would fuss around his six-year-old son who would sit on the floor and play, making piles with centime coins kept specifically for the purpose in a cake tin.

'What's your assessment?' asked Jean-Claude.

Even after eighteen years living in France Tobias's Dutch accent was still evident and was emphasised by the rapidity of his speech. 'Germany imports over a third of its raw materials, most of its butter, oil and vegetables to feed its population. Despite this, there is still a shortage of food. Hitler's promise of agricultural self-sufficiency can't be achieved because of a shortage of resources, workers and machinery. In addition the Germans' search for artificial ingredients to replace commodities such as oil, rubber, textiles and coffee hasn't been a success. It's obvious to the Nazis that if they are to stay in power, they will have to keep improving conditions for the population. That can only realistically be achieved by expanding Germany's borders.'

'So you think war is inevitable?'

'Yes, of course, inevitable.'

'What do you suggest we do to prepare?' asked Jean-Claude.

'I hope I'm wrong but a war with Germany doesn't guarantee a victory for France. German troops have marched into Paris before, and if that happened again, we could expect any gold and currency to be confiscated by the German victors. As a precaution, I've been encouraging our clients to let us transfer their gold deposits to London or New York. Around half our clients have done that.'

Tobias paused. 'Of course, the major problem for the bank is the Foundation. Both France and Britain forbid the export of works of art without a licence. The art collection will be at risk if Germany occupies Paris.'

'Can we ask the French government for a special licence to send the important pieces to London?' asked Jean-Claude.

'No, I'm afraid not. They wouldn't allow it... even with the threat of war. Of course, we must hope that, when the war comes, France is victorious.'

****

In London a week later, Philip's days were filled with meetings.

This morning's meeting was at His Majesty's Treasury. Around the long oak table were bankers, civil servants from the Treasury and the Foreign Office, some businessmen and a couple of economists. Philip had been allocated a seat near the middle of the table, it seemed obvious to him that he was not expected to contribute much to the discussion.

One of the managers from the Bank of England began the meeting. 'At the start of the last conflict, there was public panic and the banks had to be temporarily closed. The stock exchange, Hatton Garden diamond merchants and goldsmiths around Holborn were also ordered to close their doors. It's worth reminding you all that the reason behind the directive to the money market was to prevent people withdrawing currency and buying diamonds or gold, and thus causing financial difficulties with the supply of money for vital war materiel...'

Philip hoped the pompous ass wasn't intending to speak for long.

'... The question for us to consider, and so that I can send a report to our masters that they will accept, is: should there be another conflict, will it be prudent to do the same? Now I suggest I outline the basis for our discussion...'

For half an hour, the Bank of England manager outlined his ideas and then the discussion flowed one way and another.

Eventually Philip interrupted.

'I was part of the decision to close the banks and the stock exchange at the start of the last conflict. I now consider that it was a mistake.' Everyone in the room looked at him. 'The reason it was a mistake was that, when people couldn't get at their money, they assumed the worst, and there were riots in the streets. I would expect things will be calmer next time. This is because the United States has already declared its intention to remain neutral. As a result, Wall Street brokers are giddy with the prospect of the huge profits they expect can be made from a war in Europe. American companies are being told they will be able to provide both sides with the materiel needed to conduct a war. The magazine *Business Week* has just published an article entitled 'War makes it a sellers' market' and I anticipate that, the day war is declared, the stock markets in New York, Chicago and San Francisco will gain around twenty per cent—'

One of the men around the table interrupted. 'So, it's your opinion that there's no need to close the banks because there won't be a run on gold, because everyone will be buying stocks in companies that will benefit from a war?'

'I'm convinced that will be the case in America. If I'm right, it should stabilise things in Europe. I believe closing the banks would only cause unnecessary panic.'

Heads nodded in agreement around the table.

'There is one further thing I think should be considered.'

Everyone leaned forward so that they could see Philip, as well as hear any further advice he had to give.

'I suggest the government requires all people living in the UK to declare their securities with the Treasury. In the event of a war, it will give the government an estimate of the country's total worth. Armed with that knowledge, the Treasury will be able to negotiate loans from the Americans on more favourable terms.'

Once more, everyone nodded their agreement.

Half an hour later the meeting had agreed to keep the money market open.

After the meeting, Philip took a taxi to Simpson's-in-the-Strand where he had arranged to meet Michael for lunch. They took their seats at a table in one of the booths in the downstairs dining room. As the roast beef trolley was wheeled in front of them and the waiter began to carve the meet and pile up their plates, Philip declared, 'Make the most of this, Michael. Should there be a war, I suspect that Simpson's will be severely hit by a shortage of butchers' meat. Their magnificent sirloins of beef and saddles of mutton will disappear from the trolleys, not to be seen again in their full glory until long after the end of hostilities. We may not eat like this again for a long while.'

Michael smiled at his father's Englishness.

'I had hoped to go back to France for a few days and see Juliette but I've been asked to go to meet someone in Oxford so I'll have to delay Paris and go to Oxford instead. I wondered if you knew anything about it?' he said.

'I had suspected that it might have been the reason you were asked to come to London with me. With the concerns over a war, people with language skills are being recruited by all sorts of government departments. Will you go?'

'I sent a message to Juliette to say I'll be in Paris in a couple of weeks' time.' replied Michael as he covered a forkful of sirloin with horseradish sauce.

****

The usual method for recruiting someone into HM Secret Intelligence was for, one afternoon, a promising young man, usually from an Oxbridge university, to find himself invited to tea with a classics don.

Michael had not attended either university but, despite the impediment, found himself sitting in a leather armchair in a quiet oak-panelled study in an Oxford college. On the table in front of him was a plate piled high with a dozen hot buttered crumpets and a huge pot of tea that could have satisfied the thirsts of six or more people. In a corner of the room, a gramophone filled the air with horns and violins accompanying a choir singing the Sequentia of Mozart's Requiem Mass in D minor.

Michael looked at the grey-haired man dressed in dark brown corduroy trousers, slippers and a faded fawn-coloured cardigan pitted down one side with burn holes from the pipe that never left the man's mouth.

His host shouted above the music, 'Help yourself to crumpets, young man! I know how hungry you students always are!'

'I'm not a student!' Michael helpfully shouted back.

Aren't you?... Yours wasn't the prelim I marked yesterday?... Probably for the best... Your reasoning over why the Athenians made their allies pay tribute during the Peloponnesian War was lacking... Needed some quotes from Thucydides... Only gave you a *beta-alpha*...'

The man coughed and more hot ash cascaded down his cardigan. The interrogation began. Questions followed in quick succession and the answers competed to be heard above the choir in the far side of the room.

'Tell me about your family, which schools did you attend, what languages do you speak, which gentleman's club does your father belong to?'

****

After an hour, the don poured himself his fourth cup of tea, threw two heaped teaspoons of sugar into the brown liquid, stirred vigorously, noisily tapped the spoon on the side of the cup and took a large gulp of the cold liquid.

'Have you ever considered "official" work?' he asked.

'I thought that's why I was here,' replied Michael.

A pair of bushy eyebrows were raised.

'Quite so, young man, quite so, but it's for me to ask, not for you to volunteer.'

It took all of Michael's self-control to smile back at his inquisitor and not fall to the floor in convulsions of laughter.

The sixth movement of the Requiem's Sequentia – Lacrymosa – began and, as Mozart never finished it, broke off after only eight bars. The room was now strangely quiet. The interview had come to an abrupt end.

Michael found himself back on the street walking towards the train station, his hands greasy from the buttered crumpets. Doubtless he had failed the interview, though the afternoon had been an experience. Michael wondered if all university professors were as eccentric and on the train home, he wondered what relevance his father's membership of Brook's and the Reform Club had for him being of service to his country.

****

Two days later he received a letter from an anonymous government department inviting him to attend a second series of interviews, to be held at a building opposite St James's Park Underground station in London.

Before any interviews began, he was told to sign the Official Secrets Act. 'Discuss any of the stages of this interview process with anyone and you could be imprisoned,' he was told. Michael signed.

The first person to interview him beat about the bush, never quite coming to the point. There followed one interview after another, none of which seemed to have any purpose. At the end of the day, his language skills were tested.

'You speak Russian and French fluently.'

'Yes. Russian is a family language and I've lived in France since I was a child.'

'How did you come to learn German?'

'I studied it in school and recently spent almost a year with a German family.'

'And what did you do when you were there?'

'I attended a training course at the Abwehr in Berlin.'

The interviewer frowned and cleared his throat. 'Young man, we don't make jokes like that here.'

At the end of the day, he was given a medical to ensure that he was, in fact, male and didn't have flat feet.

Four days later, Michael received a further letter asking him to attend an assessment course and enclosing a rail warrant for the journey. The night before he left, he sent a message to Juliette saying he would be travelling to Scotland and would contact her on his return.

****

Michael thought Barry Buddon Army Training Camp the most God-forsaken hell-hole. He shared the draughty wooden billet with ten others. The only heat coming from a little storm stove in the centre of the barracks. It provided limited comfort to those who slept on the metal beds, each with a one-inch mattress, single pillow and two blankets. Training started at four in the morning with a two-hour hike before breakfast. Then followed lectures on map reading, survival training, firearms practice and surviving interrogation. During the afternoons, he learned how to parachute out of a plane and how to use explosives. At the end of each day, he was exhausted, but at least the food was plentiful. Even so, he lost weight.

Lying on his bed at the end of each day, in those brief moments before he fell asleep, his thoughts turned to Juliette. He longed for the end of his training when he might go back to Paris.

****

Rudolf Bauer was in Berlin reading the weather report. The following day was predicted to be warm and dry with no immediate prospects of heavy rain. Perfect for mobile operations. Five German armies, over a million men, two thousand tanks and nearly two thousand aircraft were ready to cross the Polish border.

The scheme that would give Hitler a justification for an attack on Poland had been devised. An SS unit, pretending to be a Polish army unit, would attack a radio tower four miles inside the German border. It would then broadcast Polish propaganda into the Reich.

Bauer knew it wasn't enough to broadcast anti-German propaganda. If the incident was to have a look of authenticity, it would have to appear that a small skirmish had taken

137

place near the radio tower. The Gestapo were ordered to select several concentration-camp inmates and drug them. They were to be transported to the area, dressed in Polish army uniforms and, with Polish pay-books in their pockets, shot. To the world, it would appear they were casualties of the battle from the Polish army. The attack, such as it was, would give Hitler his propaganda weapon with which to start the war against Poland.

****

When Berliners awoke to a grey, rather sultry day, with clouds hanging low over the city, and heard that German troops had crossed the Polish border, they didn't react with the same wild enthusiasm they had at the start of the Great War. Instead, they walked around in a daze, not quite believing the Führer had taken them into a war they thought he would somehow avoid.

In Paris there was no panic and people went about their daily business as normal. Everyone placed their faith in the Maginot Line, the fortifications that guaranteed the safety of France.

In London, three days after the German invasion, it was a warm September day with bright clear skies, when BBC radio announcer Alvar Lidell's measured, cultivated, calm and authoritative voice came out of the wireless, 'In two minutes the prime minister will broadcast to the nation. Please stand by.'

The glum voice of Prime Minister Neville Chamberlain spoke and ended his broadcast '… and as a consequence this country is at war with Germany.'

The reaction of Londoners was one of surprise, many saying to each other, 'Fancy starting a war on such a beautiful day.'

Then at 11.28 a.m. all hell broke loose. Church bells rang out and air-raid sirens wailed. In Battersea, a woman wearing only one shoe was seen running hysterically up and down the street. In Islington, a woman rushed to tell her friend in the next street and then rushed back home when she remembered she'd forgotten her gas mask. In Surrey, an air-raid warden drove his car around the countryside as his wife shouted through the windows 'Take cover! Take cover!' to the pigs and cows in the fields.

The air raid turned out to be a false alarm.

That evening in pubs and the better restaurants along the Strand, there was no doubt that Britain would win the war.

'Course we'll win! After all, isn't God British?' one man told another.

'And if God needs a little help there's always the Royal Navy,' someone helpfully added from the far end of the bar.

Chapter Twenty-four
Calm before the storm

September 1939

Within days of war being declared, London changed. Barrage balloons rose above the rooftops, pillar boxes were painted over with yellow gas-sensitive paint and sandbags were piled round the entrances to shops and public buildings.

Michael, already under training, was immediately conscripted into the British army. As he was already training to join the intelligence service some faceless person somewhere thought it would be a good idea that he become an officer and so he began another nine weeks of training. To Michael, now in uniform and under military law, it was a miserable decision, the time he'd planned to be in Paris with Juliette was replaced with tedious days of marching, weapons drill and having a sergeant-major shouting in his ear: 'Sir, the object of well-polished boots is that, one day, sir might hope to give some poor unfortunate lass the vague impression that yer an officer an' a geneleman. Now polish 'em again!'

As if polished boots are going to win this war...

****

His training over, Second Lieutenant Michael Tagleva once more found himself stuck in London, away from Juliette. At the start, he consoled himself by anticipating that work with SIS – the Secret Intelligence Service – would be exciting. Yet these past weeks had been one tedious day after another, which, in his opinion, didn't allow him to make any contribution at all to help Britain win the war.

His days were spent using the Emergency Powers Act to investigate German nationals living in Britain.

'They all need investigating to assess if they are pro-Nazi or not,' he was told by a senior officer.

Typically he would travel by train to places like Welwyn Garden City, and knock on doors that were opened by middle-aged men and women. Once shown into the front room, he would usually find wide-eyed children who, seeing his uniform, stood up nervously. Michael would smile as he tried to put the children at ease by handing them boiled sweets from a paper bag he kept in his pocket for the purpose.

Michael would carefully explain to the family that, on arriving in England, they had been registered as 'aliens'. Now that Britain was at war with Germany, their status had changed to 'enemy aliens'. Although he sympathised with the family's concern that they had been categorised as enemies, it was his duty to tell them that they must appear before a tribunal to decide if they were genuine refugees or Nazi sympathisers.

'How can we be Nazi sympathisers? We are Jews,' he was often told.

Michael assured them that the tribunal was a formality and they had nothing to worry about since the family had fled Nazi oppression. After half an hour he would shake hands with the husband and wife and wish them all the best.

On the way back to London, he always longed to be doing something more useful, possibly defending Belgium with the British Expeditionary Force. In Belgium, he would be closer to Juliette. His thoughts would turn to the last time they had made love and remembered her soft hair, the powder-white skin, the tiny mole on her shoulder, the way she moaned as he flicked his tongue over her nipples.

He knew that such thoughts only made the distance between them seem infinite and more painful, and he was always glad when he arrived at the office so that he could put them to the back of his mind as he wrote his reports.

****

Despite the declaration of war, the routine at the Tagleva bank in Rue Pierre Charron continued much as normal. Juliette took the daily financial report down to Jean-Claude's office.

'Have you heard from Michael?' he asked her.

'I get a letter every couple of days. He hopes to get some leave soon and come to Paris. Though I don't know when that might happen now that he's joined the army, hopefully within the next couple of months.' She smiled and left the room.

Jean-Claude picked up the report and glanced at it, but found he couldn't concentrate and walked over to the sideboard and poured himself a coffee.

Everyone in Paris was waiting for something to happen. Like so many others in the city he was preparing himself in case the worst happened, he had succumbed to the temptation of buying a few of the luxuries he expected might become scarce for the six months most people said the war would last. Bags of fresh coffee beans filled a drawer in the kitchen, four cases of champagne were stored in a cupboard in the hallway and a new pair of shoes, still in their box, sat in the bottom of his wardrobe.

Preparations to maintain his standard of living were not the only ones he'd made. He and Alain had stripped the German lettering off the television van and had driven it from its hiding place to a garage in Paris. Despite the fact that the van was now redundant and would never be used again Jean-Claude was attached to it and wanted to ensure the vehicle was safe. Perhaps after the war he would convert it to a mobile home and he and Sébastien would use it to tour the countryside, visiting small towns and eating in local restaurants.

****

The start of the war was seemingly filled with endless months of inactivity where Britain achieved very little and which people nicknamed the 'Phoney war'. Winston Churchill invited Philip and Sophie to sit in the Strangers' Gallery in the House of Commons and listen to the debate. The debate in the chamber, noisy and filled with anger, turned into a vote of no confidence in the prime minister after one member of Parliament savaged Chamberlain's leadership. Quoting the words of Oliver Cromwell to the Long Parliament, he shouted, 'You have sat too long here for any good you have been doing. Depart, I say, and let us have done with you. In the name of God, go.'

Chamberlain survived the vote, but as Philip and Sophie looked down on to the green leather benches, it was clear he'd lost the confidence of the Conservative party. Afterwards in the lobby, they met up with Churchill, who informed them that Chamberlain was trying to form a national coalition government.

'Clement Attlee, the Labour leader, has refused to join the government and I see no alternative for Chamberlain but to resign,' said Churchill.

'So will you be prime minister?' enquired Sophie.

Philip interrupted: 'My dear, we are keeping Winston from important meetings. We should leave him to get on.'

As they left their friend to the conclaves, Sophie said to Philip, 'You didn't let Winston answer my question.'

'No, my love, and for a very good reason. There are two candidates for prime minister, Winston and Lord Halifax, the foreign secretary. There will be long and difficult discussions within the Conservative party over who is to be prime minister. Winston would not wish to be seen pressing his candidature.'

'Oh, I see,' said Sophie. 'Who do you think will succeed?'

'There's no doubt that Halifax is Chamberlain's choice as his successor. However, I suspect he will turn down the offer. Halifax probably hopes he will be able to restrain Churchill more effectively by serving under him rather than as his leader. If it all goes wrong, Halifax could then expect to take over as prime minister from a position of strength.'

Sophie sighed. 'It all sounds so cutthroat, so… unpleasant.'

'Politics is. You and I saw that in Russia during the revolution,' replied Philip.

As they left the Houses of Parliament and walked towards Trafalgar Square, a car carrying the 5th Duke of Wellington sped past them, heading towards the House of Lords. The duke expected to influence events and intended to remind colleagues that Churchill was impetuous, switched parties whenever he fancied, and his opposition to appeasement would make the negotiations difficult when Britain was, inevitably, forced to negotiate a peace with Germany. It would be better if Lord Halifax were prime minister.

The Duke of Wellington's hopes were dashed when Chamberlain went to Buckingham Palace, tendered his resignation to the king and recommended that Winston Churchill should be asked to form the next government. Two days later, cheering crowds welcomed their new prime minister to Downing Street.

That day became another when all hell broke out.

Chapter Twenty-five
Dover Castle

May 1940

It was five-thirty in the morning when the telephone rang and Michael was awoken from a deep sleep. Without raising his head from the pillow, he reached over and picked up the receiver, if for no other reason than to stop the shrill noise.

'Hello,' he said sleepily into the receiver.

A female voice at the other end of the line said: 'Lieutenant Tagleva?'

'Yes,' replied Michael, wiping the sleep from his eyes.

'You're ordered to report to your unit in the Strand.'

'Now?' he queried.

'You were expected half an hour ago,' and the phone went dead.

He pushed back the covers, swung his legs out of the bed, yawned, stood up and walked to the kitchen to boil the kettle. After a quick wash, he put on his uniform and hearing the kettle whistle returned to the kitchen to make a cup of tea and spread a slice of bread with margarine and strawberry jam. Consuming both while standing over the sink, he guessed the 'phoney war' was over.

Arriving at the building that housed his unit, he found uniformed soldiers rushing from room to room with messages, papers and maps. He climbed the two flights of stairs two at a time to report to his boss.

Colonel Tim Wilson was an island of calm surrounded by a sea of panic. A tall man, easily three inches taller than Michael, he sported a thick moustache on his upper lip, had prematurely receding brown hair and a vivid scar that ran from his ear to his mouth.

'My own carelessness,' the colonel would explain, 'Got it in Palestine when I allowed a sabre-wielding Arab to take a slice out of me. He was about to have another go and – I know it was rude but his first attempt had been a touch painful – so I shot him.' Despite appearances Tim Wilson was barely ten years older than Michael.

'Afternoon, Lieutenant Tagleva. Pleased you could make it before the fun's over.'

Chuckling at his own humour, he waved Michael to a chair and sat himself on the corner of his desk.

'Let me brief you on events. Shortly after dawn, the German ambassadors of Belgium and the Netherlands were summoned to the German Foreign Office in Berlin. They were informed that German troops were, at that moment, entering their countries to safeguard their neutrality against an imminent attack from England and France.'

'I take it that we had no such plan to attack either country?' asked Michael.

'Of course not,' the colonel continued. 'The Belgium and the Dutch governments had warned us that such an attack from Germany was imminent, but with the political upheaval over Chamberlain resigning and Churchill becoming prime minister, we were too busy to take much notice. Now that German troops are trampling over bits of Europe they have no right to be in, there's a right panic on.'

'So what do you want me to do?' asked Michael.

'Of all my junior officers, you're the best at analysing problems. I want you to go to the operations room and watch as they plot German troop movements. See if you can come up with some idea of the German attack plan. In particular, their next move and, if possible, the one after that.'

As Michael stood to go, he heard the colonel say, 'Oh, and old man, I suggest you arrange for a bed to be put up in your office. You won't be going home for a couple of days, I daresay...'

As the door closed behind Michael, the colonel muttered, 'Or weeks.'

****

The operations room was one of frantic activity as reports of the German advances flowed in from Belgium, Holland and France.

As he watched from the gallery, members of the Women's Auxiliary Air Force placed blocks of wood representing infantry units and mechanised troops onto a huge map of Europe and, using long sticks, moved them around. Michael saw that German airborne troops had secured the airfields around the Dutch capital. More blocks appeared around the sea port of Rotterdam when twelve Heinkel seaplanes, each crowded with two platoons of troops, landed to attack the port.

Michael thought it didn't take a genius to see that the German plan was to entrap the Dutch government and military command.

****

Michael snatched meals of Marmite and raw cabbage sandwiches and had little sleep as he watched blocks of wood representing the best British and French forces begin to push into Belgium. At the end of the third day, Michael reported to Colonel Wilson.

'The Dutch armed forces have been cut off from the Allies. There is no prospect of any successful resistance and the Dutch cabinet has decided to surrender to avoid unnecessary sacrifices by their troops.'

'Any good news?' sighed the colonel.

'British warships are escorting three Dutch merchant ships with the Dutch gold reserves and Amsterdam's diamond stocks to London. Queen Wilhelmina is on board the destroyer HMS *Hereward*. The Dutch government sailed from the Hook of Holland on HMS *Windsor* and intends to form a government-in-exile in London.'

'I meant, was there good news on the fighting front?' said Wilson testily.

'Afraid not, sir,' came Michael's reply and he returned to the operations room.

****

The French had always considered it impossible for the Germans to move heavy tanks through the Ardennes, so when the first wood blocks showed German Panzers emerging from the forest, there was surprise and panic. French mechanised cavalry advanced into the Ardennes to stop the Germans.

The French could not cope with the speed of the German mobile units. Colonel Tim Wilson arrived in the map room in time to see the French counterattack fizzle out. The French Ninth Army surrendered, and the Second Army was seriously mauled and rendered impotent, retreating with only three functioning tanks. He watched as their wooden blocks were removed from the map.

'What do you think their plan is now?' asked the colonel.

'The breakthrough in the south is forcing the French and British armies into retreat. In the north, the Germans are racing towards the English Channel. It looks as if the objective is to trap the British and French forces between those two German forces and prevent our troops reaching the sea.'

'I agree,' said the colonel.

An orderly entered the room and handed the colonel a note.

'I've been ordered to attend a meeting in Dover with Vice Admiral Bertram Ramsay. The prime minister will be there. You know him, don't you?'

'We've met on a few occasions. He's been a dinner guest at my parents' house,' replied Michael.

'You're ordered to attend me in Dover as my bag carrier.'

****

In Paris, Jean-Claude sat at his conference table. The usual orderly routine of the bank had been disturbed since the German attack on Holland, when all telephone communication with London had been cut. Tobias had told him that cash was being withdrawn by most account holders and more than a few safe-deposit boxes had been emptied by their owners.

Jean-Claude moved to the window and looked down at the street. In the absence of any communication from the authorities, rumours fuelled anxiety. On hearing that French generals were openly stating that France was defeated, the city's citizens were in despair. He felt the foreboding shared by others in the city.

Jean-Claude contemplated the problem from different angles, as if rational thought could somehow force a positive outcome. *Surely the French army must be regrouping for an offensive to repel the Germans?* He picked up the phone to speak to Philip, but the phone was dead. The fabric of society, which he was so accustomed to, was shredding without warning and in a way he could not understand. He replaced the receiver onto the cradle. It was the first time in over twenty years that he hadn't been able to speak to his friend.

****

When Colonel Tim Wilson and Michael arrived at Dover Castle, they were informed by a military policeman that the meeting had already begun in the dynamo room in the cellars of the castle. As the door to that room opened, the colonel and Michael saw a dozen uniformed people hunched over a map of France. Vice Admiral Bertram Ramsay was pointing out something to a man in a dark civilian suit, wearing a homburg hat and smoking a cigar. Everyone in the room looked up from the map as the colonel and Michael walked in.

Michael looked at the expressions on the faces of the admirals and generals in front of him. He didn't need to be told that the presence of a simple lieutenant at such a high-powered conference was an unwelcome one, and he expected to be ordered from the room.

Winston Churchill looked over his spectacles and waved them both forward, saying, 'Colonel, thank you for coming hotfoot from London to help us with our deliberations, and Lieutenant Tagleva, you too are most welcome. The last time we met you informed me you were looking for an adventure. I trust that current events meet with your expectations.'

'They will do, sir,' replied Michael.

Churchill grunted.

As if Michael's presence in the room had always been expected, the group around the table now smiled and nodded their heads in belated welcome. Churchill returned to looking at the map and Vice Admiral Ramsay continued his briefing.

'German tanks have effectively trapped the British Expeditionary Force, which is now retreating towards Dunkirk. As you commanded, I've established an evacuation plan, Operation Dynamo. It's hasty, but its objective is to evacuate as many soldiers off the beaches at Dunkirk as possible.'

'How advanced is this plan of yours?' asked Churchill.

'An appeal has been made for all civilian vessels capable of crossing the Channel to help ferry the troops from the beaches to larger ships offshore. All available seaworthy craft in Kent are being assembled in Sheerness dockyard in preparation for making the crossing to Dunkirk. But we need time to evacuate the troops—'

A brigadier interrupted. 'If we attack southward in coordination with the French First Army under General Blanchard and reconnect with the remainder of the French forces, we might delay the Germans for a few days.'

'I don't think that would hold them for long. The French forces are already defeated,' said Colonel Wilson.

The atmosphere in the room became gloomier.

'Do we have any idea what the conditions on the ground are like?' asked Churchill.

'The retreat is being undertaken amid chaotic conditions. The roads are clogged with civilian refugees all heading away from the fighting. It's forcing the troops to slow down to a snail's pace,' said an army officer.

'At least the true situation isn't known by anyone outside this room. It would cause panic in the country,' said a brigadier.

'That won't be the case for long,' said Churchill. 'The king is to attend a special service at Westminster Abbey when the Archbishop of Canterbury will lead prayers "for our soldiers in dire peril in France". And prayers will also be said in every church throughout the land.'

'When the Germans hear about the service on the radio, they'll know we are in a mess,' muttered a general at one end of the table.

Churchill grunted once more: 'Despite any difficulties, Operation Dynamo must go ahead. It's vital we bring back as many men from the beaches of France as we can… Thank you, gentlemen, for your time.'

As the meeting broke up, Churchill indicated that Vice Admiral Ramsay, Colonel Wilson and Michael were to remain.

Once they were alone, Churchill spoke, elongating his vowels, a habit that made his radio broadcasts instantly recognisable to everyone who heard them. 'Colonel, is there *anything* your people in SIS can do to buy us time. *Every* minute saved means another soldier rescued from the clutches of this N*aaa*zi menace.'

Michael whispered to the colonel.

'Lieutenant Tagleva, if you have something to say, out with it,' said Churchill.

'This may be a stupid thought,' replied Michael.

'Let us be the judge of that, young man,' said the vice admiral.

'Sirs, if you were the German high command and heard, via a reliable source, that the prime minister and possibly the king were travelling to France to surrender, you might consider halting the attack for no other reason than to save German casualties.'

'Are you suggesting we surrender?' said the vice admiral testily.

'No, sir, quite the opposite. But if the Germans *believed* the king and the prime minister were travelling to France, they might halt their advance temporarily. If only to see what happens next.'

'We can't issue a statement saying the king and Mr Churchill are going to make peace. It would cause panic among our civilian population, not to mention our troops, who would think the war has been lost and surrender en masse,' said the vice admiral, more interested in the idea than his words suggested.

Tim Wilson looked at Michael and then at Churchill. 'We wouldn't need to issue a statement. We could use unofficial channels to deliver a message suggesting that peace is about to be asked for. The Germans might also be afraid of killing the king in error and you, sir, and thus have no one to negotiate with.'

Churchill pursed his lips and peered over the top of his spectacles. There was silence for a few moments and then he spoke. 'It's an interesting idea, and at this time I'm prepared to try *anything* that buys us even a short time. But be quite clear, this plan of yours must remain secret, secret *forever*. Any rumour that the king or I *ever* contemplated surrender must *never* become known. I would consider that a single word of this conversation mentioned outside this room would be treason, and in such an event, I'd happily act as your executioner and pull the trigger myself – you both understand me?'

'Yes, sir!' they both replied.

Churchill nodded his assent.

Wilson and Michael saluted, left the room and rushed to their car.

****

In Paris, Juliette was at a loss to know what to do. Sitting in her apartment, she drummed her fingers on the polished table. The sound was as relentless as it was loud. She constantly thought of Michael: *Where is he and is he safe?* She wanted to reach out to him, touch him, hold him, but he was far away in London. Only a few months ago, she had been deliriously happy, with everything she ever dreamed of as a child seeming to come true. Now she could only wait for news and dreaded hearing that all her hopes and dreams had been destroyed.

Then an idea came to her. She would walk to the little hill village of Passy in the 16th arrondissement, on the Right Bank and visit Madeline, her best friend. It would give her something to do, distract her for a few hours so she could forget the war and Michael's absence.

As she walked through the streets of Paris, she noticed how quiet the streets were, that there were few pedestrians and that the shutters over the windows of the grand houses were closed, as if it were a Sunday.

Over coffee, Madeline told her that many of their neighbours in Passy had packed their most valuable possessions in their chauffeured cars and limousines and had driven south towards the Loire valley, where they intended to stay until the dangers of the war were over.

'My father's decided to do the same. He says it'll be safer in the south. We're leaving this afternoon – why don't you come with us? The weather is good, and with the war, it seems like a good time to go on an early vacation to the south. Do say you'll come,' Madeline pleaded encouragingly.

'I can't just leave,' said Juliette, 'I have to work, at the bank.'

After another coffee Juliette began the walk home through the empty streets, with the shops all shut up, Michael in London, and Madeline leaving Paris she had a greater feeling of loneliness. In a street near her home, she saw a family loading their car with their belongings and noticed a man tying a mattress onto the roof of the car.

'What are you doing?' she asked.

'We are leaving. The Germans have bombed Rotterdam – Paris could be next. My mother remembers the German atrocities in the last war. We're going south to stay with my wife's family in Limoges.'

'What's the mattress for?'

'I've been told that German aircraft are firing at cars on the roads. The mattress will protect us from bullets.'

'Good luck to you,' said Juliette to the family and continued her walk home.

If everyone was leaving Paris, perhaps she had been too hasty in turning down Madeline's offer… It was too late now… She had her bicycle, but carrying a suitcase as well as peddling would be uncomfortable… *I could walk*, she thought but then looked down at her high-heeled court shoes and laughed – they wouldn't get her very far. Besides, if she left Paris and Michael came to find her, he wouldn't find her… It was better to stay.

'Michael Tagleva, I hate you for not being with me,' she whispered to the pavement. Two steps further she added, 'Of course, I don't hate you, my darling, but I do miss you so very much.'

****

On the journey back to London from Dover Michael and the colonel had begun to discuss Michael's idea.

'The quickest way to get a message to Germany would be if I walked into the Russian Tea Room and spoke to Anna Wolkoff and asked her to send a message to Berlin,' said Michael.

'Can't do that, old boy. She was arrested a week ago. MI5 knew the tea room was full of spies. It's been closed down.'

'You didn't tell me! Don't you trust me?' asked Michael.

'Trust you, old man? What a strange notion. I don't trust my own mother and you and I aren't even related. So, just remember there's always a bullet in my revolver with your name on it.'

'You're all heart!' protested Michael.

'Best not forget that when it's your turn to buy a round.'

Michael didn't know whether to smile or not. 'So how are we going to get this message to Germany?' he asked instead.

'There's one thing for certain. Berlin needs to believe the source that tells them that they've won this bloody war. Otherwise they'll never stop their tanks. I think it's time you met Rose Williams.'

Chapter Twenty-six
A Sèvres figurine

Madeline and her family drove out of the centre of Paris in their four-door Peugeot 302 sedan. A few miles outside the city, they met thousands of wagons, carts and bicycles clogging the road. The car slowed to a crawl, moving a few metres, stopping and moving another few metres before stopping once more.

Within a few miles, Citroëns, Peugeots and Renaults were littering the side of the road with worried owners standing around contemplating the prospect of walking and wondering how they would carry all their possessions.

'Why are so many cars breaking down?' asked Madeline to her father.

'It's the constant starting and stopping. It's causing the radiators to overheat. Cars aren't designed for this slow progress.'

'Will we break down?'

'We might if we don't go faster – that's if we don't run out of petrol first!' he shouted.

Madeline looked out of the window at a man on a bicycle. The few belongings he carried hung from each end of the handlebar, and around his neck was a small satchel. Madeline was fascinated to see that the tyre on the bicycle's front wheel was missing and had been replaced with corks from wine bottles.

Madeline's father cursed under his breath as the column of refugees was halted again. A French army truck was attempting to push its way against the tide of people. Blocking it was a farmer's cart piled high with hay. The peasant woman sitting on top was trying to cajole the horse to move to the side of the road. Until that manoeuvre was completed, there was no room for the army truck to pass.

Then the masses of people heard the wailing of a 'Jericho's Trumpet' siren as a German Stuka dived to attack. Everyone on the road already knew that the two-man dive-bombers had delivered bombs with remarkable precision on the refugees in Poland and were now doing the same in France. As they had done the last time and the time before, those who had been walking rushed to the side of the road and took cover in the ditch. When the ditch was full, people took shelter behind the trees that lined the road, or crouched behind trucks and carts, and some even took shelter behind other people.

Those in cars abandoned them and their luggage to join the cyclists and pedestrians. The noise from the Stuka falling from the sky became deafening. Women screamed and children closed their eyes tight and hugged their mothers, trying to block out the frightening sound. Bullets ripped through the trees and tore through the metal of the cars, sounding like small stones hitting a metal dustbin. The dust in the road leapt into the air like fountains. Inside one of the cars, a precious Sèvres porcelain figurine, wrapped in tissue and carefully packed on the top of a suitcase, lost its head.

As the aircraft screeched away, people slowly rose from their temporary shelter and surveyed the damage. The horse that had been pulling the cart lay on the road amid a scarlet puddle, and people rushed to manhandle cart and horse to the side of the road.

Madeline's father bent down to give his wife a helping hand. Pulling his wife to her feet, they searched for Madeline. They saw her still in the car: 'The silly girl didn't move to the side of the road.' Inside Madeline sat, her eyes open and unblinking as a small trickle of blood ran out of her mouth, staining her blue silk dress.

****

Rose Williams hadn't intended to work for the government. She was happy as an office girl in the advertising department of a newspaper. But as war loomed, her mother goaded her for not being patriotic and doing something creditable. Tired of her mother's nagging, she applied to join the War Office.

After a few months her intelligence and insight was recognised and she was plucked from the typing pool and found herself working at the Secret Intelligence Service for Charles Maxwell Knight, head of the super-secret unit B5 (B) responsible for counter-subversion.

Rose liked Knight and his deputy Colonel Tim Wilson. They were intelligent, uncompromising and supportive of those who worked for them. She had been with Knight when he had put forward a woman for training as an agent and a pompous civil servant had questioned his decision. Knight told him, 'I hear too often that women are less discreet than men, ruled by their emotions, rely on intuition rather than on reason, that sex plays an unsettling role in their work. My experience has been entirely to the contrary.'

Rose worked with Knight and Wilson to infiltrate the spy ring at the Russian Tea Room in Kensington. She had helped to plan the trap that had led to Anna Wolkoff being arrested. She was part of the group that had searched the apartment of a German spy and found the red book listing the 250 members of the pro-Nazi Right Club: One prince, two princesses, a duke, a marquis, two earls, five other lords, two professors, two reverend gentlemen, twelve MPs, a number of retired army officers, and sundry others with 'Sir' or 'Lady' prefixing their names. All were placed under surveillance.

Despite the Russian Tea Room being closed, the members of the Right Club still at liberty believed that Rose was still an active supporter of German ambitions and could be trusted with all sorts of information. It was a situation that Knight and Wilson found most useful.

Rose Williams walked into Colonel Wilson's office. Seeing the young girl with brown curly hair, large round eyes, thin lips, dressed in a skirt and blouse one could easily have mistaken her for a junior secretary in a small law firm. She looked like a girl that many men would consider vulnerable and in need of their protection. Michael got to his feet and extended his hand. 'Very nice to meet you, Rose,' he said.

His hand was shaken, very briefly.

****

Across the English Channel in Belgium, the north-eastern flank of the Allied armies was under heavy attack and close to collapse. The Germans, only twenty miles from Dunkirk, had 300,000 Allied soldiers trapped on the beach there. The shallow slope of the sands prevented heavy boats from getting in close and the trapped men were a sitting target.

William Mower was a northern lad from Newcastle who had never been abroad prior to the BEF being stationed in France. When his unit was ordered to retreat to Dunkirk, the prospect of going home to England didn't displease him. He hadn't seen much of France and what he had he didn't like too much. The women were pretty enough – well, the young ones were – but as they didn't understand English and he didn't speak French, communication was a bit limited.

There had been the occasion when he'd seen a pretty young lass talking to her friend in the town square where they were billeted. A member of his platoon encouraged him to introduce himself and told him the French words to say. Walking across the square, he rehearsed the phrase he'd been given over and over, trying to copy the French accent correctly. The pretty girl and her friend watched him as he strode over, and he could hear the encouraging cries and whistles from his platoon behind him. Arriving in front of the girl, he adopted his broadest smile and repeated the words he had so carefully rehearsed: *'Mamselle, je veux t'enculer.'*

The stinging slap to his face told him he'd been cruelly set up, and turning back to face his platoon, his suspicions were confirmed. They were doubled up with laughter. France seemed even more inhospitable when his sergeant confirmed that the 'Frenchies' did indeed eat snails, frogs, calf's heads, pig's feet and even bull's testicles.

His platoon had travelled to the Dunkirk area through the previous night in a lorry. It had been forced to drive very slowly, as they had orders not to turn on the lights in case they were seen by German aircraft. To make things worse, it seemed that half the French population were on the same road, walking in the opposite direction.

When William had eventually climbed out of the back of the lorry and looked out onto Dunkirk beach, he saw a scene out of hell. Peering through the smoke between the dunes and the water's edge, he could just see hundreds of dead bodies. Abandoned equipment and vehicles littered the beach, and stuck in the sand right at the water's edge were two ambulances.

Among the confusion, pigs, chickens and horses raced up and down the beach in utter panic, the last knocking to the ground any soldiers who got in their way. There was an overpowering smell of burning oil, and overhead were the angry hornet's whine of dive bombers and the screams of falling bombs. Anti-aircraft and machine-gun fire boomed a reply from the edge of the beach. Someone said something, but William couldn't hear the words above the noise. Then he saw the queues of soldiers wading out into the shallows as if waiting for a bus. Far out to sea, through the smoke, he could see some Royal Navy battleships and, between them, smaller boats shuttled soldiers from the shallows to the larger ships.

Not for the first time, William was afraid.

****

Colonel Wilson, Michael and Rose had spent an hour and a half struggling with the problem of how to halt the German advance on the troops trapped at Dunkirk. It seemed an impossible task.

'We have to persuade Hitler to order the troops to halt. Any message we send needs to be believed and considered serious enough to reach Hitler's ear. But sending one over military radio channels saying that we're surrendering isn't an option,' Wilson reminded them.

'We could use one of the enemy agents we've captured, and who now works for us, to send a direct message to Berlin,' Michael suggested.

'That won't do. The Germans would be sure to smell a rat, how would the agent know the king's and the prime minister's movements?' Rose pointed out.

'God, what's the solution,' said Michael rubbing the back of his neck. Then he whispered, 'Play the game.'

'What game?' asked Rose, confused.

'My father and I used to play a game of bluff when I was young. We used to get people to believe all sorts of daft things… let me think for a minute…'

Rose crossed her arms, tilted her head and looked at Wilson. They both remained quiet for a couple of minutes as Michael stared at one of the walls in the room.

He turned to face them. 'I've got it.'

The colonel and Rose listened to Michael's idea. It seemed crazy, too crazy, so crazy it might work. Half an hour later, after some hurried telephone calls, Michael left the office and walked up the Strand the short distance to The Savoy Hotel. Rose rushed in the opposite direction, down Piccadilly, towards The Ritz.

****

London's grand hotels – The Savoy, Claridge's, The Dorchester and The Ritz – symbolise the preservation of privilege and do their best to insulate their patrons from the world beyond their doors. Soon after war was declared, each became an oasis where, far from the prying eyes of normal people, dancing and drinking the hotel's stock of gin and angostura bitters became a patriotic activity. Within weeks of hostilities starting, the regular clientele had swelled to include wealthy refugees. The con artists and swindlers that usually hid behind the potted palms in these bars and restaurants had a new group of victims to stalk.

The exiled King Zog and Queen Geraldine of Albania, Crown Prince Leka and a variety of sisters, nieces and nephews occupied one entire floor of the Ritz and, it was gossiped, paid their bills in gold bullion. After escaping the Netherlands, Queen Wilhelmina took up residence at Claridge's and the hotel's guests could often see her, in her dressing gown, walking around the hotel followed by a phalanx of ladies-in-waiting dressed head to toe in black evening dress. Her son-in-law,

Prince Bernhard, no less eccentric, caused alarm whenever he enforced the blackout by firing his tommy gun out of his bedroom window at any nearby apartment showing an electric light.

MI5, aware of the influx of large numbers of suspect foreigners, kept a close eye on each hotel, even installing a pair of painfully handsome young men at the Dorchester to watch a group of homosexual Hungarians. By all accounts, charmed by the young men's good looks, the Hungarians were very indiscreet.

The Savoy was no different from the others. Foreign journalists set up offices in expensive bedroom suites, informers met secretly in the hotel's quiet corners, diplomats sipped cocktails in the American Bar, and everyone picked at the plasterwork to check for hidden microphones.

As Michael walked into the Savoy Grill, he saw his father waiting for him at a table in the far corner. Philip rose and shook his hand.

'Nice to see you – it's been a while.'

The waiter approached and handed them the luncheon menu for 21 May 1940. They chose *la crème vichyssoise* followed by *côtes de porc* and ordered a half bottle of wine.

After some small talk, Philip asked, 'So what have you been doing?'

'I can't tell you much, but things in France look dicey.'

When the first course arrived, they stopped their conversation so the waiter would not overhear anything of importance.

Once they were alone again, Philip said, 'I've heard that Giuseppe Bastianini, the Italian ambassador, has offered to act as a mediator between the Allies and Germany.'

'I don't think anything will come of that,' replied Michael.

'I'm not so sure,' said his father. 'I was speaking to a friend yesterday who says Mussolini has offered to negotiate a settlement that would protect European peace for a century.'

'Mussolini's too late. There's a rumour that Churchill is preparing to leave for France, with the king.'

'Why are they going to France?'

'To negotiate a peace with the Germans, I assume,' answered Michael matter-of-factly.

'Oh, then that would explain why Churchill's refused my wife's invitation to dinner. She was very upset by it. I had to spend a good half an hour calming her down this morning.'

They continued their conversation on the prospects of a peace treaty with Germany and the possible terms of an armistice for a few minutes and then changed the subject. Thirty seconds later, a man at the next table got up, walked to the head waiter's desk, paid his bill and rushed to the Italian embassy in Davies Street and the radio room in the basement.

Michael and Philip finished their lunch. Philip handed the head waiter a five-pound note as a tip for reserving a table next to the Italian diplomat.

****

At the Ritz, Rose had arranged to meet a member of the Right Club who she knew was still an active member and still at liberty but did not know that she worked for SIS.

She took him to a quiet corner of the upstairs bar.

'I've had a message in a roundabout way from the Duke of Buccleuch.'

'The Lord Steward of the Royal Household?' he asked.

Rose sounded irritated, 'Yes, yes, the same man who accompanied Lord Brocket to celebrate Hitler's fiftieth birthday. The message is important. We need Brocket to get it to Berlin urgently. Tell Brocket to use the Swedish diplomat he knows to send the message... what's his name...?'

'Bengt Berg.'

'Yes, that's the man,' said Rose.

'What's the message?'

'Britain's lost the war. The king and Churchill are travelling to France to negotiate a peace with Hitler. The trip is top secret. Very few people in Britain know of it, not even the cabinet's been told. But if the king and the prime minister are killed before they land in France and contact the Germans, the British will have no one to lead them and will fight on forever. Berlin must be told.'

'I'll go and see Brocket now,' said the man and left the Ritz.

****

Back with Rose in the colonel's office in the Strand, Michael related the conversation with his father.

'My father played his part superbly. The Italian diplomat at the next table could hardly contain himself and waited no more than a minute or so before rushing out.'

Wilson smiled, 'Could the Italian have known who you were?'

'Not a chance,' replied Michael.

Rose then recounted her meeting at the Ritz with the member of the Right Club. When she finished, the colonel told her, 'After leaving you at the Ritz, he took a cab to King's Cross and boarded a train to Welwyn Garden City.'

'So all we have to do is to wait,' said Michael.

'I don't think so,' said the colonel. 'Two messages might not be enough. We have to send the Germans as many unrelated bits of information as we can in the hope that they'll put them all together and interpret them the way we want.'

****

That afternoon in Gibraltar, Vice Admiral James Somerville received an urgent and secret radio message from the Admiralty in London. The same message was sent to Cairo to General Sir Richard Nugent O'Connor, commanding the army in the Western Desert. It advised them both to expect a *vital and secret communication* from the prime minister. Both messages were intercepted by the Germans.

The following morning, Michael composed another message, encoded it and tapped out his call sign 'FAOLAN' on the radio he'd collected from the Russian Tea Room. He waited for the response that someone was listening. There was silence. He tapped out the call sign again. Ten seconds later he heard three pips through his headphones, the signal that his call sign had been heard in Berlin. Michael tapped out the message:

Advise barrage balloons hoisted over London. Anti-aircraft guns stationed on Thames near Waterloo station, suggest planes avoid area. Winston Churchill seen leaving London for countryside. HH.

He waited. He heard the three pips again. The message had been received.

'Do you think the Germans will buy it?' asked Michael.

'We'll soon find out,' said the colonel. 'They either stop the advance, thinking we're about to surrender, or destroy our armies utterly. Britain's survival may hinge on what we've done today.'

The room went quiet as the three of them became engrossed in their own thoughts.

Chapter Twenty-seven
The order is given

24 May 1940

The German Panzer commanders had regrouped within sight of Dunkirk and were now waiting for the order to advance. When it came, they would deliver the knockout blow that would be the final destruction of the British Expeditionary Force.

At General Rundstedt's army headquarters at Charleville, Rudolf Bauer was waiting to be summoned into a meeting. He carried the file that contained the messages received from the Italian embassy in London, from a Swedish diplomat known to be sympathetic to the German cause, as well as a radio message from FAOLAN and the cryptic messages from London to various military commanders throughout the British Empire. Together they seemed to suggest that Britain was about to capitulate, that Churchill has left London and was preparing to travel to France with the king of England to surrender in person to the German forces.

Bauer leafed through the papers again. Each one on its own was insignificant, but when read together, they seemed to suggest only one conclusion. Yet Bauer was troubled; doubt gnawed at him. Could the information be relied upon? Why hadn't the British sent an official message to Berlin? That would be more usual, and if the British were defeated, then why the need for secrecy.

An orderly walked over and handed him a communication. He opened it.

Radio communication intercepted from Britain 0530

To: Aérodrome d'Abbeville

Most Secret.
Expected Lyon soonest, air protection required.

Note: Lyon is believed to be the military codename for George VI of Britain. The Aérodrome d'Abbeville is located in Buigny-Saint-Maclou, 4 km north-north-east of Abbeville in the Somme département *in France. The Aérodrome is under the control of the British air force.*

If it were true the British king was flying to France, there could be only one explanation. This could be the military confirmation he'd been waiting for. He hadn't more time to think: the doors to the meeting room opened and Bauer, together with some other officers, walked in. Inside was a long table surrounded by generals and staff officers. In the centre stood Göring flanked by generals Rundstedt and Halder, and in the middle of them all stood the unmistakable figure of the Führer. Bauer raised his arm in salute.

Hitler didn't stop speaking nor look up at the new arrivals.

'The war will be over in weeks. After that, we will conclude a peace with France and then the way will be free for an agreement with Britain. I do admire the British Empire; it brought civilisation to the world. My aim is to make an honourable peace with Britain. I only ask that London recognises the Third Reich's domination of the continent.'

Someone handed the Führer a copy of the intelligence reports. Hitler looked at it and smiled. Bauer wondered if he'd be asked to give an opinion of the messages. The thought of speaking directly to the Führer sent a tingle through him – he felt almost giddy, his mouth dry.

He watched as Hitler went into a huddle with General Rundstedt and Göring. There was some whispering between them. Göring spoke at length; Hitler nodded in agreement and seemed to come to a decision.

Addressing the room, the Nazi leader said, 'I'm ordering that the tank forces halt at the canal line. No further advance will be made until I give further orders.'

To his right, General Halder spluttered, 'But why, *mein* Führer?'

'Because in a few days we will have peace, and further advances will only serve to put our men and equipment at unnecessary risk. Until then the Luftwaffe can harry the British at Dunkirk.'

Halder began to remonstrate: 'But *mein...*'

Hitler raised his hand and glowered at the general.

The general fell silent: *The decision has been made.*

Within a couple of minutes, Bauer found himself outside the meeting room. He was in no doubt he'd witnessed history in the making.

****

On Dunkirk beach, William Mower was up to his armpits in water. He'd been standing in the water for two hours. His skin was shrivelled, his teeth chattered and he couldn't feel his toes. Among the thousands of soldiers waiting to be rescued, no one had the energy to speak much, yet a wild rumour was circulating up and down the line of soldiers that the war was over. William's thoughts turned to the carnage he'd seen on the way to Dunkirk, the piled-up bodies of civilians, the wrecked buildings and the terrible smell of roasting flesh.

William found it difficult to accept the fact that they had been defeated. His history lessons at school had only spoken of a glorious past, of battles where soldiers had fought and won against massive odds, of English invincibility. If this was defeat, he wondered if he would ever see his family again.

Through chattering teeth, he said to the soldier next to him, 'Thank God, the water's like a mill pond.'

An officer a few places in front shouted above the noise, 'Sent by the Lord because he has work for the British nation to do.'

What an arsehole, thought William as the cold water lapped against his chest.

An aircraft screamed overhead. Those around him ducked under the water for protection against the expected hail of bullets. When the officer surfaced again, William said, 'As you are on such canny speaking terms with the Lord, could yer ask him t'stop the Germans shooting at we, sir?'

A few around him laughed. William had not heard laughter for a long time and the strange noise lifted his spirits a little.

Over the next few hours, William became aware of an explosion of activity. An extraordinary sight greeted the queues of soldiers waiting to be evacuated: seemingly innumerable small ships and boats appeared out of the mist. All manner of incongruous craft arrived – barges, passenger ferries, fishing smacks, tugs, motor-powered lifeboats, eel boats, picket boats, yachts and other pleasure vessels, Thames river excursion launches and even a river fire float. They all began to take soldiers on board and ferry them to the larger Royal Navy vessels further out in the Channel.

As a small vessel came close, William was hauled into it, together with about thirty others. Having discarded most of its equipment, the boat was travelling 'light', but despite this, the boat became stuck in the sand on the falling tide.

One of the sailors said to a couple of French soldiers: 'Tha boat's stuck. You'll have to gi' out.'

The Frenchmen remained seated.

'Want 'em thrown overboard?' asked a soldier.

'No need for tha. Now git!' said the sailor pointing to the water.

Reluctantly the Frenchmen climbed back into the water. The boat was turned around and moved towards a tug that lay offshore.

William spent most of the journey to England in the tug's engine room trying to get warm and dry. Arriving at Ramsgate, he disembarked and was told by a girl in a nurse's uniform to get a 'nice cup of tea'.

Joining the queue for the hot cup of very sweet tea, he thrust his hands in his pockets so that no one would see they were shaking.

****

In London a few days later, a service of thanksgiving was held and the dean of St Paul's talked of the 'Miracle of Dunkirk' in his sermon. Sat in his kitchen in Hampstead Christopher Hatton listened to the news on the radio. He couldn't believe that the British army had not been destroyed; it had been rescued off the beaches by hundreds of small boats. Why had the German Panzer tanks halted? Why hadn't they pressed their advantage and destroyed the British army? How could this have happened?

Hatton slammed his fist onto the table. He felt sick, struck in the guts by the betrayal of the Germans. *After everything he had done for them, how could they do this to him?*

Chapter Twenty-eight
The hordes of Goths

10 June 1940

Paris was almost deserted. The French government had already left and the remainder of the population was now in full flight. The city could do nothing but wait for the inevitable. It was an open city, it would not be defended and not one single shot would be fired in its defence.

Jean-Claude was looking out of his office window at the black snowflakes filling the sky. Ash from the mountains of burning files in the courtyards of the Ministry of Foreign Affairs at the Quai d'Orsay, the Préfecture de Police and other government departments danced in the wind. The secrets of the nation were going up in smoke. Within days, possibly hours, hordes of Goths would brazenly march down the Avenue des Champs-Élysées.

Jean-Claude ordered Katherine du Bois to destroy any part of the card index the Germans might find useful. On the floor above, she and the few staff that had not fled the city were busy destroying the brains of the Bank of Tagleva. Large parts of the card index, particularly the political sections, were already empty; very soon the brain would cease to function.

There was nothing useful he could do, and so Jean-Claude left the bank and walked home. He'd arranged to meet Sébastien, Luc and Alain. He found them sitting in silence, nervous that the world they knew was about to disappear, about to be replaced by a vacuum that would swallow their hopes and dreams.

'When do you think they'll arrive?' asked Alain.

'Tomorrow, the day after, the day after that – who knows?' replied Jean-Claude.

No one spoke for a few seconds.

'What should we do?' asked Luc.

'Nothing, absolutely nothing,' said Jean-Claude. 'There is nothing to be done. We can only wait to see what happens. I suggest we meet up again when we know more. In the meantime, stay quiet and do nothing to antagonise the Germans when they finally arrive.'

Alain and Luc left. When they were alone, Sébastien gazed at Jean-Claude. He looked tired, drained of energy. Sébastien walked over and wrapped his arms around his lover and kissed him on the neck, smelling the familiar sandalwood aftershave.

'I love you. We'll be all right,' he whispered.

Jean-Claude's stomach was full of lead. He prayed that things would not be as bad as he feared.

'I love you, too,' he whispered to Sébastien and began to weep.

****

Michael had wanted to send one last message to Juliette before the war engulfed them both, but when he took a cab to the Tagleva bank to ask if he could use the bank's telephone, he was told he was too late. Communications with Paris had been cut days before.

Back in his apartment, Michael sat on his bed, engrossed in his own thoughts. He pulled out a photograph of Juliette from his wallet, stroked her cheek and lips. The smiling image with the familiar dimples looked back at him.

Juliette, my darling, I can forgive you for working for the Germans, putting those notes in my coat pocket. You're my sunshine, my princess and I will forgive you anything. I love you and I know we can sort out any differences. I will come for you, I promise, and until I do, be safe, my darling.

Chapter Twenty-nine
Ignoring the enemy

25 June 1940

Sébastien walked down the Rue Saint-Dominique towards the bread shop he hoped would be open. It was two weeks since he'd seen the first German soldiers in the city, and a fury still smouldered inside him. During those early days, he weighed up the pros and cons of exacting some sort of revenge. After discussing his plans with Jean-Claude, he concluded that, for the time being, there was little to be done other than to ignore the occupiers as best he could.

Marching down the street towards him was a platoon of Germans, their heavy jackboots sounding as one on the cobbles. Sitting astride a well-fed horse, the officer leading them wore the smug expression of the victor. Sébastien's attention was drawn to the far side of the road where two teenage girls giggled and flirted like bitches on heat at the soldiers as they marched past. He wanted to shout at them, call them whores, but knew it would be pointless.

Passing a couple of buildings, he ignored the red flag with its white circle and swastika draped over the front of the building. The Germans had quickly occupied the smarter buildings in the city. The Hôtel Majestic was the headquarters of the German high command. The Luftwaffe occupied the Ritz. The German navy took the Hôtel de la Marine. German counter-intelligence made the Hôtel Lutetia on the Boulevard Rapsail their home from home. The Gestapo established itself at 93 Rue Lauriston near the Élysée Palace, and the German commandant of Paris and his staff occupied the Hôtel Meurice.

It wasn't just the hotels that were no longer available to Parisians. The Cinéma Rex and six of the best nightclubs were now reserved for the exclusive entertainment of German troops. German officers dined at Maxim's and other expensive restaurants, and even Paris's most famous brothel, the One-Two-Two, was reserved for German officers who could indulge in increasingly exotic services the higher up the ornate staircase they climbed.

Jean-Claude and Sébastien hoped that, once inside their apartment building, the reality of the occupation could be kept at a distance, but even that hope disappeared when the empty apartment on the floor below theirs was occupied by a German Luftwaffe officer. The first Sébastien knew about their new neighbour was when the officer stepped into the lift.

'Bonjour, une belle journée,' said the German.

Sébastien smiled and responded, *'Et une bonne journée à vous,'* immediately regretting that he had spoken to the enemy. Ignoring the Germans was going to be more difficult than he had imagined. Even the clocks in Paris were co-operating with the enemy, having all been reset to Berlin time.

****

Jean-Claude knew he would have even more difficulty ignoring the enemy than Sébastien. Within days of the occupation, most of the banks in Paris received a routine visit from the Germans. So he was not surprised when he was informed that a group of officers had entered the bank demanding to be taken to the managing director. His office door opened and three SS officers walked in.

Their leader was polite. 'I am SS-Standartenführer Rudolf Bauer. My colleagues, Sturmbannführers Hoffman and Krüger. I'm here to inform you that the Tagleva bank is now part of the SS Economic and Administrative Department.'

'Are the bank's staff to be dismissed?' enquired Jean-Claude.

'No, Tagleva will continue as a bank. You and the staff will carry on your duties as before. However, all SS finances in Paris will be managed through the bank and supervised by Sturmbannführer Hoffman aided by my men. From time to time we may require your staff to aid us. When that happens, they will be informed of their new duties.'

'I see.'

'You will remain as managing director and keep your office. In future, you will find me in the chairman's office.'

Jean-Claude was shocked, but remained silent.

'I'm told that the bank owns a house in Paris that is usually occupied by the chairman.'

'It does, but the chairman is currently in London,' answered Jean-Claude helpfully.

Bauer smiled, 'I know, as the new chairman of the Bank of Tagleva, I've made arrangements to move into the house. I'm told that you usually meet with the chairman each Thursday morning... In future, those meetings will be with me... Oh, and before I forget, you will arrange for the chairman's salary to be paid, in *Reichsmark*, into my Tagleva account.'

Jean-Claude, unable to speak, just nodded his acceptance of the new arrangements.

'Good. I have a feeling we are going to get on,' said Bauer as he walked over to the mantelpiece. He looked at the French ormolu mantel clock fashioned by the Paris clockmaker Martinot. Opening up the glass front, he altered the hands to Berlin time. Turning back to Jean-Claude, he smiled as if he'd achieved a small victory.

'Now, I would like you to give me a tour of the bank.'

Rudolf Bauer waited for Jean-Claude to open his office door for him and left the room. As they arrived in the anteroom to his office, Jean-Claude's secretary, Nicole Labranche, stood and extended her arm. '*Heil Hitler*,' she said loudly.

Her outstretched arm and the enamel badge displaying the swastika pinned to her dress confirmed to Jean-Claude what he had long suspected. That Nicole had been working for the Germans for some time. It was she who had told them about the internal workings of the bank and how the German officer knew about the Thursday meeting and Phillip's house in Paris. Jean-Claude looked at her, but felt no anger for her betrayal – just pity.

They took the lift to the first floor and walked around the administration departments. Jean-Claude noticed that SS personnel were already occupying a number of desks. The bank's staff, pale and shocked, were obviously waiting for him to say something, but there was no comfort he could give them.

The lift was taken to the second and third floors. The 'buy' and 'sell' sides were inspected.

'There is one change of staff I should have told you about,' said Bauer, 'The accountant, Meijers, no longer works here. Jews are not permitted to work in banking. His office has been allocated to Sturmbannführer Hoffman.'

The group moved to the fifth floor. They found Katherine du Bois and her staff sitting on chairs near the window as SS men leafed through drawers of cards. On seeing Bauer, they came stiffly to attention. An SS lieutenant shook his head, indicating that the card index had been destroyed and was useless.

Bauer had expected nothing else. He looked towards the group of women. In the middle was an extremely attractive girl. Bauer studied her brown hair, the petite perfectly formed nose, and the large dark eyes. He watched as she noticed him looking at her and averted her gaze to the floor.

'Show me the vault,' said Bauer without taking his eyes off the girl.

They arrived in the basement to find three SS officers studying the round polished steel door of the twenty-four-bolt Diebold vault.

'Open it,' ordered Bauer.

Jean-Claude pulled out his key from his coat pocket and walked to the right of the vault's door. The vault manager took up his position to the left side of the door. They inserted their keys and Jean-Claude punched the code into the combination mechanism. The door unlocked and slowly swung open on its ball-bearing hinges.

Bauer walked inside. He viewed the racks of stainless steel, the boxes on the shelves, and indicated that Jean-Claude and the vault manager should join him inside.

'Where are the jewels once owned by the Romanovs?'

'They were taken to London by the chairman when war was declared.'

Bauer nodded – he had expected that to be the answer. 'What's in that?' indicting a large polished-oak box.

'It's part of the Tagleva art collection.'

'Open it, please.'

The box was carried to a table in the centre of the vault by the vault manager and opened. The nineteenth-century German cup fashioned out of rock crystal and enamelled in gold by Reinhold Vasters was lifted out and gently placed on the table. Bauer looked at the cup, which stood ten inches tall. It was a magnificent work of art.

He whispered to Hoffman, 'Have it sent to our fat friend, with my compliments.'

'Göring will be delighted. It should get you an invitation to his hunting lodge at Carinhall.'

Bauer smiled before turning to Jean-Claude. 'In future this vault will be for the sole use of the SS. How many keys are there?'

'There are three pairs. The set we've used to open the vault, another pair is kept in the safe in the accountant's office, and an emergency spare set in the wall safe in the chairman's... your office,' replied Jean-Claude.

'Excellent. You will hand over your keys to Sturmbannführer Hoffman.'

Jean-Claude and the vault manager handed over the keys. Bauer smiled and told them to wait outside. Once alone he opened up the lids of the boxes on the shelves and eventually found what he was looking for.

Bauer looked down into the silk-lined interior of the box and at the illuminated life of the Saxon king Heinrich. He reached in, carefully picked it up, laid it on the table and gently opened the cover.

The gold leaf and coloured letters shone up at him from the vellum pages. He marvelled at the vivid blues, reds, greens and gold of the calligraphy. To write the script and achieve such perfection, the illuminator would have chosen only the best outer wing feathers of a goose or swan to shape the pen that drew them. Bauer leafed through the pages recounting the life of the founder of the Ottonian dynasty of Saxon kings and emperors. He had found the book that was part of Germanic history. The book he'd promised Heydrich that Michael

Tagleva would obtain for him. The book would be housed in Wewelsburg Castle next to the Holy Grail and the Spear of Destiny. *He, Rudolf Baur, had found it* and imagined the glittering ceremony at the castle, attended by the elite of the SS, as he, Rudolf Bauer, presented the sacred history to the reincarnation of *Koenig* Heinrich: Reichsführer-SS Heinrich Himmler.

Chapter Thirty
The catacombs

July 1940

It had been a long day, and in The Coal Hole, the public house on the corner of Savoy Court in the Strand, Michael and Rose were nursing a couple of small beers. The downstairs bar was filled with off-duty soldiers recounting how they had spent the day with the police arresting enemy aliens and sending them to internment camps.

One of the soldiers shouted to another, 'Churchill's ordered every alien in the country to be arrested – collar the lot, 'e says!' and raised a beer to his lips.

'Quite right, too. Can't trust bloody foreigners,' chipped in a civilian from one of the benches at the side of the bar.

'Caused mayhem at The Berkeley Hotel, it 'as. Every Italian waiter's been arrested. Restaurant's had to close, no one to serve the liver and bacon at breakfast.'

A youth in uniform, no more than nineteen, shouted over the noise, 'I was with a policeman sent to pinch some German, a barber 'e was. We bundled 'im into back of the truck with t'others, and blow me, he recognised a friend from his internment during the last war. On the Isle of Man they were. On way to police station, they spent entire time talking about the good times in the camp. Did yer know, when they 'ad visits from friends, they sometimes swapped over so that friend could experience the delights of an internment camp and get some decent food an' the prisoner went home for a bit of how's yer father?'

Everyone laughed.

Another soldier added to the merriment. 'A couple days ago I was with a policeman to arrest some dumb Dora at the Waldorf Hotel. Coppers went through her belongings, found a small blue paper bag containing white powder, they did. Police sergeant said it was suspicious, sent it for analysis. Turns out it was a packet of salt from a bag of Smith's crisps!'

Laughter erupted around the bar.

Michael and Rose looked at each other and joined in the merriment. Michael had come to like Rose. Despite appearances she was tough, single-minded and, in many ways, reminded him of Juliette. He looked into his beer. He missed Juliette. If only he could speak to her, make sure she was safe, tell her he loved her. He so wanted to smell her perfume, run his hands through her hair and…

He felt a hand on his shoulder. Rose was smiling at him.

'Thinking about Juliette again?'

Michael nodded.

'Don't worry. If she's half the girl you say she is, she'll be OK.'

Michael looked up and smiled. 'I'm sure you're right.'

Their conversation was disturbed by Chris Smith. The ginger-haired youth with a face covered in freckles, poked his head around the door and indicated they were needed.

Michael and Rose got up and walked over to him.

'There's a flap on. You're both ordered back by the colonel.'

****

Ten minutes later they were sitting in Tim Wilson's office.

'The police have picked up a couple of Germans they think might be spies. These were found on them.'

The colonel passed them a couple of pieces of paper.

'Five-pound notes?' said Michael.

'This is one of twenty, all of them forgeries. We've been ordered to find out as much as we can about them and find the forger.'

Back in his office, Michael pulled out a genuine note from his wallet and, using a magnifying glass, compared the two. The forgery wasn't perfect. The feel of the paper was right, but the curve on one of the letters on the forged note wasn't rounded enough and the image of Britannia's clothing was different from the original. Nevertheless, he guessed it would have been good enough to fool most people.

Michael yawned. He was dog tired. *It's too late to do anything now. May as well get some rest and start early tomorrow*, he said to himself.

The following day was his mother's birthday and he'd promised his father that he'd stay at his parents' home so that they could have breakfast together and wish her a good day.

It was with relief he arrived home. For the past ten nights, he'd slept on the camp bed in his office. He was looking forward to the comfort of fresh cotton sheets and resting his head on soft duck-down pillows. He opened the front door, stepped inside and pulled the blackout curtains together before switching on the light in the hallway.

The study door opened. 'A long day?' enquired Philip.

'It's been a long ten days and I'm bushed,' and Michael walked to the staircase.

'Good night,' said Philip watching his son climb a couple of stairs before turning around.

'Father, I don't suppose the phone line is working from the Tagleva offices between London and Paris?'

'You *are* tired. You've forgotten there's been no phone link with Paris since Dunkirk.'

'Oh, yes, I remember, how silly of me. I wasn't thinking. Thought I could get a message to Juliette.'

'And if you could, what would it say?'

Without turning, Michael continued to climb the stairs to bed. '563, 14, 9 to 12,' came the reply.

Philip watched the retreating figure until it disappeared and then walked back into his study.

****

Jean-Claude was standing at one end of the Métro station platform as the train arrived. The Paris Métro train had five cars and the one in the middle, painted red, was reserved for those who'd bought first-class tickets. The German occupiers always travelled, as if by right and for free, in the middle car.

Jean-Claude had bought a standard-fare ticket hoping to avoid rubbing shoulders with the Germans.

After arriving at his Métro stop, he had some distance to walk. There was, however, one advantage to walking. It allowed him to check that he wasn't being followed.

Within seconds of ringing the bell at Tobias Meijers' apartment block, he was being greeted by the former chief accountant and his family.

'How are you, my friend?' asked Jean-Claude once they were alone.

'We're doing fine. I miss work. It's boring with nothing to do.'

'I'm sorry. I heard how the Germans ordered you to leave the building. Had I known it was going to happen, I would have tried to stop it.'

'There was nothing you could have done. I'm Dutch *and* a Jew. I have no legal protection. Anyhow I had expected it.'

'Nevertheless, as far as I'm concerned you're still an employee of Tagleva bank.' Jean-Claude handed over an envelope. 'I've brought your month's salary. I've also added six five-franc Napoléon coins.'

Tobias knew that the gold coins were meant to be saved for a time when the family might be forced to buy things off the black market or use them to bribe an official.

'I'll try to come back each month with your salary. And when all this is over, you must come back to the bank,' said Jean-Claude. 'Do you have any plans?'

'Of course, we will stay in Paris. The Germans are still taking control of the city and until they have they won't have time for small fry like me. Besides, we don't have anywhere else to go. If needs be, we will just disappear.'

'Where to?'

'I've spent the past weeks exploring the catacombs below the city – they are truly amazing. It's a maze with more than two hundred kilometres of tunnels running from Montparnasse to Porte d'Orléans. Some people have lived in the tunnels for years. If we need to, I plan to take my family below ground.'

'How do you gain access?' asked Jean-Claude, intrigued.

'Down manholes.'

'Don't the police monitor such things?'

'Yes, of course. When they find one entrance, they seal it, but within a few days, another manhole is opened and people are told where the new entrance is.'

'But if you know about the catacombs, then the Germans will, too.'

Tobias smiled. 'Yes, and they've already begun to use some of the tunnels for their own storage. But for the moment, they're afraid to go too deeply into them in case they get lost, and anyway, many tunnels are so well hidden it'll take the Germans years to find them all. Of course, in the long-run they know they must control the catacombs – otherwise they will have a resistance they can't control.'

Jean-Claude spent another half an hour with Tobias and, after saying goodbye to him and his family, left the apartment, deep in thought. Tobias's talk about the catacombs had given him an idea.

****

Philip Tagleva arranged to meet Walter Abraham at The Coach and Horses in Hill Street, an eight-minute walk from the American embassy in Grosvenor Square.

The two had become friends when Philip was in the United States to open the Bank of Tagleva in New York and Walter had helped him with the official paperwork. That had been fifteen years ago. When Walter began to work at the American embassy in London, their friendship had been quickly rekindled.

Philip arrived at their table with two pints of *Warwicks' Nut Brown* beer.

'English beer is so much tastier than any American beer,' declared Walter, having developed a taste for the room-temperature brew.

After they had both taken their first sips, Philip said, 'I hear Ambassador Kennedy thinks Britain's defeated and we should make peace with Germany. If he's right, we might all be drinking German Pilsner soon.'

'Kennedy thinks it's folly for Britain to continue the fight with Germany and is telling Washington so,' confided the diplomat.

'And you, my friend, what's your opinion?' asked Philip.

'As a diplomat, I don't have an opinion. As an American citizen with Polish-Jewish grandparents, I have a very strong opinion.'

Philip raised his eyebrows questioningly.

'That the dumb cluck needs to grow some balls and urge you Limeys to whip those Nazi asses.'

Philip laughed and raised his glass in a mock toast.

'Tell me,' said the diplomat, 'while it's always a pleasure to meet up with you, I suspect this isn't a social call.'

'You're right. I was hoping I could use the services of the US State Department to get a message to Paris. The message is innocent enough, but it would mean a lot to me.'

'Can I ask you what the message says?'

Philip told him. Walter thought for a couple of minutes.

'If Ambassador Kennedy knew I was doing this, he'd send me home in disgrace. But Ambassador William Bullitt in Paris might welcome it. If for no other reason that he hates Kennedy. No promises, but I'll see what can be done.'

'Thank you, my friend,' said Philip and they took another sip of their beers.

Chapter Thirty-one
The Bank of England

August 1940

The following morning, Colonel Tim Wilson walked into Michael's office and sat down. 'It seems that forged bank notes have been turning up like confetti all over the place for the past six months. They've been found in Portugal, Spain, India and Egypt. It's not just five-pound notes either, forged ten- and twenty-pound notes have also been found. You and I have a meeting at the Bank of England in an hour.'

Arriving at a side entrance of the bank, they were escorted by a porter down a long corridor, up a flight of stairs and half-way down another corridor. Michael was disappointed. He had expected a more imposing interior, but the corridors were just like any other government office building. Arriving at a door, identical to dozens they had passed, the porter knocked lightly and opened it. Inside was a small meeting room devoid of any pictures or decoration. Waiting for them was a tall man of around fifty dressed in a dark suit, with a balding head and thick horn-rimmed spectacles.

'Thank you for coming. My name is Mark Johnson,' said the man breathlessly.

They shook hands and were waved towards some seats around a small table.

'Gentlemen, we don't have much time, so I will quickly explain the bank's dilemma. You are probably already aware that the first responsibility of the Bank of England is to maintain the financial stability of Britain and the Empire. As a consequence, the bank takes any threat that could undermine that stability very seriously. Forged notes are one such threat. Over the past months, we have become concerned that forged bank notes have been appearing in various parts of the world.'

Michael noticed that Johnson was slightly agitated and formed the impression that the man was nervous, which surprised him. He imagined, after everything his father had told him, that Bank of England staff were calm at all times, even in the worst crises.

Johnson took a deep breath before continuing: 'Forgery of the currency is nothing new. People have been trying to copy the realm's currency since medieval times and the bank takes great pains to make it as difficult as possible. For instance, our banknotes are made from cotton paper. During its production, we incorporate watermarks and other devices to make the production of counterfeits difficult and very expensive to reproduce.'

Johnson poured himself a glass of water from a carafe on the table, took a sip and continued: 'It's been obvious to us for some time that the Germans are trying to counterfeit Britain's bank notes.'

'Why do you think it's the Germans? Couldn't it be a British forger?' asked Michael.

'A good question. The answer is that the quality of the paper being used is exceptional. None of the usual counterfeiters we know of could afford a large quantity of that superior material. The printing also suggests that a great deal of time and finance has gone into the engraving... Our experts have concluded that the costs alone suggests a sophisticated and well-financed operation. In the current circumstances, that would indicate the Germans.'

'So how can we help?' asked Wilson.

'Currently the forgeries are being detected quite easily, even by foreign banks. While the paper is very good, the printing hasn't reached a quality good enough to deceive an experienced bank clerk.' Johnson paused as if to think what he would say next. 'But a situation has occurred that might change that. We don't print the banknotes here at the Bank of England, but at regular intervals, the printing plates are brought back to the bank to be inspected for damage and cleaned. This ensures that the quality of the printed notes remains consistent. In this past week, we've had two of these plates here at the bank for cleaning.'

Johnson rasped as he took another gulp of air. 'Yesterday we discovered that one had disappeared – the five-pound note plate.'

'What do you mean – *disappeared*?' said Wilson.

'Just that – it's vanished! We've searched everywhere and have concluded that it's been stolen.'

'Stolen?' exclaimed Wilson.

'Yes, stolen,' rasped Johnson again.

'So much for the expression "As safe as the Bank of England"...' said the colonel.

Johnson looked away and bit his right thumb nail.

'What do the plates look like?' asked Michael.

Johnson looked up. 'Originally, all English notes were made from hand-engraved or etched flat copperplate. While that process produced high-quality reproductions, the softness of the metal wore over time, which necessitated frequent re-engraving. Even the most talented engravers struggled to replicate the original. Many years ago an American arrived and offered the bank the technology to produce thousands of identical banknotes using hardened steel. His system uses a cylinder, twenty inches long and fifteen inches in diameter. It is one of those we believe was stolen.'

Johnson rubbed the back of his neck with his right hand.

'If the Nazis get hold of the cylinder, they will be able to flood the world with perfect copies of the five-pound note. If that happens, no one will be able to trust the currency, and it will increasingly become worth less and less. Eventually, we won't be able to finance the war. The Nazis will have defeated us.' Johnson paused. 'There is one other thing. One of the bank's employees has also gone missing. He was a porter and responsible for transporting the plate around the building.'

'His name?' asked Michael.

'John Knight.'

'How long has this John Knight worked for you?' asked Wilson.

'About a year.'

'If you can give us his address and any details of other staff who had access to the plate while it was here, that would be helpful.'

'All the information we have is in this file.' Johnson passed over a brown envelope. 'But I'm afraid you'll find that John Knight address is a false one. As soon as we knew the plate had gone missing we sent people to it, but the landlady said she'd never heard of him.'

Wilson picked up the file. 'We'll contact you if we need any further information.'

Colonel Wilson and Michael left the building.

****

Juliette was irritated with the German orderlies working on the fifth floor. They would seek her out to make trivial enquiries regarding the card index, not because they wanted answers to a problem but to strike up a conversation and invite her out. She knew that some women in Paris were flattered and encouraged by the attention paid them by the occupier, but she wasn't one of them. *Better,* thought Juliette, *the Germans should visit the bordello at Rue de Provence where there would be any number of girls ready to cavort in a room decorated as a Moorish harem or a Roman bath. Those girls would smile sweetly, flatter them, laugh at their stupid jokes and let them fuck them before taking another lover prepared to pay for their company.* She was grateful when a friend told her that the Germans feared disease, particularly venereal diseases, and would cough loudly whenever a German soldier came close. It usually had the desired effect.

To escape the confines of the fifth floor, and the German orderlies, she got into the habit of taking her lunch in a café on the Rue Marboeuf. She was enjoying her coffee and the solitude when a young man approached and stood before her. As he looked down at her; she coughed hard.

'That's a nasty cough you have, *mademoiselle*,' said the man with an American accent. 'May I join you?' – without waiting for a reply he slid onto the bench beside her.

Juliette thought the man's approach rude and unwelcome and she was about to ask him to sit elsewhere.

'Scott J Coleman, by the way. Nice to meet you,' and he extended his hand.

She chose to be polite and shook his hand briefly. At least he wasn't German.

'Nice to meet you, too. My name's Juliette Villeneuve. Can I ask what the "J" in your name stands for?'

He laughed. 'Nothing, it's an affectation bestowed on me by my parents.'

Juliette thought it a stupid thing, but warmed to the stranger.

'You work for the Tagleva bank, don't you?' he asked.

Juliette was suddenly scared. How did this man know? He must have been following her. Perhaps he was German after all, even a member of the Gestapo...

As if reading her mind, he said, 'Don't worry, I'm not German. Actually, I work at the American embassy.'

She felt relieved and intrigued but decided to remain on her guard.

'I have a message for you.'

'A message... for me? Who from?'

He looked into her eyes. 'The message is "563, 14, 9 to 12". Can you remember that?'

She nodded.

'Goodbye, *mademoiselle*. I wish you well and I don't expect we'll meet again.' With that, he got up and left.

As she returned to the bank, the message was all that Juliette could think of. All afternoon the numbers she'd been given by the American tumbled around her mind. On more than one occasion, she wondered if she had got the sequence muddled up. At the end of the day, she rushed home and pulled out her copy of *Anna Karenina* from the bookcase, turned to page 563, her finger traced down to line 14 and then along to the words 9 to 12 and read... 'and he loves her'.

She closed her eyes, breathed in and savoured the moment. She hugged the book to her, never wanting to release it. Some of the tension left her body and she began to cry. After some minutes she went to the window, opened it and blew Michael a kiss.

'I love you, too, my darling,' she whispered to the wind.

Chapter Thirty-two
A race against time

August 1940

The delight that Jean-Claude had once experienced from his work had been replaced by a dread of the schizophrenic environment in which he now found himself, which was at the same time both familiar and alien. Under his protection the Tagleva staff adapted to their new relationship with their German masters and Jean-Claude took it upon himself to ensure that the occupiers were satisfied with the work done for them. Productivity fell, as people camouflaged themselves with work processes, busied themselves with trivia and he did nothing to prevent it.

On the fifth floor, Katherine du Bois and her staff had been ordered to restore the card index to a usable resource. Progress was painfully slow, despite supervision by a particularly irritable SS sergeant. Cards went missing, reference numbers were incorrectly allocated and the three-mistake rule, so rigorously enforced in the past, was never mentioned.

On the third floor the staff in the 'buy side' and the 'sell side' departments were used by the SS to keep track of their own investments. Companies or property acquired by the occupiers sometimes had the names on the deeds of ownership changed from Mandel, Blum, Abram and the like to Schmidt, Richter and Krüger. A special note of the previous owners was always secretly recorded.

The occupier contributed to the staff being unproductive by the many regulations they imposed on the city. The nightly curfew required everyone to be home between nine at night and five in the morning. Those found on the streets without a curfew permit would be arrested and harshly punished. Reduced public transport meant that the greater the distance from the bank a member of staff lived, the earlier they had to leave work – that is, if they were to undertake essential food shopping and other errands before the curfew started.

Jean-Claude looked at the clock on the mantelpiece. It was a nice day, he had little to do, so decided to walk home to enjoy the last couple of hours of sunshine before being shut up for the night in his apartment. He walked down Rue Pierre Charron, turned left into Avenue George Cinque, and took a deep breath of fresh air as if trying to remove the stale air from his lungs.

Halfway down the street, parked in the road, he saw a van. He stared at it. The driver climbed down from the cab and Jean-Claude walked over to speak to him. 'Is this a television van? I think I saw one like it at the Olympics in thirty-six.'

The driver looked at him. For the past few days, he'd done nothing but carry heavy boxes of equipment from one place to another. He was tired, bored and thankful to have someone friendly to talk to.

'It is. We're setting up a television station in the city. Broadcasts start from the top of the Eiffel Tower in a week or two.' He waved a hand in a vague manner as if giving directions to a stranger.

'Will you be filming in Paris?' enquired Jean-Claude.

'Ever since the Führer was filmed touring the city, people in Berlin can't get enough news of Paris. There are plans to show news from Paris each week all over Germany, and from the top of the Eiffel Tower news from Germany will be broadcast, so that our troops in Paris have news from home.'

Jean-Claude gave the man a cheery farewell, and hurried home to tell Sébastien.

****

In the Strand, Michael and Wilson were briefing Rose on their meeting at the Bank of England and were pondering the loss of the printing plate.

'I don't understand how a porter can just walk out of the Bank of England with a circular plate for printing bank notes.

Their security must be awful. People should be shot for such incompetence,' said the colonel.

'How do you think they'll get it out of the country?' asked Michael.

'Most likely a small fishing boat, a submarine off a deserted beach somewhere. If only we knew where John Knight is... But we'll probably never find him, anyway, it's probably not even his real name,' said Wilson.

'John Knight you said?' exclaimed Rose.

Wilson nodded.

'A John Knight was a member of the Right Club. I'm sure there was, where's the list of members of the Right Club we got from the Red Book?' she asked.

Michael went to his office, returning a minute later with a file of papers. Rose snatched the file from him, extracted the list and began to run her finger down the list of names. She turned the page, then another, then a third.

'Here it is. John Knight, works at Bank of England, home address, Ealing.'

'And that's a different address from the one he gave to the Bank of England. That looks like our man,' said Michael.

'And remember Frank Cyril Tiarks, a director of the bank, and Montagu Norman, its governor, are members of the Anglo-German Fellowship,' added Rose.

'Perhaps we should arrest them, too,' said Michael.

'Let's not be too hasty, chaps, it doesn't mean that Tiarks or Norman are traitors or even linked to the theft of the printing plate,' cautioned Wilson. 'Montagu Norman was a member of the Anglo-German Fellowship because he had to deal with the president of the Reichsbank, Hjalmar Schacht, who also happens to be a member of the AGF. And, the last thing I want is you two oafs – particularly you, Michael – going in and upsetting important people without reason. *I'll* go and see Tiarks and Norman. You two go to Ealing and look around John Knight's rooms. See what you can find out.'

****

Michael and Rose parked the car at the end of the street in Ealing. It was almost empty except for a group of boys, in short trousers with their socks around their ankles, kicking a football against one of the houses. Since the start of the war, London had become an exciting place and the boys were having fun. Yesterday they had watched men paint white lines around trees, lamp posts and everything an unwary pedestrian was likely to bump into in the complete darkness of the blackout. The boys told them, at every opportunity, 'Luv-a-duck, mate, you've missed a bit.'

Watching the painters had been a distraction from the main focus for their mirth, the air-raid wardens – the volunteers who checked for light seeping out of the blackout curtains at night. Whenever the wardens gathered in their hut to try out their whistles and wooden rattles, which would warn the population of a gas attack – a rehearsal the wardens undertook with great seriousness – the boys would loudly chant outside the hut:

> Underneath the spreading chestnut tree,
> Mr Chamberlain said to me,
> If you want to get your tin-hat free,
> Join the blinking ARP!

The fun for the boys was not the chant, nor the torment they inflicted on the wardens, but out-running them as they gave chase up the street.

Watched by the boys, Michael and Rose walked to number fifteen and knocked the door. It was opened by a woman in an apron, holding a yellow duster. Seeing Michael's uniform, she folded her arms and looked down both ends of the street to check which net curtains were twitching.

'Lawks, wardens complain about me Charlie dis mornin' an' now bloody army's turned up. Don't you lot have better things to do? With all this comin' an' goin', the neighbours are beginnin' ter talk. Know what I mean?'

Michael smiled. 'Good afternoon, madam, we're not calling about your son, Charlie. We're looking for a John Knight.'

'The tenant? What's 'e done? Anyhow 'e's not in, hasn't been for days.'

'Can we see his room?' asked Michael.

'Dunno. All I know is 'e owes me ten shillin' in rent.'

Michael took out a ten-shilling note from his wallet and handed it to the landlady, who quickly tucked it into the front of her apron and stepped aside for them to pass.

'Top of stairs, second door on da right.'

The room was small, tidy, with a single bed, chest of drawers, wardrobe and washbasin. A few personal belongings made the room homely. Rose opened a drawer and began to rummage through neatly folded shirts. Finding nothing, she moved to the next drawer.

Michael sat on the bed, opened the drawer in the bedside table and looked inside. Pills, a comb, a couple of postcards of leggy girls in stockings and suspenders. Michael picked one up and began to admire the artwork.

'You're meant to be looking for clues,' came a reprimand from the other side of the room.

'Just trying to get to know my enemy,' said Michael with a smile.

He replaced the picture, closed the drawer and looked at Knight's bedtime reading. The two paperbacks – *Wild Strawberries* by Angela Thinkell and *Poirot Investigates* by Agatha Christie – looked new. He picked up the hardback, *My Man Jeeves* by P G Woodhouse, priced at two shillings. It was well thumbed, the spine was broken in a couple of places and the dust jacket torn. Michael leafed through the volume and was about to close it when he noticed a small pinhole. Turning a couple of pages he found another and then a third.

'Come and have a look at this,' he said to Rose.

Together they studied the book and found a dozen more pinholes.

Michael and Rose leafed through the other books on the table but there were no pinholes. Quickly searching the rest of the room and finding nothing more of interest, they left.

****

197

Rose drove back to the Strand at breakneck speed. On more than one occasion, the tyres complained loudly as they clipped the pavement when making a turn. Rose ignored her passenger pressing his foot into the floor where a brake might have been.

Arriving at the office, Michael was thankful to be able to get out of the car alive. As he did, he smiled at Rose in an effort to show he hadn't been scared. Rose smiled back at him, telling herself that next time she should drive even faster.

The two of them studied every page of *My Man Jeeves* and every letter with a pinhole was identified.

'Give me a while and I'll tell you what the message says,' said Michael.

'How do you know?' asked Rose.

'I expect it's similar to a code I was shown by the Abwehr in Berlin.'

A few minutes later, Michael announced, 'I've cracked it!'

'What does it say?' asked Rose

'"Deliver at 18278 brocket vital importance."'

'"Brocket" could mean Lord Brocket. He's also a member of the Anglo-German Fellowship,' said Rose.

'But what does "18278" mean?' mused Michael.

'… It's a time and a date… six o'clock, twenty-seventh of August,' answered Rose.

Michael looked at the calendar on the wall. 'That's today, and it's already ten past five.'

They ran from the office, almost colliding into Colonel Wilson.

'Wooah, careful, you two,' he shouted. 'And where the hell are you chaps off to in such a hurry?'

'Brocket Hall,' Michael shouted back.

Rose drove the car along the Strand, making a sharp turn down Savoy Street. The tyres screeched as it turned onto the Victoria Embankment. Racing along the Embankment, she turned into New Bridge Street and nearly knocked a policeman off his bicycle. The car raced towards Camden, through Chalk Farm, Highgate, Tufnell Park, Barnet, and for the first time, Michael willed Rose to drive faster. Eventually the car screeched to a stop in front of the open gates of Brocket Hall. They looked up the driveway towards the house.

'What do we do now?' asked Rose.

'Pay Lord Brocket a visit, I guess.'

Rose pushed the accelerator flat to the floor. The car sped up the winding drive, over the flint bridge, and skidded to a halt at the front entrance amid a cloud of dust.

A butler appeared at the door. 'Can I help you people?' he asked testily.

'Where's Lord Brocket,' said Michael.

'I'm afraid His Lordship's not in residence. He's at Bramshill House, his estate in Hampshire.'

'When did he go to Hampshire?'

'Ten days ago,' replied the butler, irritated by the impertinent inquisition regarding the whereabouts of his employer.

Rose saw a face in the window.

'Who's inside?' she asked.

'An acquaintance of His Lordship. He's holding a meeting. His Lordship gave permission for such a meeting before he left.'

Michael brushed past the butler and rushed inside. Turning left, he approached the door that led into the main drawing room and, flinging it open, saw the man in the centre of the room pointing a pistol at him. The man fired. Michael heard the sharp retort of a Luger pistol. The bullet embedded itself in the wall beside him and a shower of plaster covered his hair. Thankful that the man was not such a good shot, Michael crouched down expecting him to fire again. Instead, the man ran to another door at the far end of the room and disappeared.

Michael stood up and gave chase, leaping over a coffee table and running as fast as he could to the same door. Opening it, he found himself in an ornate dining room; the man was standing, twenty feet away in front of the fireplace, pointing the Luger at him. Michael ran forward and leapt at the stranger. Flying through the air he hit his quarry in the midriff just as the Luger was fired for the second time. The two men crashed into a small Regency side table with a pink marble top set on very fine tapered legs, one of a pair Lord Brocket had recently purchased. It was now matchwood.

Winded by Michael's tackle, the man gasped for air. Michael grabbed him by the jacket and punched him in the face, breaking his nose, a rush of pain jolted through the man's body. Tasting his own blood, he became desperate to escape and grabbed Michael by the hair. As his head was wrenched backwards Michael loosened the grip on his adversary, in that split second the man saw an opportunity to escape and hit Michael on the left ear with the Luger. Despite the searing pain, Michael managed to bring down his fist onto the man's face once more. There was a sharp cry of pain, the struggle was given up and the Luger dropped onto the Persian carpet.

Rose and the butler arrived. Retrieving the Luger, Rose pointed it at the bleeding body on the floor.

'Who is this man?' she asked the butler.

'He introduced himself as John Knight. He's not been at the Hall before. He was to meet another guest.'

'Who?' she asked.

'I don't know. Mr Knight didn't tell me.'

'For a butler, you don't know much, do you?' said Rose sarcastically.

'His Lordship has many visitors. In recent times, not all have given their names,' replied the butler defensively.

Surveying the damage, the butler groaned. 'What will His Lordship say about all this – the holes in the walls, the table, and everything?'

Michael hauled John Knight to his feet.

'Please, don't let him bleed onto the carpets,' begged the butler.

Through the pain in his left ear, Michael gave the butler a withering look and hauled his prisoner to the car.

Rose searched the rest of Brocket Hall as best she could. She was looking for the printing plate and for any other visitors but, except for the other servants, found neither.

Arriving at the car, Rose noticed Michael nursing his bruised face while keeping his prisoner subdued in the back seat. She climbed into the driver's seat, adjusted the mirror so that she could keep an eye on the back seat and noticed a small dark red stain underneath Michael's left shoulder.

'Are you wounded?' she asked.

'Not badly, it's just a scratch,' came the reply.

Rose drove quickly back to the Strand where John Knight was passed over to the military police. Michael walked to his office where Rose helped him remove his jacket and shirt.

Inspecting his shoulder she was relieved to see the bullet had broken the skin just enough to make it bleed badly but hadn't entered the shoulder. *He's been lucky.*

'Will I live?' asked Michael as he gently took hold of Rose's hand, squeezed it and looked into her eyes.

Their gaze lasted a full second. Nothing needed to be said. Michael's look had communicated the message.

'Live? Not if you don't let go of my hand and get those thoughts out of your head. You're feeling sorry for yourself because you're in pain. It's not me you want, you know it isn't, and anyway I refuse to be something temporary. You trust her to wait for you and you should do the same. Without trust, you can't have love, it just isn't possible. So let go of my hand and I'll blame this moment of stupidity on that bump on your head. And we won't mention it again.'

Michael let go of Rose's hand. 'I'm sorry,' he said softly.

Rose soaked a gauze pad with Dettol and pressed it onto his cut face. As the antiseptic liquid stung, Michael took a sharp intake of breath. 'Don't be such a baby,' smiled Rose, dabbing the wound some more.

****

Despite John Knight's nose having been covered with an adhesive bandage he was still uncomfortable. His hands were handcuffed to the chair he had been sitting in for what seemed like hours. The room was hot and smelled of boiled cabbage. Patches of perspiration stained the armpits of his shirt and the dried blood from his broken nose had stiffened it. Something sharp, the head of a nail probably, protruded very slightly above the seat. It was a constant distraction. It was all he could think of as it necessitated continual changes in position. At the door stood a military policeman, presumably to ensure he didn't try to escape. Even if he could, he wouldn't have tried – his face was sore, his right eye was bruised and almost closed, he had a splitting headache and he just wanted to sleep.

Sitting behind a large desk was Colonel Wilson and Michael. For what seemed an eternity they had been asking him the same questions, over and over again.

'What's your name? What were you doing at Brocket Hall? Who were you meeting? What's your job at the Bank of England? Who ordered you to steal the plate? Where is it? Who else at the bank is involved? Who did you give it to?'

As each question was asked, it echoed around the green-tiled walls and made his head thump more.

Knight stayed silent.

Tim Wilson looked at him and raised his voice: 'Don't play stupid with me. I haven't got time for this. You're a traitor. Helping the enemy in time of war is a capital crime. We hang traitors but if you tell me everything I want to know, perhaps I can have a word with the judge and save you from the hangman.'

Still he remained silent.

Wilson sighed. 'You will tell me everything I want to know. I have all the time in the world. So why don't you make it easy for yourself. Then you can have some sleep.'

'I had to do it. They gave me no option,' came the muffled reply.

'Who gave you no option?'

'The Nazis.'

'Then tell me everything,' said Wilson.

'You're too late. It's left the country by now.'

'What's left the country?'

'The thing you're looking for… the plate.'

'How was it taken out of the country?'

'I don't know.'

'Who did you give the plates to?'

'I didn't know his name. I hadn't seen him before.'

'What did he look like?'

202

'I don't know, a big man, wore spectacles. I never saw him before.'

'You don't know much, do you?' shouted Wilson.

The colonel got up from his seat and walked round to Knight, bent down and through clenched teeth whispered in his ear.

'You're telling me nothing. Perhaps I should save my time and just have you shot now and get it over with quickly.'

Wilson didn't wait for a reply. He walked to the door and noisily threw it open and left the room. Michael got up from his seat, walked round and placed a comforting hand on John Knight's shoulder.

'I'm sorry the colonel has such a bad temper. He's not nice when he's angry. If only you could tell me something that would let me help you, then I could speak to the colonel and perhaps things would go easier for you. I'll try to help you, but you have to help me first.' Michael paused. *'Wie heißen Sie?'* he asked softly in German.

'Ich heiße Müller, Leopold Müller.'

Chapter Thirty-three
Preparations

August 1940

Jean-Claude arrived home in time to avoid breaching the nine o'clock curfew. The apartment was strangely quiet and dark. He found Sébastien sitting in the fading light, looking out of the window over the city and towards the Eiffel Tower. Jean-Claude walked to the kitchen, poured two glasses of Pernod, added a little water, which turned the liquid cloudy, and returned to the sitting room. He handed Sébastien one of the glasses and sat down beside him. They both stared out of the window in silence watching the final rays of daylight fade.

Eventually Jean-Claude whispered, ever mindful of their Nazi neighbours, 'If you're worried about anything, perhaps I can help.'

'I'm not worried. I resigned from *L'Illustration* this morning,' Sébastien replied.

'Want to tell me about it?'

Sébastien smiled. In the years they had been together, they had had no secrets. He had always shared his innermost thoughts with Jean-Claude, told him about all the crazy things he'd done in his youth and the ambitions he still held. Jean-Claude had never been judgmental, never told him he'd made a wrong decision, was always enthusiastic about his future plans, sympathetic about his problems and always prepared to give advice if asked.

'The magazine's editor, Jacques de Lesdain, supports everything the Germans are asking to be published. He's collaborating with them. The magazine's becoming a voice for the occupiers and I don't want to work for anything like that.'

'And why should you? It would be a waste of talent. What will you do instead?'

'Perhaps I'll set up my own newspaper, tell everyone the truth.'

'I would prefer you didn't do anything so dangerous. If you were arrested and sent to prison, I'd get very cold at night.'

Still looking into the darkness, Sébastien took a sip of Pernod and whispered, 'So what news have you?'

'Not much. Katherine told me that the Germans have given up on restoring the card index. It seems they have other ideas for the space. They've cleared away the filing cabinets and installed what looks like a printing machine.'

'What do they want that for?'

'No one knows, but the Germans seem very excited by it all. The floor's guarded by two soldiers twenty-four hours a day and all Tagleva bank staff are forbidden to enter the fifth floor. Even I can't go there.'

'What happened to the people who worked there?'

'I've reallocated them to other work. My old secretary got the promotion she wanted – she now works for Colonel Bauer. I'm relieved – she's been spying for them for some years. It's how the Germans knew so much about how the bank and the Foundation worked. I have a new secretary, a girl called Juliette.'

'Thank you for your understanding about *L'Illustration*. You always make a problem seem so very small... Do you think the Germans will persecute us like they persecuted Helmut or use our love for each other to try to control you'

'They may, who knows, we'll have to wait and see what happens. If they believe I'm useful to them they'll leave us alone. We must be seen to co-operate but keep the flame of resistance alive.' replied Jean-Claude.

'It won't be without its dangers... Shall I turn on the light?' whispered Sébastien.

'No. Why don't we have an early night?'

'Mmmmm, I'd like that.'

****

The following morning, Colonel Wilson and Michael briefed a brigadier on the information they had gained from Leopold Müller's interrogation.

'Müller's mother's English, married to a German and he holds a British passport as well as a German and came to England two years ago. His mother upset the Nazis when she wrote some letters to the newspapers criticising the anti-Jewish race laws. They weren't printed, of course, but nevertheless she was arrested by the Gestapo. There was a quick trial and she was sent to the women's concentration camp at Ravensbrück, which provides forced labour for the German electrical engineering company, Siemens & Halske.

'Around eighteen months ago the Germans approached Müller, telling him that they would release his mother if he worked for them. Naturally he agreed. Using contacts within the Anglo-German Fellowship and false papers, a job was found for him as a porter at the Bank of England under the name John Knight. The Germans wanted information on the state of the British economy, particularly on how a war would be financed. It was easy for Knight to find this information. The porters at the Bank of England are responsible for destroying documents such as notes taken at meetings, which are discarded once the official record has been typed. John Knight removed any information he thought would be of interest to the Germans before it was destroyed. When the possibility of stealing a printing plate arose, the Germans considered it an opportunity too good to be missed. One evening Müller hid the plate in some rubbish that was usually left on the street corner for the refuse collectors. No one thought it unusual.'

'What happened then?' asked the brigadier.

'After work he retrieved it from the rubbish on the street and took it to Brocket Hall where he handed it to a contact.'

'And I don't suppose we're lucky enough to know who the man was?'

'I'm afraid not, he hadn't met the man before and they didn't speak more than a few words. We think he's a spy we haven't identified yet.'

'How do you think he will get it out of the country?' asked the brigadier.

'We think he'll use the services of a neutral country, sympathetic to the Nazis, to send the plate out of the country in their diplomatic bag.'

The brigadier sighed. 'There are any number of neutral countries that would help the Nazis by smuggling it out of the country.'

'The Spanish and the Portuguese are the most likely. Diplomats from both embassies are being closely watched but no leads to date,' said Michael.

'Is Lord Brocket involved?' enquired the brigadier.

'We don't believe so. He admitted that some people were to meet at the Hall but thought it was to discuss "making a just peace with Germany". By the way, he's asking if he will be compensated for the damage to his walls and the broken table,' said Wilson.

'I'll be buggered if he will – he's lucky he's not been arrested for treason.'

Michael supressed a chuckle; the Brigadier glowered at him.

Turning his attention to the colonel, the brigadier asked, 'So what happens next? I have to brief the prime minister in the next hour. The news that our currency might soon be worthless is likely to make Churchill explode. I would like to be able to sugar the pill somehow.'

'We have every available agent working on it. Some diplomatic bags have been secretly searched and certain diplomats have had their travel "inexplicably" delayed but we can't keep that up for long. We *are* doing our best, sir,' Wilson replied.

'Well, your best might not be good enough. We're running out of time. Get me results!' said the brigadier as he stormed out of the room.

****

The following morning Jean-Claude and Sébastien were having a light breakfast of coffee and a shared croissant.

'As you're no longer working at *L'Illustration*, I was wondering if you could do some things for me?' Jean-Claude enquired.

'Ask away.'

'I've seen some orders that will soon be issued by the Germans. In future, the majority of French agricultural products will be shipped to Germany. In a few days, meat will be rationed and, in the next few weeks, rice, milk, butter, cheese, coffee and other products. And it won't be just food – leather is to be reserved exclusively for German army boots. All shoes for civilians are to be made of canvas with wooden soles.'

'You want me to buy you some more shoes?' asked Sébastien.

Jean-Claude laughed. 'No, I have enough shoes, but the restrictions on food are just the beginning. So if you come across dried pasta or rice, buy it. No, I'm more concerned that the Germans have ordered owners of large cars to take them to the Hippodrome de Vincennes. They are to be evaluated for forced purchase at the race track there. In a short time, the only vehicles on the streets will be German.'

'You have plans?' asked Sébastien, unable to hide his excitement.

Jean-Claude smiled. 'I do and I have a feeling we may find a use for the television van after all. It's fooled the Germans before and could again. Go and see Alain and Luc. I want the three of you to buy as much petrol as you can – you may have to use the black market. Then store it with the van or in another garage close to it. If you can, find some spare tyres and buy those, too.'

Sébastien nodded as Jean-Claude continued.

'After that I want you to purchase two bicycles. It'll cost you a lot of money as everyone is doing the same, so make sure you bring them into the apartment. Don't leave them on the street – they'll just be stolen.'

'Anything else?' said Sébastien, excited by the prospect of doing something positive against the German occupiers.

'Yes. Go and see Tobias. Ask him if he can find space in the catacombs and then arrange to move Samuel Finkenberg's workshop underground. I'll see you back here just before the curfew – and don't take any unnecessary risks.'

****

Later that morning Sturmbannführer Bernhard Krüger was briefing Bauer on the progress they'd made installing the printing press on the fifth floor. Bauer was half-listening as he looked at his reflection in the gilt Napoleon III mirror. He adjusted his collar. His thoughts turned to his childhood, when the moneylender had come to the door demanding payment of the interest on the family's meagre loan. He remembered his mother weeping with the shame. Now, he seemed to see the moneylender kneeling on the floor before him.

You've come back to see me, Jew, to admire my new uniform. What's that? Yes, you should be afraid, very afraid. Speak up, what did you say, Jew? You ask why I persecute you and your children and your children's children? Jew, I am not to blame for your misery. How can I be? It was you who fashioned me, you who shaped me, you who made me what I am. What? You say I am too harsh? You, who made yourself rich by stealing the bread from children call me cruel and arrogant? Jew, why must I listen to you? I've heard enough of your excuses and your cries. Stop haunting me. Now leave me. Oh, and before you go, Jew, remember that what I have now you will never take away from me, and if you try, I will crush you underfoot like a cockroach. You ask that of me? No, it would be best if you and your like were to disappear. You are surprised, Jew? Why should you be surprised? You are vermin.

The vision disappeared and Bauer turned around to hear Krüger say, 'We expect the plate to arrive in a couple of days. Once installed, it should be able to start printing within a month. Britain may be about to surrender, but we will still need to destroy the British economy so that the pound is worthless. We calculate that, if Britain's dominions – Canada and Australia – and their other colonies have to finance the war themselves, they will be reluctant to continue the conflict.'

'Excellent. When the plate arrives, store it in the vault,' ordered Bauer.

The meeting over, Krüger saluted and left the office.

Bauer sat in his chair to consider the future. The Führer had been promised that, within days, the RAF would be destroyed and Britain would be forced to make peace. Within weeks, the Germans could be in London. Bauer picked up the file to continue work on the orders to the SS for the occupation of Britain. The arrangements that Heydrich had asked him to compile.

The organisation and function of the military government of Britain

Objective:
To centralise and safeguard Britain for future exploitation. Everything but normal household stocks is to be confiscated for the future use by the Reich. All firearms and radios are to be handed in to Reich authorities. Those failing to turn in these items are to be immediately executed. If considered necessary, to ensure compliance by the population, hostages should be taken.

All paintings and other works of art in museums and private collections are to be assessed, and those deemed of value to the Reich are to be marked for transportation to Germany. Art considered to be degenerate is to be destroyed.

The following organisations and institutions are to be immediately disbanded:

- All Jewish organisations
- Political parties
- Trade unions
- Fee-paying (public) schools
- The Church of England (a powerful tool of British imperial politics)
- The Boy Scouts (known to be a source of information for British Intelligence)

Public libraries are to be closed

Bauer picked up the *Die Sonderfahndungsliste GB*, the list of those to be arrested or executed. It was 2,000 names long. At the top of the first page was Winston Churchill. There followed members of the government, newspaper editors, trade unionists, priests, Aldous Huxley, H G Wells, E M Forster, J B

211

Priestley, Noël Coward, Bertrand Russell, Harold Laski, Lady Bonham Carter, Lord Baden Powell...

Turning to the final page, Bauer added 'Count Philip Tagleva, Countess Sophie Tagleva and Michael Tagleva' to the list.

Bauer put down the pen. Such was his excitement he was finding it difficult to concentrate. He looked, once more, at the card that had arrived that morning. It was his invitation to attend the ceremony at Wewelsburg Castle when he, Rudolf Bauer, would present to Heinrich Himmler the sacred book that he had recovered from the Tagleva vault detailing the life of King Heinrich. During the ceremony Himmler would place around his neck the Knight's Cross with oak leaves, swords and diamonds that Heydrich had told him was already being fashioned for him in Berlin. It would be the pinnacle of his career. He would return to Paris with a second silver oak leaf on his collar, indicating his promotion to SS-Oberführer.

He was too distracted by thoughts of the ceremony to concentrate on work. He put the papers in his desk drawer and locked it. Walking into the outer office he instructed his secretary that he was going out and to take messages.

Stepping into the corridor he saw the girl he'd seen on the fifth floor coming out of Jean-Claude's office. Her back was towards him.

'Good afternoon, *mademoiselle*,' he said.

The girl turned around, obviously startled. She was more attractive than he remembered. He looked at her brown hair, large eyes and youthful complexion. In that split second, he decided he would invite her to spend the evening with him. He was excited, alive and wanted someone to share his good fortune. They would dine at Maxim's. He pictured himself with her on his arm and the other officers in the restaurant raising their glasses of champagne in admiration of him. Afterwards, if she were agreeable to him, he would make love to her. She was bound to say yes; they always did.

'*Mademoiselle*, I know we have not met but I would like to repair that oversight. Would you do me the honour of having dinner with me tonight, at Maxim's?'

Juliette looked at him. 'I'm sorry, *monsieur*, but I'm engaged to be married and must refuse. I hope you will forgive me.'

'Would your fiancé object to you spending time with a lonely soldier?'

She looked down at the third finger of his left hand. 'Would you be upset, Standartenführer, if your wife went out to dinner with another officer while you are doing your duty in Paris?'

'Your fiancé need never find out.'

'True, but I would know,' she smiled disarmingly.

Bauer would not beg, he never begged.

'Another time,' he said and politely clicked his heels, bowing his head very slightly.

Bauer watched as she walked down the corridor. He half-expected, hoped, she would turn back to look at him, but she didn't.

Her mind would be changed when he was promoted to Oberführer. One way or another, he would have her.

Chapter Thirty-four
The concierge

7 Sept 1940

Christopher Hatton received confirmation from his contact that the printing plate had left Britain. It had been taken by boat to the neutral Republic of Ireland, to the German embassy in Dublin and, the following night, had been flown to Portugal in the diplomatic bag.

He thought back to that day at Brocket Hall. It was chance that he'd been looking out of the window and seen the car drive over the flint bridge. While the army lieutenant had talked to the butler at the front entrance, he'd taken the opportunity to grab the plate and rush as fast as his weight would allow into the dining room. He was halfway down the servant's corridor that led to the kitchen when he had heard the unmistakable sound of Luger shots. He guessed what was happening when he heard a crash of furniture and a struggle. It had given him the time to rush out of the Hall via the tradesmen's entrance, through the kitchen gardens and to the trees beyond. It was luck and his usual caution that had persuaded him to park his car at the back entrance. He remembered having to wipe the sweat from his forehead and take gulps of air from the open window to recover from the exertion as he drove to London.

Now in the calm of his house, he was enjoying an after-dinner brandy. He didn't fear the authorities would find him; there was nothing to connect him with John Knight. If one was needed, he could always find an alibi within the Right Club. Someone of importance who would swear he was nowhere near Brocket Hall at the time.

Nevertheless there was one thing that gnawed at him. He was sure he'd seen the young officer somewhere. It had only been a fleeting glance, but the face was familiar, he recognised the features clearly… but where had that been? He shook his head, trying to improve his memory… Perhaps it wasn't important.

His thoughts were interrupted by the air-raid siren and he walked upstairs to get a better view of the destruction of London. Opening the blackout curtains, he looked over the darkness of the city and watched as searchlights pierced the sky. A minute later the distinctive drone of German aircraft could be heard overhead, followed by the distant thud of anti-aircraft batteries opening up.

He sipped his brandy and watched with increasing excitement as a wave of incendiary bombs fell, flashed, quickly became pinpricks of dazzling white burning sulphur and turned yellow as buildings began to burn. Soon the horizon of the city was ablaze with fires – scores of them, perhaps hundreds. He felt neither fear nor horror, because there was something inspiring in the savagery of it. He took another sip of his brandy as a new wave of planes, like bumblebees in a blind fury, droned overhead. Bombs fell and immediately above the fires, the sky became red and angry as a cloud of orange smoke created a ceiling in the heavens over the city.

It was the most brutal, most beautiful thing he'd ever witnessed.

****

A few minutes after four o'clock the following morning, Jean-Claude got out of bed, washed and dressed. Once the curfew was lifted at five, he cycled to Porte de Montreuil in the 5th arrondissement. He took the precaution of stopping a couple of times to catch his breath and ensure he was not being followed. Forty-five minutes later, he cycled into the courtyard of Samuel Finkenberg's apartment block. Parking his bicycle against the wall, he looked up at the red brick walls four storeys high that contained perhaps fifty apartments. In common with so many apartment blocks in Paris, the courtyard was constructed from four older buildings that had been adapted and altered to become one. The result was a building with multiple entrances, reconfigured stairways and some unused spaces that only served to confuse the visitor.

The concierge appeared from her *loge*, identified by the uniform worn by every concierge in Paris, a long black dress and blue apron with a large pocket in the front. She looked at Jean-Claude. '*Bonjour, monsieur*,' she said politely.

Like thousands of others all over the city, the concierge was the boss of the building. Through the glass door of her small ground-floor apartment near the entrance, she saw the comings and goings of the tenants, busied herself keeping the public areas clean, acted as mailbox, messenger and childminder. She knew every tenant's business, those with money problems, those who were ill, the malingerers, those who brought in a late-night visitor and she knew all the other concierges in the district. Ask any resident what they thought of their concierge, they'd tell you, 'She's a bitch!' – there was nothing that could be done and so it was best to remain on her good side and be generous on Saint Sylvestre's Day when the 'voluntary' gratuity for her services was handed over. It was the only way to ensure that mail wouldn't go astray and one's reputation wouldn't be tarnished by malicious gossip.

The concierge was the first person the police talked to when they had questions about a tenant. Aware of their importance, the Germans had ordered them to report the arrival of any new tenant within twenty-four hours and any visitors who stayed longer than a single night and to remove any anti-German graffiti from their buildings. The co-operation of the city's concierges was guaranteed by making it plain that failure to do so might result in imprisonment, or worse.

Jean-Claude smiled back. '*Bonjour, madame*,' he replied.

Climbing the stairs, he wasn't worried that his visit would be reported to the police or the Germans. For years, the concierge had undertaken a number of special tasks for the Tagleva bank and was paid a regular and very generous wage for her troubles.

As he entered Samuel's apartment, his wife and children came from the kitchen to greet him. Jean-Claude smelt a delicious aroma coming from the kitchen. Not having had breakfast, he suddenly felt hungry.

Samuel smiled. 'You can smell my wife's *cholent*, the Sabbath stew. It's our traditional midday meal and the only hot dish of the holy day. My wife prepares it on Friday, and every time the lid is raised, wonderful smells fill the entire apartment. In the old days when I was a child, my grandmother used to make it. We were poor and didn't have a large oven so my brothers and I would take the pot to the baker's oven in the village. Other families would do the same and the baker would give me, the youngest child, a metal tag with the number of our pot, and when it was cooked, my father and brothers would collect it and bring it to the house before the Sabbath began.'

'It smells delicious. What are the ingredients?' enquired Jean-Claude.

'Traditionally meat, potatoes, barley beans and *kishke*, a sausage stuffed with the intestines of a cow and other tasty foods. It tastes wonderful unless the idea of a cow's intestine bothers you. My mother would add dumplings because, as my grandmother told her, the quickest way to a husband's wallet is through his stomach.' He roared with laughter. 'At the end of the Sabbath, and after eating so much stodge, my father, brothers and I had to go to the synagogue to pray for our stomachs to recover' – and he roared with laughter again.

Then Samuel's face took on a serious expression. He looked towards the kitchen and leaned forward, motioning Jean-Claude to do the same.

'I'll tell you a secret. A measure of who is a good Jew is whether you like *cholent*. It's a test the Nazis haven't tried yet, so keep it to yourself and don't tell them!' and he leaned back in his chair and laughed some more.

They were interrupted by Samuel's wife entering with a tray of hot tea and a small plate with two biscuits. Placing it on the table, she smiled at Jean-Claude and returned to the kitchen. Samuel indicated to Jean-Claude that he should help himself to a biscuit.

There was some noise from the apartment above. 'You must excuse our neighbours getting up from their bed. For the next hour, they will drag chairs over their floor as they prepare their breakfast. Then it will go quiet again as they don't speak to each other when they eat. Then after they've eaten, they will begin their chores and it will sound like the German army's on manoeuvres. That's because they walk on the wooden floor wearing clogs!' and he chuckled.

'It's good to see you in such good humour,' said Jean-Claude.

'For the minute, thank God, things are quiet. And we might as well use this time to laugh because it won't be long before the Nazis will find ways to make life unnecessarily difficult. I've heard some people say that the French authorities will prevent it, but I doubt it. The French have their own interests to protect and speaking up for a few Jews, particularly foreign ones like us, won't be a priority.'

Samuel's smile disappeared. A weight seemed to press down on his shoulders and they became rounded as his eyes were cast down. In that moment, Jean-Claude saw a sorrow – the years in Germany when the family would measure the success of a day being one where they woke and were able to lay their heads back on the same pillow at night. Jean-Claude glimpsed the depth of Samuel's pain.

'Are you safe here for the time being?'

'Having the Germans in Paris is a shock. We thought we had escaped them. Now there seems no escape. But if we keep ourselves to ourselves we hope to escape notice for as long as possible. My wife's talked about going to the unoccupied zone in Vichy, but I've told her that Vichy will be no safer. The Germans will tell the Vichy government what to do and they'll ask how high they need to jump to obey. No, I've decided we will stay in Paris where there are opportunities to hide and where we have friends like you to help us, though I fear they will find us... eventually.'

Jean-Claude smiled. 'That's the reason for my visit. You've been told of the arrangements if things become difficult?'

'Yes, we all understand them.'

'Did you manage to move your printing room into the catacombs?'

'The two men who came to help me were very efficient. Over a few hours we managed to take everything we needed to the secret room under the streets. It's now disguised by a brick wall and very well hidden. It's where I'll take my family when the Nazis decide to become objectionable.'

'Good. In the meantime, are you able to do me another service? I need some documents,' said Jean-Claude.

'Of course.'

Twenty minutes later, the two men hugged each other and said goodbye.

'When the documents are ready, I'll get a message to you,' said Samuel. Jean-Claude shook his hand once more and left the apartment.

****

Philip Tagleva, appointed as the prime minister's personal financial advisor, sat at the meeting table at the Bank of England. Like the others around the table, he knew the meeting meant it was a crisis.

Colonel Tim Wilson was briefing them about the theft of the printing plate. '... I'm afraid the trail has gone cold.'

There were furrowed brows, one person played with a pencil, another polished the lenses of his spectacles, a third leaned back in his chair and looked at the ceiling.

'Should we start to recall the five-pound note and issue another?' rasped Mark Johnson.

'That would take many months and, during wartime, would indicate to everyone that there's a problem,' came a reply from the far end of the table.

'I agree, it would cause unnecessary speculation,' said another.

'What are the likely effects of thousands of forged five-pound notes being in circulation?' asked the colonel.

Philip began to explain: 'The major ill-effect that printing money has on the economy is that it increases prices, which in turn leads to inflation. Within a short time a large amount of counterfeit money would mean every bullet, aircraft or pair of soldier's boots would become increasingly more expensive. However, the short-term result of counterfeit money for goods and services we import from other countries is worse. They would get sick of selling us goods for what might end up as worthless sheets of paper. The end-result would be that the country's creditors, such as the United States, would demand payment in another currency or in gold.'

Philip paused and then continued: 'For example, to illustrate the seriousness of the situation, during the Great War it wasn't the British and French armies that defeated Germany. Germany had to surrender suddenly because it had printed so much money to pay for its bullets that the currency had become worthless.'

'So the theft of this plate is serious,' said Wilson.

'It's catastrophic,' said Johnson.

****

After Jean-Claude returned from seeing Samuel, he stored the bicycle in his apartment, had a coffee with Sébastien and walked to the Tagleva bank to arrive at his usual time. Walking down the Rue Pierre Charron, he saw a military motorcycle parked outside and recognised it as a Zündapp KS750 with a sidecar. The Germans loved the vehicle because it allowed for fast transport of two personnel and could carry light equipment. As Jean-Claude came within a few feet of it, a sergeant stepped from the sidecar and onto the pavement. Leaning inside the sidecar, he lifted out a cylindrical package. As he stood up and twisted to lift the package, his jackboot caught the kerbside and he fell backwards. Landing on the pavement, he cried out in pain and let go of the cylinder. It slowly rolled along the pavement coming to rest against Jean-Claude's feet. Jean-Claude bent down and picked it up. Part of the thick brown cloth that wrapped the cylinder had been pulled away and he could see through to the engraved metal inside.

'I think that belongs to me.'

Jean-Claude looked up to see the Standartenführer in front of him with his hand outstretched.

Jean-Claude looked at the cylinder and then back at Bauer.

'Oh, of course.' Jean-Claude passed the cylinder over.

Bauer passed it to the orderly standing behind him. 'Have it placed in the vault,' he ordered. The soldier turned and walked inside.

The sergeant was on his feet now, standing to attention, waiting for the reprimand he was bound to receive.

Bauer ignored him, looked once more at Jean-Claude, then turned and walked back inside the bank. The sergeant let out an audible sigh of relief, climbed into the sidecar and was quickly driven away.

Chapter Thirty-five
'Surely they must come soon'

In his office, Jean-Claude was thinking through what had happened outside the bank. When he'd picked up the package, he'd found himself looking at a familiar picture: Britannia, holding a staff, surrounded by heraldic mantling and surmounted by a crown and knew he'd seen the reverse image on the top left-hand corner of an English five-pound note. Jean-Claude suddenly realised that the cylinder would be used on the floor above his office to print hundreds of millions of pounds of counterfeit money. They would destroy the economy of Britain and lose it the war.

His thoughts were disturbed by Juliette entering his office with some papers for him to sign. Taking them from her, he signed them immediately. It was the first time he'd signed anything without reading it first. She looked at him. 'You look tired. Can I get you some coffee?'

'A carrier pigeon would be better,' he muttered.

'*Pardon?*'

'Oh nothing. I was just wishing I could speak to Philip Tagleva. Get a message to him, that was all,' he replied with a smile.

She left the room.

****

At the end of the day, he left the bank with the other employees, Jean-Claude was still deep in thought. He only noticed Juliette when she was already by his side. *Strange*, he thought, *she lives in the opposite direction.* They turned the corner and were out of sight of the bank before she spoke.

'This morning you said you wished you had a pigeon.'

They stopped walking as Jean-Claude thought back. 'Yes, I remember… but I don't understand?'

'I think I know where I could find a pigeon, to take a message to London.'

At that moment, a Luftwaffe officer appeared around the corner. They ceased talking and Juliette placed her hands around Jean-Claude's neck, pulled him towards her and kissed him firmly on the lips.

Jean-Claude smelt her Mais Oui perfume by Bourjois, felt the softness of her lips and the gloved hand gently touching his neck. Once the officer had passed, she let him go.

'I'm sorry, better to be seen kissing than talking.'

'Quite so,' he replied.

'If you can make the message short, perhaps ten words, I'll see if my pigeon will deliver it. See you tomorrow, and thanks for the kiss.'

'My pleasure,' mumbled Jean-Claude as he watched her walk up the street.

****

That night Christopher Hatton couldn't sleep. He was troubled and the sounds of the bombing in the distance kept him awake. At eleven, he gave up the struggle, got up, dressed and walked from his house onto Hampstead Heath where he watched the city burn. *Surely*, he thought, *Britain can't suffer much more of this bombardment.* For two hours, he stood looking towards the city, returning home to bed only when he could no longer hear the drone from the bombers.

The following morning, like everyone else, he listened to the BBC broadcast:

> The German air force unleashed a wave of heavy bombing raids on London, killing hundreds of civilians and injuring many more… About 300 enemy bombers attacked the city for over an hour and a half… The Ministry of Home Security said the scale of the attacks was the largest the Germans had yet attempted… Our defences actively engaged

the enemy at all points... The Air Ministry has confirmed that eighty-eight German aircraft were shot down, against twenty-two RAF planes lost.

How could the statistics be true? He had seen it for himself last night. The Luftwaffe was bringing complete destruction to London. It had defeated the air forces of five nations and was bringing the RAF to its knees. Surely, Britain couldn't hold out for much longer. Within weeks the Germans will be in London. Then he would have what he had been promised, the grand house in London, another in the country, he deserved nothing less. Then, those who had called him fat and a fool would eat their words. He would make sure of it. They would learn he was their master. Surely the Germans must come soon.

****

Two days later, Philip's secretary walked into his office.

'I have a gentleman outside who says he's from the American embassy.'

Walter Abraham was ushered into the office. As they shook hands, Philip felt the firm grip that would remind him of their meeting for the rest of the day. Sitting down, he noticed Walter's crimson tie woven with the legend 'VE-RI-TAS', indicating that he had attended the United States' oldest and best institution of higher learning, Harvard University.

'Philip, thank you for seeing me,' said the American with his familiar New York accent and broad smile. 'We've received a message from our embassy in Paris. I don't need to remind you that passing it on to you is contrary to embassy rules. If Ambassador Kennedy found out, I could be in *deeeep* trouble.'

'Walter, once again I appreciate the risk you are taking and you have my assurance that no one will find out about your involvement.'

Walter handed him a white envelope.

'I know you're busy so I'll bid you good day.'

Philip shook Walter's hand again and the American left. As the door to his office closed, Philip clenched and unclenched his hand to get the circulation moving again. He slit open the

225

envelope with a paper knife and took out the single sheet of paper and read the message:

Value of Plate in Diebold five Jewels.

Philip read the message three times. He thought for a few moments, picked up the phone. Fifty minutes later, he was in a meeting room at the Bank of England with two of its directors and Colonel Wilson.

Mark Johnson spoke: 'Now that the Germans have the plate, the situation's hopeless. My fear is that, within a year, the entire foundation of the British economy will be ruined.'

Half an hour later, Philip escorted the colonel out of the building. Arriving on the pavement of Threadneedle Street, he said to Wilson, 'Perhaps things aren't quite as hopeless as my colleagues at the bank believe. I have an idea that you might find interesting. Do you have time for a cup of tea?'

Chapter Thirty-six
When hell freezes over

September 1940

Air Commodore Stephenson was holding a briefing with four of his wing commanders at RAF Bentley Priory and had instructed the switchboard to disturb him only in an emergency. So when the phone rang, he picked up the receiver. The flying officers watched as the air commodore first listened to the caller and then began to roll his eyes. Eventually he replied: 'I don't know who you are, except you are most likely a lunatic. So, let me explain in simple words you might understand. Each day and night the Germans fly planes over the country and drop bombs on our cities. We are using every available aircraft to try to stop them. At this point we are losing so many aircraft and pilots that we are in danger of losing the war. So you decide that this is a good time for you to *borrow* a plane? Get this into your tiny mind. Hell will freeze over before I agree. I suggest you go back to the funny farm that's obviously discharged you in error, and let me get on with fighting the war.'

The phone was replaced onto its cradle. The four officers in the room smiled at how expertly their commanding officer had dispatched the caller.

Twenty minutes later the phone rang again.

Irritated by yet another interruption, the air commodore picked up the phone. 'What is it this time?' he growled.

The flying officers waited with growing anticipation to hear the expletives their boss would use on whoever had interrupted him, particularly if it was another request to borrow a plane.

Eventually the air commodore spoke: 'Yes, Prime Minister... of course, Prime Minister... I will make one available, Prime

Minister… immediately, sir… yes, Prime Minister… good day sir.'

The phone clicked and Winston Churchill's voice was replaced by a familiar voice. 'Air Commodore, it's Colonel Wilson again. Now that hell has frozen over, could you have the plane you've kindly agreed to lend me available to fly three nights from today. I will give you what details I can when we meet.'

As the receiver was once more replaced onto the cradle, one of the airmen whispered to another, 'The chief caught that flak mid-fuselage.'

****

In Paris, Rudolf Bauer was pleased the city was generally peaceful since its occupation. There were the odd signs of resistance, graffiti mainly. People were writing 'V' for *Victoire* everywhere. The sign had been chalked on walls, café chairs, and tables. One had even been scratched onto the door of a German staff car. *Only to be expected. It allowed ordinary people to feel they were doing something, however pointless, to protest against the occupation* he thought. Nevertheless he intended to stop these acts of vandalism and ordered three SS officers and a representative of the Gestapo to meet with him. After some discussion, the Gestapo man said, 'Mostly these chalked V's are scrawled by children.'

Bauer replied, 'Then arrest a few young boys and make an example of them. It will concentrate the minds of the others, and make sure that people hear about it.' The Gestapo man nodded his assent. 'Now, I want to discuss a much more serious problem than graffiti chalked on walls.'

Bauer opened a file on his desk and read aloud:

'In the last few weeks, the police have reports that the following documents have been stolen: Two passports, a Wehrmacht driving permit, three identification cards, two work permits, a number of curfew passes, and a security identification document for the Heinkel Airplane Factory.'

He closed the file. 'These thefts can only mean one thing. There's a forger in the city. I want that forger found.'

'What do you propose?' asked one of the SS officers.

'Firstly, I want it known among our troops that there will be severe penalties for losing official documents or their identity passes. Then in three nights' time, I intend to flood the city with police and troops. All civilians walking the streets, even in the company of a German officer, during the curfew will be stopped and questioned. Any civilian walking the streets not accompanied by a German officer is to be brought in for questioning. The exercise will continue throughout the following day. Anyone found in possession of forged documents is to be arrested and taken to Gestapo headquarters for questioning. That same day there will also be raids in certain districts of Paris. Every apartment block, every office, every shop, café and storeroom is to be searched. Initially we'll concentrate on the 13th arrondissement.'

'Any reason for that specific area?' asked the Gestapo man.

'Yes, a few days ago the police in Bercy reported that a butcher and a baker had been handed forged food stamps. It's our only lead. I want the forger and the printing press found.'

****

In London, Colonel Wilson was giving Michael his instructions.

'You have your plane. Three days from today, you'll be in Paris, but are you sure about the plan? One message seems a flimsy amount of evidence that the plate is in the Tagleva bank vault in Paris.'

'My father and I have been over it a dozen times.'

'How can you be sure the message is genuine?'

'Believe me, it is,' said Michael.

'Very well, old boy, if you say so. I just don't want you getting into any hot water for no reason.'

'I won't. I'll be wearing some civilian clothes I bought in France before the war so I won't look out of place. If I'm stopped, I'll show my Nazi party membership card. The one I was given in Germany – that'll convince most people to not detain me. In any event, I don't expect to be in Paris long enough to get into any trouble. I'll be home in a few days.' He paused... Actually there is one thing I'd like to know before I leave.'

Wilson nodded.

'You knew that I'd been in Germany and that Mr Churchill had asked me to collect information, but how did you know that I wasn't so impressed by what I'd seen that I wasn't a German spy, a double agent and all that?'

'We didn't. When we discovered that your hosts were the SS and the Abwehr had recruited you, we had you watched. You were under constant surveillance from the minute you arrived back in Paris. We knew you were passing information to the Germans. However, it soon became clear to us that you were also the key to identifying a group of British and French collaborators that had evaded us. By following the information you gave them as it passed from one person to another, we were able to identify a number of German spies here and in Paris that we hadn't known about. What we didn't know was whose side you were *really* on. We decided that one way to find out was to get you back to England where we could keep a close eye on you. We thought you were working for the Germans up to the time you admitted having been trained by the Abwehr at your interview in London.'

'I didn't think anyone took me seriously.'

'Oh, you were taken seriously, old boy, very seriously.'

'So what would have happened if you had found I was working for the Germans after all?'

'That was the easy part, old man. One night we'd have arrested you. As a serving officer you were, by then, under military rule. We would either have turned you so that you worked for us, under close supervision, and send the Germans false information, or if that didn't work, we'd put you against a wall and shoot you.'

'So, it was after Dunkirk you knew you could trust me.'

'Trust you. Now don't start getting delusional. We've had you watched the whole time... just in case.'

'I never noticed anyone... oh, my God... you mean Rose?'

'A talented girl is Rose. The old girl can smell a traitor at a hundred yards. Even told us of the pass you made at her after Brocket Hall. That did give us a laugh.'

Michael wondered how many people made up 'us'.

'Well, I won't ask if you trust me now.'

'If you succeed in this next task, we might consider trusting you,' smiled Wilson.

Michael smiled back. 'So to change the subject and save me further blushes, if things do go wrong, who do I blame for recommending me for the Intelligence Service and putting me into your clutches?'

As if reluctant to reveal the answer, Wilson hesitated. 'I suppose you have a right to know who's giving you your adventure. There were three names on the recommendation: Winston Churchill, Noël Coward... and your father's.'

****

The plane was waiting, its propellers turning and ready to fly Michael to France. Tim Wilson and Rose had come to see him off.

'Take care, old man, and when you return, I'm buying the first pint of beer at The Coal Hole,' said the colonel.

'If you're buying the beers, I'll swim the English Channel to get back home.'

He turned to Rose and held out his hand to shake hers. 'Thank you for keeping an eye on me, and out of trouble,' he said.

Still holding his hand, she planted a kiss on his cheek. 'My pleasure, take care and make sure you come back safely.'

Michael smiled at them both, turned and climbed up the short ladder into the plane. The door closed and Wilson and Rose watched as the aircraft taxied towards the runway, sped away and disappeared into the night sky.

Wilson turned to Rose, 'Well, old girl, it's back to work for us... we have a spy to find.'

****

The Bristol Blenheim usually carries a crew of three: a pilot, a navigator and the telegraphist who doubles up as an air gunner if the aircraft is attacked. On this flight, Michael had taken the place of the telegraphist.

While most pilots regarded the Blenheim as a pleasant aircraft to fly, little did Michael suspect that it was a less-than-adequate plane to cross the English Channel. But it was the only aircraft an angry and embarrassed air commodore would make available. With little to do than to let the pilot fly the plane, Michael settled into his seat and closed his eyes.

****

As they crossed the French coast, a couple of anti-aircraft batteries opened up, but with no searchlights, they fired harmlessly into a black sky and the Bristol flew on, undamaged, towards its destination.

Fifteen minutes later, Michael was thinking through what he had to do when he arrived in France. His thoughts were disturbed by another anti-aircraft battery coming to life. The first shell exploded harmlessly to the port side. Then there was another explosion. The Blenheim shook violently, the tail dropped sharply, and immediately the plane climbed 300 feet. Michael was thrown against the bulkhead and banged his head. He winced with the pain.

The pilot struggled with the controls. 'The throttle won't go back!' he shouted to the navigator.

The plane reached the top of its climb and then began to descend and roll to the right. The pilot was losing control. The aircraft wasn't responding. He was commanding the aircraft to bring its nose up and to turn left but the Blenheim was doing the exact opposite. As the steering failed, the wounded plane continued its roll. The pilot looked in panic at the instrument panel; the gauges were spinning. The aircraft banked about thirty-eight degrees and was now in danger of rolling over onto its back. If that happened, it would spiral into the ground. The pilot slammed the throttle closed. He had no idea what made him use the throttle; nothing in his training would have suggested it. But after a few agonising seconds, the right wing slowly came back up.

The plane had been fatally wounded. The pilot knew it and also knew it was not high enough off the ground for the crew to bail out and have time to open their parachutes safely. They were going to crash. The pilot had no option but to hang onto the controls and try to glide the aircraft to the ground. The tendons in his neck straining against his skin, his knuckles white, he watched as the indicators on the gauges in the cockpit continued to spin behind their glass protectors. He struggled with the oscillations that were carrying the nose up and down in an irregular undulating wave.

Dear God, I'm going to die. I'm twenty-three-years old and I'm going to die. I only met my girlfriend two weeks ago. We plan to marry, have three beautiful children, and damn it, I'm going to die before I've even…

Seconds before the plane hit the ground, the pilot noted the speed, twice that for a normal, safe landing.

'I think we're gonna make it!' he shouted encouragingly.

He knew that, at this speed, the tyres would explode on contact with the ground or the undercarriage would collapse and the plane would disintegrate. Twenty-five feet above the ground, the right wing banked more than twenty degrees. The left wing dropped and it took but a fraction of a second for it to tear into the muddy field. At the same time, the landing gear gouged a trench through the wet soil. With no weight on the tail the Blenheim pirouetted onto its nose. The windows of the cockpit burst and the pilot felt a rush of cold air as shattered glass lashed his face.

The pilot awoke lying in a field with cuts to his face. He felt sick. He could see that his left shoulder was level with his ear and knew his shoulder was dislocated. His back throbbed from a compression fracture of his spine, and the tendon that controlled his right thumb was severed. Turning his head, he managed to look around him. The navigator was lying ten feet away. He called out to him but received no reply.

****

Michael had not been thrown clear of the plane. He was still strapped into the seat and hanging upside down. He was bruised, his head hurt from a bump he'd received and one of his ears was cut and bleeding. He stayed quiet for a few seconds, checking for bones that might be broken and for internal injuries. After a minute, he knew he was not badly wounded.

Releasing himself and finding a hole in the fuselage, Michael carefully crawled out of the plane and discovered the navigator, his breathing was irregular and it was obvious the navigator was in a bad way. He saw the pilot a few feet away.

'Are you hurt?' he asked.

'My shoulder's dislocated and my back aches like buggery, but I guess I'll live. How's the navigator?'

'Quite bad, I'm afraid.'

The pilot gripped Michael's wrist with his one good hand. 'There's not much you can do here and we didn't risk everything for you to get caught. The Germans will know we've been shot down and will be swarming around here soon. You don't have much time. If you can, destroy the plane and then bugger off and go fight the war for us.'

Michael saw the sense of it but hated the thought of abandoning the pilot and navigator.

'Do you know where we are?' asked Michael.

'I guess a few miles outside Meaux – it was the last place we flew over. Now go, and good luck!'

Michael retrieved the small leather case from the plane that held his civilian clothes. He pulled a flare from its holder on the bulkhead, pulled the tape, waited for the sparks to catch the powder and threw it into the plane. Flames began to take hold of some spilled fuel.

He checked on the navigator once more. He had stopped breathing. Michael ran towards the trees at the edge of the field and hid in the undergrowth. It was just in time as he saw a couple of trucks come down the road, and watched as German soldiers disembarked and began to search the area.

****

Christopher Hatton listened to the BBC's morning news report. He scowled at the exaggerated success over the German bombers. How could the RAF ever beat the Luftwaffe?

He thought back to the time when he'd watched wave after wave of planes fly over the stadium at Zeppelin Field as he sat among the other foreign VIPs.

'My God!' he cried out loud. The boy who had sat next to him, the boy with the golden hair, the boy he'd poked in the ribs because he was obscuring his view of the parade. The boy in the stadium and the officer who had burst into Brocket Hall were one and the same. *His name... What was his name...? The SS man in charge of the section had told him his name... Michael... Michael Tagleva – that was it and he was due to attend a ceremony at Wewelsburg Castle. It must be him. His arrival at Brocket Hall could mean only one thing. He's a traitor, working for the British. He must be exposed.*

Hatton would get a message to Berlin; they must be told. He would send the message that night.

****

The first hotel in Europe to provide every bedroom with a telephone, electricity and en-suite bathroom was the Hotel Ritz in Paris. The Luftwaffe had made it their headquarters.

A courier walked into the building and delivered a despatch reporting the crash of a Bristol Blenheim near Meaux. The pilot was injured and was in hospital; the navigator dead. The third member of the crew, the telegraphist, was missing, presumed to be on the run in the countryside. Two infantry platoons were searching the surrounding area.

The officer on duty read the message and passed the information on to his superior. Judging by the reports of the crashed plane, the Luftwaffe officer assumed the fugitive British airman was probably wounded, and dressed in his RAF flying suit, he would be captured quickly. There was, however, one strange note at the bottom of the report. An expensive pair of gentleman's leather gloves had been found near the wreckage with a label from a shop on the Rue Delambre in Paris.

Chapter Thirty-seven
'Forgive me, Father, for I have sinned'

Michael had watched from the hedgerow surrounding the field as the Germans began to search the area around the plane. Once it was safe, he ran down the nearby road for perhaps a mile, until he saw the silhouette of a farm building a few hundred yards away. Carefully walking up the pathway to it, he waited to find out if anyone had seen him. Opening the barn door, he slipped inside and allowed his eyes to adjust to the darkness.

The barn was full of farm equipment and he sat down next to an old cart to work out what he should do next. Rubbing his ear, he felt the grit of dried blood. He would be quickly stopped if he had blood on his face. He also needed to change out of his flying suit and boots and into the civilian clothes he'd brought to disguise himself. He was exhausted but thanked providence that the Bristol had crashed near Meaux. As a child, he'd often holidayed in the region with an English couple he had adopted as grandparents. With luck, he could be in Paris in a few hours. He leaned against the cart and closed his eyes, just for a moment.

****

Michael awoke with a start to the sound of cattle passing the barn. Daylight streamed through the gaps in the wooden door. He cursed himself for falling asleep. Crawling over to the door, he peered through a hole to see a farm hand taking some cattle for milking. *Damn it*, he said to himself. It would be more dangerous to move around the countryside in daylight and not be recognised as a stranger.

Once the farmhand had passed, he searched the barn. There were some rusty ploughs, a broken wheel and a feeding trough for cattle partly filled with rainwater from a hole in the roof. At one end of the barn, he found a couple of barrels, and at the other a metal bowl and a piece of broken mirror. He filled the bowl with water from the trough and placed it on top of one of the barrels. Positioning the broken mirror against the bowl he looked at himself. The face that looked back was bruised, dirty and needed a shave.

Removing the flying suit he carefully washed away the dried blood from his face. Opening up the small attaché case, he extracted a razor and shaved as best he could with cold water and no soap. He used a little of the foundation cream Rose had given him to disguise the bruises from the fight at Brocket Hall. He ran a hand through his hair to tidy it. Once satisfied with the way he looked, he took out a pair of trousers, jacket and boots from the suitcase. The clothes were crumpled but they would have to do. Once dressed, he hid the flying suit in one of the empty barrels and the suitcase and the flying boots in the other.

Carefully opening the door, he strode down the track to the road. No one saw him.

If the pilot was correct and the plane had crashed on the outskirts of Meaux, he should soon be able to find the Canal de l'Ourcq. It supplied Paris with half the water needed to clean the sewer system and street gutters, and to supply water to parks and fountains. If he walked down the towpath, it would eventually lead him into the centre of the city.

Michael had been walking down the road for ten minutes when he saw a figure cycling towards him. He thought of hiding but it was too late and it would look suspicious, and anyway the cyclist was a woman. As the cyclist came closer, he saw it was not a woman but a priest. He had been mistaken because the priest had unbuttoned some of the thirty-three buttons of his cassock, each one representing a year of Jesus's life, and was sitting astride the bicycle. As the cassock billowed in the wind it had given the impression of a skirt.

A hundred yards in front of Michael, the priest slowed down and turned into the garden of a small cottage. Leaning the bicycle against the wall, he pulled a small bag from the wicker basket and knocked on the door. It was immediately opened by an old woman and he disappeared inside.

Michael looked around. There was no one else on the road. He walked to the front of the house, picked up the bicycle, mounted it and peddled away. Riding down the road, he spoke into the wind: 'Forgive me, Father, for I have sinned and I am heartily sorry for having offended you, but the Lord knows my need is greater than yours. In penance, I'll light a candle in Notre Dame cathedral!'

****

Twenty minutes later a message was radioed to Luftwaffe HQ at the Hôtel Ritz and the Oberleutnant read it and went to speak to his superior.

'*Herr Major*, the fugitive airman's not been captured near Meaux. There are reports that a flying suit and boots have been found hidden in a farmer's barn, together with a small suit-case containing a razor. The farmer's being interrogated but denies knowing anything. There's also a separate report of a priest's bicycle being stolen. The local *gendarmerie* questioned the priest and confirmed that, at the time of the theft, he was administering the last rites to a member of his flock.'

'If the airman's not wearing a flying suit or boots, what *is* he wearing? Did the first report say that there was a pair of civilian gloves found in the aircraft?'

'Yes, sir.'

'Bring them to me.'

An hour later, the gloves were delivered. The officer examined them. They were good quality, the leather particularly soft. Inside he found the label from the shop on Rue Delambre. Then he pulled back the hem of the gloves and found a name tag. He recognised it as the type sewn into children's clothing by the English aristocracy when sent off to boarding school. He looked at the tag: 'MICHTAGLEVA'.

'So, we have an airman that's dressed in civilian clothes, riding a stolen bicycle. We aren't searching for an airman in an RAF uniform – we're looking for a spy and this label would seem to suggest his name. Inform the Gestapo and the French police. We'll see if they have any ideas.'

'Yes, sir.'

Chapter Thirty-eight
A raid

The following day

After leaving Samuel's apartment Alain walked down the road towards the café where he had arranged to meet Luc. In the secret pocket in the lining of his jacket were the two curfew passes he'd collected from Samuel. He turned the corner of the street and stopped. Halfway down the street was an Opel Blitz, the three-ton truck used by the Wehrmacht. On the pavement, two *gendarmes*, dressed in their distinctive uniform of black jackets, blue jodhpurs and knee-high boots, were stopping pedestrians and inspecting their papers. From the back of the truck, half-a-dozen soldiers jumped onto the street and rushed into an apartment building. Alain turned and quickly walked back to Samuel's block. Entering the concierge's apartment, he told her what he'd seen. He then left, walking in the opposite direction to the German truck.

The concierge collected the clothes horse that leaned against the side of a chest of drawers and positioned it in the courtyard in front of her apartment door. Leaving a red duster on one of the wooden slats of the horse she went back inside, returning with a metal bowl of washing. As she walked towards the clothes horse, the bowl slipped from her grasp, fell to the ground and rolled across the cobbles. The noise of the metal on the flagstones echoed around the courtyard walls.

Four floors above, Samuel looked out of the window. Seeing the clothes horse with the red duster, he collected his wife and children and rushed them out of the apartment and down the stairs to the floor below. At the end of a short corridor, behind a false wall hidden from immediate view, was an old staircase once used by a resident to smuggle his mistress into his apartment. They rushed down it.

The Finkenbergs arrived at the bottom of the steps as the Germans entered the courtyard and waited a few seconds for the concierge to collect her keys that would open any apartment the soldiers might wish to inspect.

Samuel's family came to a door in the outer wall that had long ago been bricked up as they heard the German's boots walking across the courtyard to the staircase that would lead them to the apartments in their block. Samuel reached down to a metal ring in the floor, pulled at it and the flagstones lifted. He ushered his wife and children down to the cellars and from there to the catacombs, the flagstone trap door was closed behind them.

Opposite Samuel's apartment lived two women. Once Samuel and his family had left one of them walked into the apartment and cleared away the cups from the kitchen table into the sink, and began to wash them.

German boots could be heard climbing higher up the building. Doors were opened and apartments inspected. There was a loud bang on the Finkenbergs' door and demands for entry. The woman put away the last of the cups in the cupboard and walked to open the door. Three uniformed soldiers rushed in. One demanded her identity card. She handed it over, showing that she lived in the apartment alone. The soldiers looked at the toys on the floor, and demanded an explanation – did she really live alone? She explained that, to earn money, she ran a small nursery looking after other residents' children while they were at work. The Germans searched the apartment and, finding nothing of interest, left. Half an hour later they were searching the building next door.

****

Alain found Luc in the café where they had arranged to meet and sat down at the table.

'There are Germans and police everywhere. What's going on?' asked Luc.

'I don't know, but they are searching every apartment block. They would only do that if they were on a fishing expedition. We should avoid any trouble and get home as soon as possible.'

They were about to leave when two *gendarmes* entered the café. Each policeman went to a different table. One approached Alain and Luc.

'Your papers,' he demanded.

Alain and Luc handed over their identity papers. The policeman studied them.

'You both live on the other side of Paris. What's your business in this area?'

'I'm visiting a sick relative,' said Alain.

The policeman turned to Luc. 'And you?'

'I came to keep my friend company.'

'Wait here – you two are coming with me for further questioning,' said the *gendarme*.

Across the café, the other *gendarme* was questioning a boy of about fifteen. The boy was told to turn out his pockets. He hesitated. The *gendarme* pulled out his truncheon. The boy put his hands into his pockets and pulled out a few centime coins, a handkerchief and a stick of white chalk. He laid them on the tablecloth. The *gendarme* looked at the stick of chalk and then back at the youth. Suddenly the youth lunged forward and pushed the *gendarme*. Caught off balance, the policeman staggered backwards and fell over a chair and, as he fell, knocked over a table. Coffee cups cascaded off the table and smashed all over the floor. Everyone in the café was startled by the noise. The youth made a dash for the door that led to the kitchen. The policeman threw down Alain and Luc's papers onto the table and gave chase. Once both policemen had disappeared into the kitchen, Luc scooped up their papers and they left the café by the front entrance, hearing another crash of crockery as they reached the pavement. Turning right, they rushed up the road. At the corner, they stopped to look back to see if they were being chased. They saw the boy, limping and with a bloody nose, being frogmarched towards a German truck.

'That was a lucky escape,' said Luc.

'For us, I guess,' replied Alain.

****

As Michael cycled down the canal's towpath past the tall poplar trees and the quiet waters of the canal, the war, the plane crash and even the reason he was in France seemed like another world. He had to get off the bicycle a few times and walk as the towpath petered out or disappeared entirely, but he always managed to locate it again. After four hours, he arrived on the outskirts of Paris.

More used to a bustling city with streets full of traffic, Michael was surprised how empty the streets were. No longer were they the welcoming boulevards he remembered. Instead they were wide, unfriendly, empty and forbidding. Those people who were about kept a distance between each other that seemed like a gulf. The atmosphere caught Michael by the throat, and he had the sensation that everyone was looking at him, as if they knew who he was and that he should not be in Paris.

As he stopped at a crossroads to get his bearings a gust of wind blew something against the front wheel of the bicycle. He leaned down and picked it up – it was a small booklet. He flicked through the sixteen pages informing German soldiers how they might spend their leisure time in the French capital. There was information about the museums, reviews of various cabaret shows, and a list of the restaurants and shops where Germans were welcomed. There was practical advice for getting around Paris with a Métro map, some useful phrases in French and even letters to the editor where soldiers shared their bad experiences. Michael thought the information might be useful and began pedalling holding the booklet in his right hand.

It was only a couple of roads later that he saw a road block and German troops stopping cyclists and pedestrians and inspecting their papers. He managed to turn into a side street without being seen. He tried to visualise a map of Paris and the streets that might help him avoid further traps.

****

Guillaume Reynard was irritated. He felt alienated, disconnected from the once-familiar world in which Frenchmen saw a policeman as a guardian of the Republic.

Ever since the Germans had occupied Paris, many of its citizens had considered him a collaborator. He could put up with the disapproving looks from most of the population. What made him particularly angry was the fact that lowlifes had suddenly gained immunity from arrest and prosecution simply because they worked for or were useful to the Germans. Pimps, petty crooks and others he would have arrested before the war now addressed him by slapping one hand down on the opposite bicep and raising the other in a fist. Having to tolerate the macho display of the erect penis of the *bras d'honneur* twice yesterday had put him in a bad mood.

He had expressed this opinion to his sergeant and, to add insult to injury had been rewarded by being ordered to work a double shift and on his daughter's tenth birthday. Instead of being at home to celebrate the happy day with his Chantelle, he was on duty checking identification papers.

Positioning himself at a corner where he could stop a pedestrian or cyclist when it was too late for them to turn around, he looked up the street. Just then a cyclist turned the corner. He held up his arm to stop the rider. As the cyclist drew close, he noticed he held a copy of the German guide to the city. *Must be an off-duty German.* Still, his orders were to stop everyone not in uniform, occupier or not.

'Your papers,' he demanded.

The man passed over a card. Guillaume looked at the heading: *Nationalsozialistiche Deutsche Arbeiterpartie.* He'd not seen too many Nazi party membership cards. He looked at the man in front of him. The blond hair, blue eyes, square jaw and broad shoulders represented the stereotype of the occupier. Yet his years as a policemen told him that there was something not quite right. He looked at the man's clothes. They were typical of French fashion. *How and why would a German acquire such clothes, and what are those small cuts on his face that he's disguising with a little makeup?*

Guillaume moved his right hand to his holster, carefully unbuttoning the leather strap and wrapping his hands around the handle of the pistol. He was about to draw it when the man spoke.

'*Monsieur*, are you a true patriot of France?'

The accent belonged to a Parisian; the man was not German. So why would he be in possession of a Nazi party membership card that had been issued in Munich.

'Of course, what of it?'

'Then I will confess everything to you. Then you must decide where your duty lies. I'm a British soldier and yesterday I flew into France from England on a special mission. You can arrest me and take me to the Germans and doubtless they will reward you for capturing me. You will be a hero to the *Boche*. They might even promote you, and all Paris will know what you have done for the occupier. Or you can let me cycle away in the knowledge that you have helped deliver a blow for the freedom of France.'

Guillaume looked at the man. In all the years he had been a policeman, he had never heard a confession like it. His duty was clear. He should arrest the man. He didn't know why, perhaps it was the thought of Chantelle at home crying because her father could not be at her birthday party, perhaps because he was angry at his sergeant, perhaps because he loved France. He released the grip on his pistol and handed back the card.

'Your papers are in order. On your way before I change my mind. If I were you, I'd avoid cycling down Rue La Fayette and as much of the 1st and 2nd arrondissements as you can. Another *gendarme* might welcome promotion.'

The man mounted his cycle and rode away.

Guillaume looked up the street. There was a couple walking towards him. He would stop them.

Chapter Thirty-nine
The riddle

That evening

The curfew had almost begun and Jean-Claude was in his apartment. When he'd arrived home, Sébastien had told him that Tobias Meijers had been caught by a German patrol as he emerged from a manhole leading from the catacombs. Tobias had tried to escape but as he ran up the street, the Germans had fired. Witnesses said that he lay in the street, writhing in agony, as the soldiers stood around laughing as they waited for a van to take him away. After twenty minutes, he lost consciousness and soon after died in the street. The Gestapo arrested his wife and children. Jean-Claude was angry and had a leaden feeling on his shoulders, as if the weight of the world was resting on him and there was nothing he could do to relieve the pressure. He couldn't remember feeling so lost… so powerless… so vulnerable as he thought of the centimes in the tin at the Tagleva bank that would never be played with again.

Looking through the large windows towards the Eiffel Tower, he tried to gain a feeling of being at one with the city. Instead his thoughts turned back to the start of the occupation and the self-disgust and despondency he had felt when there had been no street fighting, no act of symbolic resistance. The city had rolled over and allowed the Germans to tickle its tummy. Out of nowhere, they had come strutting down the Bois de Boulogne, Champs-Élysées and over the Pont Neuf, in their green uniforms and jackboots, infesting the city like flies crawling all over the corpse. Now a friend and his family had disappeared into the darkness. Jean-Claude knew it was only the beginning, that there would be more pain to be endured before the nightmare was over.

Sébastien walked into the room with two hot steaming cups. Handing one to Jean-Claude, they both looked out of the window to the city beyond.

'I love you,' whispered Jean-Claude.

'I love you, too,' replied Sébastien.

They were disturbed by a sharp knock on the door.

Jean-Claude sighed. It was most likely to be the Germans; all *good* Frenchmen were tucked up in their apartments. They were probably going to question him about Tobias. He put his cup down on a side table, closed the curtains, turned on a lamp and walked towards the front door. On the way, he glanced at the wireless dial to ensure that the needle was not set to receive broadcasts from the BBC.

Opening the door, it took a couple of seconds to register the face. 'My God, come inside, quickly!'

Jean-Claude and Michael hugged each other.

****

Rudolf Bauer was reading the daily security report. He was angry that the raids in the Latin Quarter hadn't been more successful. Only one mimeograph machine, used to print off leaflets, and some stencils had been found but it wasn't the forger. Overnight there had been more Vs chalked on walls throughout the city. One youth had been captured with some chalk in his pocket, and another dozen teenagers arrested, plucked off the streets at random. They were now imprisoned in the cells at Gestapo headquarters.

The following day he would visit the interrogation floor and give each of them a good thrashing. He would enjoy the exercise, and it would relieve some of the anger he felt at not capturing the forger. When released, the youths would be an example to others to stop making their chalk marks. It would also show their parents how merciful he was by not deporting them to Germany.

It was a shame the person emerging from the sewers had been killed; he might have proved useful had he been interrogated. But it was unlikely he had been the forger; that would have been too lucky. Bauer would order more raids over the next few weeks; time was on his side. He would find the forger, eventually.

****

Michael had bathed and was feeling refreshed. Wrapped in Jean-Claude's dressing gown and cradling an Armagnac, he related how he had survived the plane crash, stolen the priest's bicycle, evaded a few roadblocks, been stopped by the *gendarme* and entered their apartment building when a German officer left it and allowed the front door to close too slowly.

'So your father got our message?' asked Jean-Claude.

'Everyone had given up ever finding the printing plate. Any minute The Bank of England expects thousands of forged notes to rain down on the country instead of bombs. To discover that it's in the Tagleva vault was like a miracle. All we need to do now is to work out a way of stealing it back from the Germans.'

Jean-Claude looked at him and sighed. 'I'm not sure you will have much luck. The Germans have it locked in the basement vault and the building is run with Teutonic efficiency by a Standartenführer Rudolf Bauer.'

'Rudolf Bauer!' exclaimed Michael.

'You know him?'

'I do. He was my host when I visited Germany before the war. He's ambitious, ruthless and a bully. It also gives us a problem. If the plate is recovered, it must be done in such a way that no one at the Tagleva bank can be blamed. If Bauer even suspected that someone there was involved, he'd take the greatest pleasure in having everyone in the bank arrested, interrogated and sent to a concentration camp.'

'With one exception, my old secretary Nicole Labranche. She won't ever be sent to a concentration camp. She's been working for the Germans for years. Now works as Standartenführer Bauer's secretary. Gives the *Heil Hitler* salute to anything that moves and struts around the building as if she owns it and telling people what to do.'

Michael smiled. It was the one piece of information he'd longed to hear.

****

Christopher Hatton finally arrived at the orphanage.

He'd spent time coding the message that would expose Michael Tagleva to be a traitor and radioed it to Germany. It was inconvenient that the pre-arranged time was so late into the evening, but changing the time regularly was a necessity, it avoided detection by the British authorities. Once he'd sent the message, he shut off the radio's power. The message ensured that, one day, Michael Tagleva would be shot. But for now, Hatton was in a hurry to spend a pleasurable hour at the orphanage.

The nurse had been irritated at the late hour of his arrival. The children were already in bed, she tutted, but he paid her the usual amount and she pocketed the money and went to find Dorothy.

Hatton took his coat off and sat down in the comfortable chair. As he waited, he polished his glasses with his handkerchief. Once done, he picked up the colouring book on the chair beside him and leafed through it, pausing only to look at the crayoned pictures of Snow White and the Seven Dwarfs from Disney's 1937 film. He glimpsed at the wall clock, trying to calculate the time when the nurse would arrive with Dot. As he waited, he became slightly breathless and wiped his hands on his trousers.

The drone of the air-raid siren began. *Damn it!* he thought. He hoped the nurse would still bring the girl to him. He would be annoyed to have to wait for the sirens to sound the continuous two-minute wail signalling 'Raiders passed'.

He heard the German bombers grinding overhead and the boom of the anti-aircraft guns and the *crump, crump, crump* as heavy bombs tore buildings apart. *Surely the nurse isn't going to keep me waiting?*

Suddenly there was a massive explosion outside, the windows were blown inward and the blackout curtains fell to the floor. Hatton fell, too, and was covered in glass. He stood up to move further away from the window. At that moment, there was another explosion and the wall of the room fell inwards.

When he woke, he felt stiff, his legs hurt, his ears rang and he couldn't move. He was covered in bricks and masonry that was crushing his chest. He tried to focus his stinging eyes. One of the lenses of his spectacles was broken, but above him, he could make out the stars. By a miracle, he was alive. His mouth was dry with the taste of brick and dust, and he wished he could have a drink of water. He lay there for what seemed like hours. When he heard the bells of the fire engine through the ringing in his ears, he knew it wouldn't be long before he was rescued.

****

The nurse was about to wake Dot when the sirens started. She helped the children get up from their beds, put on their dressing gowns and collect their favourite teddy or rag doll, and walked them to the safety of the crypt in St Luke's Church opposite the orphanage. The children huddled together on the few mattresses or tried to sleep leaning up against a wall. The nurse hated the crypt. The only light came from a dim bulb in the centre of the ceiling, the toilet facilities consisted of an iron bucket, and the floor around it was always awash with urine. As they settled down, a couple of the children began to cry, more from the discomfort and the cold than from the fear of German bombs.

When the sirens sounded the all-clear, the nurse told the children to return to the orphanage. The older ones helped the younger children climb the stairs, hauling their teddies and comfort blankets back to the orphanage. The nurse stayed to tidy up.

Arriving where the orphanage used to be, the children looked impassively at the pile of rubble. In the distance, Dorothy spied the familiar features of Mr Hatton lying in the rubble. 'Dot, come, help me,' she heard him call.

For the first time, she wasn't afraid. She knew he couldn't hurt her.

He called out to her again.

The other children crowded around Dorothy as if to protect her. A few remembered the times when they had been woken by the nurse. They stared at the figure lying in the rubble and gripped their teddy bears more tightly to themselves.

'Help me, Dot, I'm in a helluva lot of pain,' Hatton croaked again.

Dorothy turned and walked away.

****

Hatton watched through his one good spectacle lens as, one at a time, each child turned their back on him, until only one girl remained. He knew her name was Emily. He called out to her. Emily looked at him, screwed up her face and poked out her tongue, turned and rushed to catch up with the others.

Alone, Hatton began cry. His leg and chest hurt and his right eye was blinded by blood that ran down from the cut on his head. When he was rescued, he would have the children punished. *How dare they not help me!* He would think of a special punishment for Dot: *She's the ringleader.*

Then he smelled the gas. The main must have broken.

Rescuers would come soon. *Where the hell are they?*

It must have been a spark from a broken power cable that ignited the gas. The explosion ripped through the ruined building. Hatton felt the rubble rise up beneath him and then collapse. Falling twenty feet, bricks, mortar and dust crashing around him, he landed on the floor below breathless and choking. His glasses were lost and now everything was blurred. He couldn't feel his legs. He feared his spine might be broken, but the real pain came from his right hand, crushed and trapped by a steel girder that had fallen across the wrist. He cried out with the agony of it. *Surely the rescuers must come?* Then the smell of gas became overpowering. In the gloom of the rubble he saw an electricity cable sparking. He watched in horror as the gas ignited and the flame rushed towards him. Trapped by the girder across his wrist, he screamed, trying to take away the pain as his flesh turned black and began to melt.

Chapter Forty
The vault

Two days later

An hour before curfew ended, a grey van from the Paul Nipkow television station drove along Rue Pierre Charron and parked outside the Bank of Tagleva. Out of the cab jumped a blond man who walked up to the front doors and banged loudly on them. A minute later, an SS private poked his head around the door.

'The bank's closed. What do you want?'

'We've come to set up the film equipment.'

'What film equipment?' said the private scratching his head.

'To film the Reichsminister's visit, for the newsreels.'

Two men pushed past him carrying boxes and a camera.

'What Reichsminister, what visit? I've not been informed about any Reichsminister. I'm ordered not to admit anyone out of hours. The bank opens at eight,' said the SS private, thoroughly confused.

'So I'm to inform Reichsminister Göring that, because the night watchman wasn't informed, he can't be filmed for the Reich newsreel?'

Irritated at being referred to as the night watchman, the private replied testily, 'I will check with my superiors.'

'Do that, but we can't wait long. Important people will start to arrive in the next half hour – see, here are the orders.' The blond man passed the confused private a paper. He looked at it as two men began to position a camera on a tripod a few feet from the main door.

He read the paper. It was an itinerary for Reichsminister Göring's visit and he would be arriving within the hour. Looking at the bottom of the page, he recognised the signature: 'Standartenführer Rudolf Bauer'.

He was already on extra duties for being dressed improperly and he didn't want to get into more trouble by unnecessarily disturbing a superior.

'I guess it'll be all right then,' said the soldier, handing back the paper.

'Good,' smiled the blond man.

'If you smartened yourself up a little, perhaps we can have you in the film guarding the door when the Reichsminister arrives. Your parents and all Germany will see you.'

Delighted at this new turn of events, the private pulled his jacket straight and went to collect his belt as another box of equipment was brought into the lobby and the door to the bank closed.

As soon as the soldier disappeared, Michael picked up a small leather bag and, with Alain, rushed to the stairs that led to the vault, leaving Luc in the lobby. At the bottom of the stairs, they arrived at the security door. Similar to prison bars, it was designed to delay a thief from accessing the safe deposit boxes by creating a cage around the vault. From his trouser pocket, Michael pulled the key that Jean-Claude had given them, inserted it into the lock and turned it. The grill doors opened and Michael and Alain walked in and faced the twenty-four-bolt Diebold vault.

Alain looked at the polished steel door, tall enough for a man to walk through. 'Bloody hell, how are we going to open that?'

'You're going to help me,' said Michael. 'First we must disable the time lock. It's set to open after a pre-set number of hours have passed. Currently it'll open at nine o'clock.'

Alain looked at his watch. 'It's four-forty now. If we wait until nine, the SS will be here to open it for us.'

Michael smiled. 'When my father worked for the Bank of England, he was stuck in a lift between floors and had to be rescued. He said it was the most embarrassing thing he'd ever experienced, and ever since, he's had a fear of being trapped in a small space. So when this vault was fitted, he asked the makers to give him a special key that, in an emergency, could bypass the time lock and release anyone trapped inside. When the war started, my father took the key with him to London.'

From his jacket pocket, Michael produced a six-inch-long piece of metal fashioned in the shape of a hexagon with threads carved into two of the six sides. He held it up for Alain to see.

'This is the key that bypasses the time lock, and it goes into one of these holes here,' Michael pointed to six small holes that formed part of the Bank of Tagleva crest on the front of the vault door. Inserting the key into the middle one, Michael turned the key. A soft *ping* was heard.

'There, that's the time lock switched off.'

'If you hadn't shown me, I would never have noticed that hole. I thought that it was part of the decoration,' said Alain.

Michael smiled again. 'Now you'll have to help me. To the right of the vault door is a box that I'll have to punch the combination number into. On your side, you will have to turn this key, which Jean-Claude hid from the Germans. The key must be turned at the same time as I punch in the code.' Michael showed Alain where to insert the key and how to turn it correctly.

'Only turn it after I've started to punch in the code and keep the key turned until I tell you to release it.'

Michael started to punch in the code and, seeing him nod, Alain turned the key. Then Michael nodded again and Alain released the key.

They waited for a few seconds but nothing happened. The door remained firmly closed.

'Let's try it again,' said Michael.

Alain turned the key once more as Michael simultaneously, and for the second time, punched in the code. The vault door remained stubbornly closed.

'Damn it! I was afraid of that,' said Michael.

'Afraid of what?'

'That Bauer would order the combination to be changed. I was hoping that, if he thought he had all the keys and the vault could only be opened when he was in the building, he might not have bothered.'

'So, if we can't open it, that's it, we've failed,' groaned Alain.

'We have to try,' replied Michael.

'The code's eight digits long. You can't try every combination. We'll be here for days,' Alain said anxiously.

'We have to try. We've got one more chance,' repeated Michael.

'"One more chance"?' said Alain nervously. 'What do you mean "one more chance"? What happens if it doesn't open on the third try?'

'Alarm bells will ring all over the building and at the local *gendarmerie*.'

'Oh, God, we can't risk that – we'll be caught!' *That's when the firing squad arrives…*

'Let me think for a moment,' said Michael as he placed his head in his hands.

****

Upstairs, Luc was setting up the camera and lights. The SS private was being kept busy. Luc asked him to play the part of the Reichsminister arriving at the bank.

'It'll help me position the camera and set up the lighting. I need to make sure there are no shadows that'll spoil the film. Move here,' said Luc, manhandling the soldier to a position in front of the doors to the bank.

He returned to look through the camera. 'No, that's not right,' and he walked over to the soldier once more and moved him to another position. Once Luc returned to look through the camera lens again, he audibly cursed at having so short a time to set up the equipment.

'Do you know how demanding a Reichsminister can be?' he asked the soldier.

'No,' said the soldier.

'Oh, very demanding. Not all of them mind you – Goebbels and Himmler are wonderful to film.'

'Have you filmed the Führer?'

'Many times.'

'That must make you so proud. I would love to meet the Führer.'

Luc walked over to the soldier, moved him two inches to the left, and adjusted his collar. 'I want you to look to your left as if greeting the crowds,' said Luc as he clasped the soldier's head and jolted it to the left. 'And don't forget to smile.'

****

Below them in the vault, Michael said to Alain, 'We'll try it one more time.'

'That's not a good idea,' came the nervous response. 'Why don't we just leave? We've tried, done our best and it's not worked.'

'Look, if it doesn't work, I have my revolver. We'll rush upstairs and shoot our way out. There's only one guard on the ground floor. It will take the two guards on the fifth floor a couple of minutes to get to the ground floor. By then, we would have made our escape. We have to try once more,' said Michael firmly.

Alain slowly nodded, and on Michael's signal, he turned the key and prayed: *Our Father who art in heaven…*

Michael simultaneously punched in the code: 20041899.

Alain held his breath waiting for the bells and sirens to ring out. His heart hammered and he could feel the walls closing in, sealing off any escape to freedom. He pictured the firing squad aiming their rifles.

The mechanism came to life, the bolts *clunked* back and the door was released and slowly opened on the steel ball-bearing hinge.

Alain exhaled loudly. 'How did you guess the code?'

'From what I know of the man I gambled Bauer would use the twentieth of April eighteen ninety-nine, Hitler's birthday.'

Michael walked inside the vault and looked around the shelves of boxes. There was nothing resembling the cylindrical metal plate that had been described to him. He opened up a few boxes and, not finding what he was looking for, closed them again. Then in the far corner he noticed what looked like a brown paper parcel. He walked over to it. It was the cylinder. He picked it up and, through a tear, saw the engraving of Britannia. Placing the plate back where he'd found it he walked over to his bag and carried it into the vault. Extracting a small glass bottle, he snapped the top and positioned it on the grille-like shelf above the metal cylinder and watched as the clear liquid began to drip onto the cylinder.

Within a few seconds, the nitric acid began to eat into the metal and an orange cloud rose as it reacted with the metal to form nitrogen dioxide. Michael waited a minute to ensure the engraving was ruined. Once he was satisfied the plate was useless for printing, he picked up his bag and walked out of the vault.

Alain was relieved when he saw Michael emerge. His legs no longer seemed to be his own and he'd begun to tremble; he thought he might vomit and could taste the bile that had begun to collect in his mouth.

'Is it done?' he whispered.

'It is. Let's close the door and get out of here.'

They began to push the door closed, but when it was just halfway Michael stopped pushing.

'One moment, I want to check on something,' and he disappeared inside.

What now? Alain thought to himself, feeling a desperate need to visit a toilet. Michael reappeared.

They sealed the vault, reset the time lock, closed the metal cage, and climbed the stairs to the lobby.

They found Luc explaining to the SS private the intricacies of television production and the private was doing his best to look as if he understood.

On seeing them, the soldier asked, 'Where have you two been? I thought you were outside with the van.'

Ignoring the question, Michael asked him, 'This *is* 22 Rue Marbeuf?'

'No,' said the private. 'Rue Marbeuf is the next street along.'

'Oh, God,' shouted Michael to the others, 'we're in the wrong bloody building. Quick, pack up the equipment – we don't have any time to spare!'

The private watched as the boxes were quickly repacked and the three men left the building. He followed them as they bundled everything into the back of the television van.

'So I won't be on television?' he said to Luc.

'Afraid not, next time – don't call us, we'll call you!' shouted Alain as he slammed the back doors shut, rushed to the front and climbed into the cab.

The SS private stood in the middle of the road, watching the television van move down the street and disappear from view. As it turned the corner, a green staff car turned into the road and came to a halt a few feet behind him. Rudolf Bauer got out of the car and walked up to the soldier, who came to attention.

'Why are you in the street?'

'I was awaiting the arrival of the Reichsminister.'

'Reichsminister, what Reichsminister?'

Not waiting to hear the answer from the imbecile, Bauer strode into the Tagleva building.

****

Having driven the television van back to the garage, each of them went home using different routes. Jean-Claude downed a quick coffee and walked to work, arriving at the Bank of Tagleva soon after the doors were officially opened. He was not looking forward to the next hour. In his office, he found Juliette sorting through some papers.

'Good morning, sir,' she said.

'It is, but I have to apologise. I've left some papers in my apartment and I'll need them today. I was wondering if you would go and collect them for me?'

'Of course, I'll leave now.' Jean-Claude handed her his apartment keys.

'Where are the papers?' she asked.

'Oh… you'll find them on the coffee table in the living room, I think.'

Juliette donned her coat and hat, picked up her gloves and left the Tagleva bank.

****

Fifteen minutes later, Juliette pushed the wrought-iron and glass door and walked into the white marble lobby of Jean-Claude's building on the Rue Le Tasse and took the lift to the fifth floor. Once inside the apartment, she went in search of the papers. Opening one door, she found herself in the living room. Her immediate impression was that the décor was sophisticated. Two large curved Art Deco walnut-and-leather sofas sat either side of a glass coffee table on a fawn and cream Persian carpet. The windows were draped in heavy silver-coloured curtains. But she was not alone in the room. Admiring a painting on the far wall was a man dressed in a dark suit. She was surprised – she hadn't expected anyone to be in the apartment. And this wasn't Sébastien. '*Pardon moi, monsieur,* but I…'

The man turned around.

Her hand went to her lips. 'My God… Michael…' she whispered.

She felt dizzy and had to steady herself. Michael rushed over, took her by the arm, led her to one of the sofas and sat down beside her.

'Where have you come from? I've missed you so much. Why aren't you in London?' Tears began to form in her eyes.

Michael held her. They stayed like that for some minutes, kissing each other, looking at one another, laughing at her tears. He stroked her hair, she his cheek. After what seemed an age, she pulled herself away from him and asked, 'What are you doing in Paris?'

'I can't tell you, but it has to do with the message you sent to my father.'

'So you got it. I waited outside the American embassy every day until the same diplomat who gave me your message appeared. In return for sending the message, I agreed to have dinner with him.'

'Just dinner?' enquired Michael.

She giggled at his jealousy. 'Just dinner. Once I told him I was engaged, he was the perfect gentleman. So you guessed the message was from me.'

'Signing it "Jewels" did confuse my father until I explained it was my nickname for you.'

'So he knows what your nickname is for me... Did you tell him my nickname for you?'

'I did not,' said Michael blushing a little.

Juliette giggled. Then she looked around. 'I'm so upset. I can't stay. I'm meant to be collecting some papers, I'll have to go back to the Tagleva Bank once I've collected them,' and she began to cry at the thought of leaving him so soon.

Michael pulled out an envelope from his jacket. 'These are the papers Jean-Claude left.' He gave her an envelope with her name clearly written on it. 'Go on, open it. It's addressed to you.'

She opened it and read:

Juliette, I'm sorry you are unwell.
I suggest you take a few days off work to recover.
J-C

She looked at the note, slightly confused, and then back at Michael. 'So, there are no papers for me to collect?'

'No.'

'So we can be together all day?'

'All day and all tomorrow, too,' said Michael.

He stood up, held out his hand and led her to the spare bedroom where a bottle of chilled champagne and two glasses stood on a silver tray.

****

Bauer was in a good mood. The printing press on the fifth floor was ready. The paper had arrived the previous morning, and today a test would be made to print a perfect English five-pound note. While he waited in his office for the vault's time lock to be released, he read through the security report from the night before:

Two black marketeers arrested. Three men detained after curfew and without passes.

More graffiti has appeared on walls around the Hôtel Majestic.

The suspected spy from the crashed Blenheim is still at large.

An incomplete and jumbled message from an agent in London has been received that seems to identify a traitor to the Reich. The name of the traitor was not understood due to radio interference, probably by British intelligence. The transmission came to an abrupt end before the agent could sign off correctly. This may indicate that the agent has been captured by the British. The agent will be told to repeat the message tomorrow night. Another incorrect sign off would confirm the agent's capture.

At exactly nine o'clock, Bauer put down the report, and walked to the basement accompanied by Hoffman and Krüger. He watched as the thick steel door of the vault swung open. Walking inside he smelt a strange acrid smell he couldn't identify. Somehow the cylinder looked different. He looked at the cylinder, the paper wrapping was burned. He picked it up. The engraving was clearly of an English five-pound note, but Britannia's face and shield were melted and some of the lettering had disappeared. He stared at it more closely. It took him a few seconds to understand the enormity of what he was looking at. *How has this happened? It's impossible.*

He looked on the shelf above and saw the empty bottle of acid. The liquid had dripped onto the plate and destroyed it. *Where did it come from? It wasn't there before. Someone must have entered the vault. Who has done this?* Anger boiled up inside him, too much for him to control. *Whoever has committed this crime will suffer, horribly!* He put down the cylinder and rushed out of the vault. Followed by Hoffman and Krüger, he took the lift to the fourth floor and burst into Jean-Claude's office.

'What have you done?' screamed Bauer.

'Done? I don't know what you're talking about,' answered Jean-Claude.

Bauer leaned forward, his hands clenched tightly at his sides, his knuckles glowing white, his face flushed red, the veins standing out from his temples, his eyes bulging from their sockets and his mouth contorted into a grimace.

'I'm angry, and I guarantee that you will not like me when I'm angry. What's happened to it? How did you destroy it?'

'Standartenführer, I don't know what you're talking about,' replied Jean-Claude.

'The plate in the vault, the one we were going to use today, it's been destroyed, it's useless!' screamed Bauer as he thrust his face towards Jean-Claude.

'I don't know anything about a plate. And anyway, I don't have keys to the vault. All the keys were handed over to you and Sturmbannführer Hoffman.'

'Then you must have more keys. You must have some hidden keys. Last night the vault was opened and the printing plate destroyed. I'll have you shot! I'll have everyone in the Tagleva bank shot!' Bauer screamed.

'But Standartenführer, no one could have gained access to the vault last night, even with keys, if the time lock was on. It wouldn't have been possible to open the vault until nine o'clock this morning.'

Bauer turned to face the two officers that stood behind him. 'Was the time lock on?' he shouted.

'You yourself supervised it being set last night,' replied Hoffman.

Bauer remembered doing so.

Jean-Claude added, 'If the time lock was set, then no one could have entered the vault, it's impossible. And anyway, you told me that you intended to reset the entry code. If you did then I don't know the new code. No one at Tagleva bank would know the new code, except for you and Sturmbannführers Hoffman and Krüger.'

Bauer stared blankly at Jean-Claude for a full five seconds. The truth fully dawned on him that the plate had been destroyed and there was no one to blame.

He turned and marched out of Jean-Claude's office. The two SS officers followed him down the stairs and into the basement once more.

Bauer ordered the vault opened again. The plate was re-inspected and both Hoffman and Krüger agreed it was now useless.

Bauer leaned against one of the shelves and rested his head on his arms, shut his eyes and cursed inwardly. Then he thought of the illuminated manuscript recounting the life of the Saxon king Heinrich, the founder of the Ottonian dynasty of German kings and emperors. The book he was to present to Heinrich Himmler at Wewelsburg Castle in a glittering ceremony attended by the elite of the SS. Opening the box the sight that greeted him was unbelievable, shocking. Unable to comprehend, he closed his eyes, then he opened them again but all he could see was the blue silk lining where the book had once been.

Chapter Forty-one
'We're safe now'

Two days later

Nicole Labranche was sat at her desk when an envelope for the attention of Standartenführer Bauer marked *urgent and secret* was delivered by courier. She didn't open the letter and therefore didn't see the note inside was from Gestapo headquarters asking Bauer if the word *Michtagleva* had any significance. Instead Nicole looked at the envelope and placed it in the basket with the other communications that had arrived that day... *now was not a good time.*

****

Bauer was in the chairman's office at the Bank of Tagleva in the dress uniform he had expected to wear at Wewelsburg Castle. The white belt and the silver aiguillette, denoting that he was an aide-de-camp to Adolf Hitler, contrasted with the blackness of the uniform. The Iron Cross, first class, of which he was so proud, hung from his left breast.

He waited for the arrival of the officers who were coming to arrest him. His crime was not the destruction of the plate stolen from the Bank of England, which would have won the war for Germany. His real crime was not being able to present to Himmler the illuminated manuscript recounting the life of the Saxon king Heinrich.

The arresting party entered Bauer's office. They too were all dressed in black.

Bauer stood up. '*Heil Hitler!*' he saluted.

The salute was not acknowledged. Instead they looked at him impassively. Bauer put on his white leather gloves, wearing his greatcoat over his shoulders so that it would not detract from the uniform he put on his cap and looked at his image in the mirror. The reflection was resplendent, and he paused a moment to admire it before walking from the room. As he walked down the staircase, the fear that coursed through Bauer's veins never reached his face. His jaw remained firm, his eyes steady as if he were about to inspect troops. As he left the Tagleva building for the last time, he turned to look at the building and reflected for the briefest of moments on what might have been.

He climbed into the back of the car and looked straight ahead as it drove up the Rue Pierre Charron and on towards Berlin. He knew he was looking into a dark pit, an abyss. He wondered if his fate would be a bullet in the back of the neck or the agonising death by hanging by piano wire from a meat hook in the ceiling. The punishment he had himself inflicted on those arrested during the Night of the Long Knives all those years ago.

He hoped, prayed, that Himmler would be merciful, that it would be a bullet in the back of the neck.

****

In London the following evening, Sophie and Philip finished dinner and climbed the stairs to say goodnight to the children. They found Matislav lying on his bed reading a book. On the wall above his bed hung the green felt hat, with its white feather, Michael had brought from Bavaria. In her bedroom Halinka was at her desk finishing an essay on the 'Importance of the Silk Road to the development of European civilisation' for her school homework. Both children kissed their parents goodnight.

As Sophie and Philip walked along to the nursery, Sophie whispered: 'Those children went through a terrible experience with the bombing of the orphanage. Thankfully the Foundation's managed to place them all in new homes.'

Arriving at the nursery, Sophie placed a finger on her lips and gently pushed the door open. Inside they heard a little girl's voice: 'We're safe now, Teddy. We have a nice new mummy and daddy and we're going to be very happy and I promise no one will ever hurt you again. Good night, Teddy.'

Kissing the little bear goodnight, Dorothy pulled it towards her and closed her eyes. Sophie quietly closed the nursery door, a tear running down her cheek. As the pair walked downstairs, Philip wrapped an arm around her waist.

****

In Paris, the cork flew out of the bottle of champagne. Jean-Claude poured the liquid into glasses, which Sébastien handed to Michael and Juliette.

'*Vive la France,*' said Jean-Claude, and they all raised their glasses.

Jean-Claude looked at Michael and asked, 'When Bauer recruited you as a spy, what did he expect you to do for Germany?'

'Two things: Obtain any information I could from the Tagleva card index about Britain and France's economic ability to go to war with Germany. Bauer knew the card index was one of the best sources of information in Europe. The second thing he wanted me to do was to steal the book of the life of the Saxon king Heinrich.'

'But why did Bauer think you would steal such a valuable thing from your own family?'

'He had promised Heydrich he could obtain the book for Himmler. Bauer thought that, if I became a fanatical follower of the Nazis, then I would steal it to please him. I guess it's why he arranged the unusual ceremony at Wewelsburg Castle and risked letting me leave Germany even after his steward, Kurt, told him of his suspicions. Bauer's ambitions blinded him to the logic of Kurt's argument because he didn't want to risk not obtaining it. The book was Bauer's path to everything he craved for.'

'But why did Himmler want the book in the first place?'

'Himmler believes he is the reincarnation of the dead king, and the book was to become one of the holy treasures at Wewelsburg Castle.'

Jean-Claude smiled. 'Bauer was livid when he found the plate destroyed and the book gone, but he didn't know how the vault could have been opened. He ordered a minute inspection to find a secret way to unlock the door. The Germans spent hours looking for one but didn't find it and, having changed the combination, assumed no one could have gained entry. The destruction of the plate was declared to be an accident.'

'Does anyone know about the television van?' asked Michael.

'No one has said anything about it. After all the fuss and Bauer's arrest, I assume the SS guard was too afraid of the consequences if he admitted to having allowed people to enter the bank. As for the book, the Germans think that it was taken to London before the war started and Bauer lied about finding it or that Bauer had stolen it for himself. So, as you promised, no one at the Tagleva bank was implicated.'

'By the way, what's happened to the book?' asked Michael.

'It's hidden in Samuel's workroom in the catacombs.'

'And Samuel and his family are safe?'

'Yes. For the moment, the Germans have enough to do consolidating their hold over France than to hunt for Jews. Samuel and his family have moved back into the apartment. They'll be safe for the time being, and they can quickly disappear if things get more difficult.'

'I must congratulate you, Uncle Jean-Claude. You have the beginnings of an effective anti-German resistance group!'

'True, but there's still a lot to do. The chief task is to get organised so that, when the time is right, we can resume the struggle. The occupation has only just begun and the people are still numbed by it. But the Germans know that their occupation of France must become more brutal if they are to hold onto France and in turn the people will become angry at the deprivations imposed by the conqueror. It will be then that the people will rise up and fight them... Why not stay until that time comes and join in our fight against the Germans?'

'Nothing would please me more, but I can't. I'm a serving British officer. I must get back to London and continue the fight from there,' replied Michael.

'And I'm going with him,' said Juliette.

Michael smiled at Jean-Claude as he wrapped his arm around Juliette's waist. 'Using the travel documents Samuel is making for us, we plan to travel south through Vichy and into Spain or Portugal. It won't be without its dangers but, with luck, we should be back in London within a few weeks.'

Jean-Claude beamed at them both. 'I'll be sorry to see you both go, but I understand that it's what you have to do. Though when the time comes for you to leave, can I offer you a lift as far as the Vichy border in a television van?'

Detail on historical events, quotations, characters and the facts behind the story.

Quotes attributed to historical figures

Quotations attributed to Adolf Hitler and opinions given by George Geoffrey Dawson and the 5th Duke of Wellington while accurate may have been taken out of the actual time frame or context in which they were made.

The quotation attributed to Winston Churchill with reference to King Edward and Mrs Simpson in chapter two of *I Spy the Wolf* is reproduced by kind permission of Curtis Brown, London on behalf of The Estate of Winston S. Churchill © The Estate of Winston S. Churchill.

The quotation at the start of the novel attributed to William 'Willie' Gallacher Member of Parliament for East Fife is taken from his book *The Chosen Few* published in 1940 and is reproduced by kind permission of Lawrence and Wishart, London.

While the planning meeting at Dover Castle for the evacuation of troops of the BEF (British Expeditionary Force) from Dunkirk happened as recorded, the private conversation between Winston Churchill, Tim Wilson and Michael have been imagined for the purpose of the story.

German Television 1935–1944

The first regular television service in Germany began in 1935 and was initially broadcast for ninety minutes, three times a week. During the 1936 Summer Olympics, broadcasts up to eight hours of television a day were shown in Berlin and Hamburg. Following the Olympics, there were plans for a huge expansion of television, but at the start of the war these were changed in favour of radio. Very few receivers (televisions) were ever privately owned, and thus broadcasts were only seen by the Nazi party elite. But, programmes could be viewed by the German public in television parlours by paying a one *Reichsmark* admission. The Berlin station continued to broadcast throughout the war and the station in occupied Paris broadcast from the top of the Eiffel Tower until the city's liberation by the Allies.

As mentioned in *I Spy the Wolf* one of Germany's most popular shows prior to and during World War II was *An Evening with Hans and Gelli*. The description of the makeup used to transmit a suitable image to a television screen is also factual.

Operation Bernhard

Was the codename used for the secret Nazi plan to destabilise the British economy and was the largest counterfeiting operation in history. The Bank of England learned of the plot as early as 1939. By the end of the war the forged notes were considered to be 'the most dangerous ever seen'. The plan was directed by and named after Sturmbannführer (SS Major) Bernhard Krüger, who eventually set up a team of counterfeiters selected from inmates at Auschwitz concentration camp. It is believed that most of the notes produced ended up at the bottom of Lake Toplitz near Ebensee and were discovered by divers in 1959. But examples have turned up in Britain for many years.

Locations and events

The events at Zeppelin Field and Kristallnacht in Augsburg are accurate. The details of Wewelsburg Castle and Brocket Hall are accurate. The huge swastika mosaic laid in one of the reception rooms of the German embassy at 9 Carlton House Terrace, is rumoured to remain to this day and is now covered by a thick carpet.

German penal code

The details of paragraph 175 of the Nazi German penal code and 'The Amendment for the Prevention of Offspring with Hereditary Diseases' mentioned in the story is correct. Between 1933 and 1945, an estimated 100,000 homosexuals were arrested in Germany by the Nazis. Most served time in regular prisons or were incarcerated in concentration camps.

There are no known statistics for the number of homosexuals who died in the camps but estimates of the numbers murdered range from 10,000 to 25,000. The paragraph 175 of the Nazi law proscribing homosexual acts remained in force in Germany until June 1969.

Britain after a German invasion

The information relating to the treatment of Britain following Germany's successful invasion of the UK, *Die Sonderfahndungsliste*, and the list of individuals to be arrested, and the organisations to be disbanded are taken from papers discovered by the Allies after WWII.

The Anglo-German Fellowship

The organisation existed just prior to World War II and had a pro-Nazi leaning. Its stated aim was to build up friendship between the United Kingdom and Germany. Members included the Governor of the Bank of England, Montagu Norman; Frank Cyril Tiarks, a director of the Bank of England; and Geoffrey Dawson, editor of *The Times*. 'Corporate membership' was available for leading companies, and amongst these, it's alleged, were Price Waterhouse, Unilever, Dunlop Rubber, Thomas Cook & Son, the Midland Bank, and Lazard Brothers.

The Right Club

Led by the MP Archibald Ramsay, the Right Club had close ties to the Nazis in Germany. At its early meetings, the 5th Duke of Wellington acted as chairman. The Right Club focused on opposition to a war with Germany up to and including acts of treason. At the outbreak of war, many of its members were detained in Brixton Prison under the Defence Regulations. In his autobiography, *The Nameless War*, Ramsay argued: 'The main object of the Right Club was to oppose and expose the activities of Organized Jewry.'

L'Illustration

The weekly French newspaper began publication in Paris in 1843. During World War II, *L'Illustration* became a voice for Marshall Petain's collaborationist government. Following the Liberation of Paris in 1944 it was shut down.

Details on historical characters mentioned

To satisfy readers who wonder 'what happened to…' I include a few details on the historical characters mentioned in the story.

German

Hermann Göring

After helping Adolf Hitler take power in 1933, he became the second-most powerful man in Germany. Hitler's right-hand man went to great lengths to surround himself with beauty, looting some 5,000 of the world's most fabulous works of art to adorn the walls of Carinhall, his country retreat near Berlin. He was convicted of war crimes and crimes against humanity at the Nuremberg trials and was sentenced to death by hanging, but committed suicide the day before the sentence was to be carried out.

Heinrich Himmler

Reichsführer of the SS. Himmler viewed the SS as an 'order' along the lines of the Teutonic Knights. He became convinced that he was the reincarnation of King Heinrich I who lived in the 10th Century and is generally considered to be the founder and first king of the medieval German state. As facilitator and overseer of the concentration camps, Himmler directed the killing of some six million Jews, homosexuals, and others who he believed to be racially inferior. Captured in 1945 by the British, he escaped trial by committing suicide.

Herschel Grynszpan

After assassinating Ernst vom Rath, Herschel was imprisoned by the French near Paris. One month after the German occupation of France, Grynszpan was flown to Berlin. During the war he was moved to various locations, including Flossenburg and Sachsenhausen concentration camps. It's believed he was murdered by the Gestapo in Magdeburg Prison.

Reinhard Heydrich

SS-Obergruppenführer (General). Many historians regard Heydrich as one of the darkest figures within the Nazi elite. One of the main architects of the Holocaust, he formalised the plans for the 'final solution to the Jewish Question' and the murder of six million Jews. Heydrich was assassinated in Prague in May 1942 by a British-trained team of Czech and Slovak soldiers. German intelligence falsely linked the assassins to the village of Lidice. On the orders of Adolf Hitler, the village was razed to the ground, all the men and boys over the age of sixteen were shot and its women and children deported to concentration camps.

Bernhard Krüger

Under the codename Operation Bernhard, he was responsible for producing forged pound notes amounting to £600 million (approx. $7 billion 2017). After the war, Krüger was detained by the British and then turned over to the French. He was released in 1948 and returned to Germany to work for the company that had produced the special paper for the banknote forgeries. He died in 1989.

French

James Couttet

At the age of sixteen and a half, he was the world downhill skiing champion in 1938. In the first competitions of the post war era, he dominated the sport and led the French Alpine skiing team in the Winter Olympics in 1956. He died in 1997.

Jacques Lesdain

French journalist and the editor of *L'Illustration*. After the liberation, he fled France and was tried in absentia by the French courts and sentenced to death for treason. He fled to Rome where he worked for *L'Osservatore Romano*, the Vatican's newspaper, between 1958 until 1968 and under the papacies of Pius XII, John XXIII and Paul VI. He died in 1975.

Austrians

Wilhelm Miklas

The third President of Austria from 1928 until the Anschluss in 1938. During the war, he was placed under house arrest. He died in March 1956 in Vienna.

Kurt Johann Schuschnigg

Chancellor of the Federal State of Austria when Nazi Germany annexed Austria (Anschluss) in March 1938. He was arrested by the Germans, kept in solitary confinement, and eventually interned in various concentration camps (Sachsenhausen and Dachau). Liberated in 1945 by the advancing United States army, he spent much of the rest of his life working as professor of political science at Saint Louis University. He died near Innsbruck in 1977.

English

The 8th Duke of Buccleuch

It was a matter of personal delight to Hitler that the Duke, the Lord Steward of the Royal Household to King George VI, and thus a prominent member at the court of Britain's Royal Family, attended his fiftieth birthday celebrations. Buccleuch opposed any war with the Nazis, and even after war had been declared urged a truce that would allow Germany to keep all the lands Hitler had up to that point occupied in Europe. An embarrassment to the king, he was sacked in 1940. He died in 1973 and is buried among the ruins of Melrose Abbey.

Neville Chamberlain

Prime minister of the United Kingdom from May 1937 to May 1940, Chamberlain is best known for his appeasement policy and for signing the Munich Agreement in 1938. After Adolf Hitler invaded Poland, Chamberlain led Britain through the first eight months of World War II. He died of bowel cancer in 1940 aged 71.

Sir Winston Churchill, KG

Politician and prime minister of the United Kingdom from 1940 to 1945 and again from 1951 to 1955, Churchill is regarded as one of the greatest wartime leaders of the 20th century. Churchill was also a historian and won the Nobel Prize for Literature. He was the first person to be made an honorary citizen of the United States. His achievements are too many for this book to detail.

Noël Coward

Playwright, composer, director, actor, and singer known for his wit and flamboyance. At the outbreak of the Second World War, Coward volunteered for war work. He worked with the British Secret Service using his influence to persuade the American public and government to help Britain. Coward died of heart failure at his home in Jamaica in 1973.

George Geoffrey Dawson

Dawson was the editor of *The Times* between 1923 and 1941. A member of the Anglo-German Fellowship he was a prominent proponent of appeasement policies with Nazi Germany. After Adolf Hitler came to power, and while editor of *The Times*, he forbade any mention in the newspaper of German anti-Semitism. He died in November 1944 in London.

Anthony Eden, 1st Earl of Avon, KG

Resigned as Foreign Secretary in protest at Neville Chamberlain's appeasement of Mussolini's Italy. He was reappointed to the position during the Second World War. Having been Churchill's undisputed deputy for fifteen years, he succeeded him as Prime Minister in 1955. He died in 1977 at the age of 79.

Lord Halifax

When visiting Nazi Germany for the first time as British foreign secretary Halifax nearly created a diplomatic incident. Thinking Hitler to be a footman Halifax began to hand him his overcoat. Halifax was saved by someone throwing a hoarse whisper in his ear 'Der Führer, der Führer'. After Neville Chamberlain resigned in 1940, Winston Churchill kept Halifax on as foreign secretary to give the impression that the British government was united. He died in 1959. In 1968, one historian wrote, 'To history Halifax was the arch-appeaser. This is now recognised as a mistake. His role was complicated.'

Charles Henry Maxwell Knight

An English spymaster, naturalist, and broadcaster – and reputedly a model for the James Bond character of M – he rose to be head of the section responsible for infiltrating agents into potentially subversive groups in Britain. He died in 1968.

Lord Londonderry (Charles Vane-Tempest)

A cousin to Winston Churchill who referred to him as a 'half-wit', Londonderry regularly visited Germany. He met with Hitler on several occasions and Hitler considered the aristocrat of real influence. When Hitler informed him that Germany would invade both Czechoslovakia and Poland Londonderry immediately passed this information on to a member of the British government. He was not taken seriously and rearmament in Britain was not accelerated. As a leading member of the Anglo-German Fellowship, he attracted the popular nickname 'The Londonderry Herr' from the popular press. He died in 1949.

Arthur Ronald Nall Nall-Cain, 2nd Baron Brocket

Brocket was a committed member of the Anglo-German Fellowship and a Nazi sympathiser. Even after the outbreak of war, Brocket continued to work for a negotiated peace settlement and tried to arrange talks with Hitler. Throughout the war he was known to have had contacts with Hermann Göring through a Swedish intermediary called Bengt Berg. It's been alleged that during the Blitz, he lit fires on his Hertfordshire estate to guide German bombers towards London. He died in 1967.

Admiral Sir Bertram Ramsay

With the collapse of the British and French armies in 1940, Ramsay was put in charge of 'Operation Dynamo' – the evacuation of British and French troops from the beaches of Dunkirk. He oversaw the successful plan that brought back to Britain more than 300,000 men. He was killed in a plane crash on the way to attend a conference in Brussels in 1945.

Archibald Ramsay MP

In 1939 Ramsay founded the secret society called the Right Club. Unknown to Ramsay, MI5 agents had infiltrated the Right Club and in 1940 the police raided a flat owned by a member of the Club and discovered nearly 2,000 classified documents. Included in the documents is what became known as 'Ramsay's Red Book' containing the names and addresses of members of the Right Club. However, the Home Secretary refused to publish the names, stating that publication might unfairly smear innocent people. In 1941 the *New York Times* claimed Ramsay had been a spy for Nazi Germany and Ramsay sued for libel. The newspaper's owners were found guilty, but the jury awarded Ramsey a single farthing (1 cent) in damages. He died in 1955.

Frank Cyril Tiarks

He was, with his wife, a member of the Anglo-German Fellowship and prominent members of the British Union of Fascists. Among his appointments included a directorship of the Bank of England (1912–1945), a partnership in J. Henry Schröder & Co., and a director of the Anglo-Iranian Oil Company, and High Sheriff of Kent. He died in 1952.

Fifth Duke of Wellington

Arthur Charles Wellesley was a member of several right-wing and other anti-Semitic groups. These included the Anglo-German Fellowship, the Liberty Restoration League and Right Club. He died in 1941.

Americans

Robert Worth Bingham

Ambassador to Great Britain in 1933, he pushed for stronger ties between the United States and Great Britain. He vocally opposed the rise of fascism and Nazism in the 1930s. He was succeeded in the post by Joseph P. Kennedy, Snr. He died in 1937.

William Christian Bullitt, Jr.

Fluent in French and an ardent Francophile, Bullitt was made US Ambassador to France in 1936. He rented a *château* at Chantilly and reputedly owned over 17,000 bottles of French wine. After the German invasion of France, he was the only ambassador of a major nation to remain in the French capital. He died in Neuilly, France in 1967 and is buried in Woodlands Cemetery in Philadelphia.

Adelaide Hall

The American-born, UK-based jazz singer and entertainer arrived in Paris in the fall of 1935. She was hugely popular during World War II and became one of Britain's highest paid entertainers making more than seventy records for Decca and was the first black artist to have a long-term contract with the BBC. Her London nightclub, The Old Florida Club, was destroyed during an air raid in 1939. Hall made a cameo appearance in the 1940 Oscar-winning movie, *The Thief of Bagdad*, in which she sings 'Lullaby of the Princess'. She died in 1993.

Joseph Patrick 'Joe' Kennedy Sr.

Kennedy supported a policy of appeasement with Germany and argued strongly against the United States giving military and economic aid to the UK. On the first day of the blitz on London Kennedy was walking with an aide through Green Park, gesturing towards Buckingham Palace he said: 'I'll bet you any sum that Hitler will be sitting in there in two weeks.' Kennedy was asked to resign his post shortly afterwards by the British government.

According to Harvey Klemmer, one of Kennedy's embassy aides, Kennedy habitually referred to Jews as 'kikes' or 'sheenies' saying that 'as a race they stink and spoil everything they touch.'

Today Joseph Kennedy is largely forgotten in favour of his children John F. Kennedy and Bobby. After he suffered a disabling stroke in 1961 he developed aphasia and lost all power of speech and was confined to a wheelchair until his death in 1969.

Russians

Anna Wolkoff

Anna's father had been the Russian embassy's naval attaché until the revolution in 1917. After the Russian Revolution the family were granted political asylum in Britain and the Wolkoff family opened the Russian Tea Room in South Kensington. Anna, however, established a small business as a milliner in Regent Street. Her clients included the Duchess of Gloucester, Wallis Simpson and the wives of senior politicians. MI5 believed she was spying for Germany and her actions began to be monitored. After she developed a close relationship with Wallis Simpson (the future wife of the Duke of Windsor) MI5 believed that both women were passing state secrets to the German government. Anna was arrested in 1940 and charged under the Official Secrets Act with passing official documents to Germany. Her trial took place in secret and she was sentenced to ten years, imprisonment. Soon after leaving prison she was killed in a car crash.

About the author

Stephen Davis began his writing career aged twenty-seven with a column in the *Western Mail* in South Wales. A regular contributor to business magazines, he is also the author of two business books, as well as a sought after speaker and broadcaster on business issues.

The Tsar's Banker was his first novel. *I Spy the Wolf* the second in the series that follows the fortunes of the Tagleva banking family between 1912 and 1946.

"A thrilling novel painted in glorious period and geographic detail with the real life conspiracy theory of Dan Brown and the glamour of Ian Fleming at his best. It compels you to turn the pages to find out how Philip Cummings and the British Empire are embroiled in the destiny of Tsarist Russia. I loved it."

Caspar Berry – Poker Advisor on Casino Royale.